Check It Out Now!

Bob Stone

*This book has only been possible thanks
to the generous people who contributed
their time, money, advice and stories.*

*This is for them, for the millions whose stories
continue every day, and the countless loved ones
whose stories are remembered in our hearts.*

Part One
Overture

Chapter One

It was a Friday when Liam found out that Michael was dead. It ruined what was otherwise looking like quite a good weekend, even though he hadn't seen the man he had once thought of as one of his best friends in nearly forty years.

Liam had been looking forward to this weekend. The weather was promising, and he had finally finished a rewiring job that had been going on for far too long. The job was in a farmhouse owned by an old guy called Huw, who didn't really want the work doing in the first place but had been told to do it by his insurers. Judging by the way he dressed and the state of the house in general, he didn't look like he was in the habit of spending money on anything very much and had an annoying habit of appearing by Liam's side, apparently out of nowhere and making helpful suggestions about how the work could be done cheaper.

"You don't want to use them bulbs, boy," was one such suggestion. "They've got 'em cheaper in Lidl." Liam hadn't liked to point out what false economy this was. He'd done enough jobs for people like Huw to understand that they always knew best, though obviously not well enough to do the job themselves. He had come across some places where Huw had clearly had a go at doing it, and quite honestly, it was a surprise he was still alive to have an opinion on it now. There were some sockets that were still made of brown Bakelite and one or two light fittings that were several decades older than Liam himself, which these days was saying something. The only benefit to working for Huw was that it had been a very long time since anyone had called him 'boy' and meant it, but with Huw's somewhat advanced age, it wasn't necessarily a compliment. At least the work was finished now and whatever else might kill the old farmer (if he wasn't immortal), it wasn't likely to be electrocution.

Liam wasn't looking forward to presenting the final bill, however. He had no expectation that it would be paid in full with no argument or discussion. He fully expected every single item and charge to be dissected and examined before any money changed hands. That was a problem for another day. In the meantime, there was a weekend to look forward to.

Liam could just about remember the days when he looked forward to the weekend as a time of socialising, parties or long drinking sessions. If he thought back, there were probably a great many weekends entirely absent from his memory for exactly that reason. These days, now he had reached the grand old age of fifty-seven and could see sixty peering at him from round the next corner, he looked forward to the weekend simply as a time when he wasn't working. For two whole days, he could get up when he wanted, eat what he fancied whenever he fancied eating it and watch Midsomer Murders marathons if he was so inclined. He wasn't so inclined very often, but it was nice to know he could do it if he wanted.

Since he and Nic divorced, there was no one to tell him what to do and when to do it; he could just please himself. She'd taken back her surname of Marsh and he had taken back control of the TV remote. Sometimes, he relished it, and sometimes, it bored him rigid, but at least he had the choice.

He had only half expected to have this weekend free because Huw's helpful advice and assistance had made him fear that the job was going to over-run and there was another job lined up for the following week (a much simpler one, thank God). He'd managed to ignore Huw and finish the rewiring by early Friday evening, so the weekend was all his. He had a couple of bottles of wine in the fridge and had found a few classic DVDs in a local charity shop and two days of slobbing about in his jogging trousers and Half Man Half Biscuit sweatshirt beckoned. And then, just as he was getting into his van and waving Huw a fond farewell, he happened to glance at his phone and saw a message from Andy and suddenly the weekend was in bits.

It wasn't like Andy to text. Normally, if they had anything to say to one another, they would phone and could go for months without doing that either. They met up maybe five or six times a year for a drink or a curry (often both) and did all their catching up then. It was only in recent years that they even had done that. They had left university and gone their separate ways in the late eighties and, in those dim and distant days before mobile phones and social media, had simply moved on with their lives and lost touch.

A chance meeting had reconnected them and they were now firm friends again, or at least as firm as it got. All the same, they could go for weeks, sometimes months, without speaking at all. Liam had never really got his head around the necessity most people seemed to feel to be in contact *all the time*, as if their lives didn't exist without the validation of telling someone about every single thing that happened to them as soon as it happened.

It was only in the last couple of years that Liam had bowed to pressure and opened a Facebook account. He mainly used it for the business (out of necessity) but very seldom posted anything personal (out of choice). His daughters kept trying to get him to go on WhatsApp and have a 'family group', but he didn't fancy that at all. He also knew that Freya and Del were in a group with Nic, which made Liam even more reluctant to go anywhere near such a thing. It hadn't been a particularly acrimonious split, more like sad and resigned, but he still didn't particularly want to get involved in a constant string of messages about things that didn't necessarily concern him.

When he first saw the lines of apparently random letters in Andy's text, he didn't recognise it as a link to a Facebook page. It was the words in the text that caught his eye.

        Shit Liam. You seen this? I think
            it's Michael Smart

9

Liam tapped on the link, and it opened a Facebook page, which did indeed belong to someone called Michael Smart. It was hard to tell if it was *the* Michael Smart because the tiny picture next to his name was a photograph of a dog, a border collie from the look of it. He read the most recent post on the page and immediately saw why Andy had started his text with '*Shit*'.

```
This is Becky, writing on Michael's
  behalf. I can barely find the words to
    write this, but I'm devastated to say
  that Mike has lost his fight. He fought so
  hard and for so long, but at 3am today, he
slipped away in my arms. Thank you to everyone
 for the messages and cards you have sent over
   the past few months. They have been a great
    comfort. I will let you all know when the
                funeral is.
            RIP Mike My Love xxx
```

Liam stared at the post for several minutes before noticing that the date on it was about six months earlier. He scrolled down a bit and saw a photograph attached to the post. It was of a man dressed in hiking gear, sitting on a rock up a mountain somewhere on what looked like a sunny day. He was wearing a woolly hat and sunglasses, and his face was lined and gaunt, but it was unmistakably the right Michael Smart.

Liam sat in the cab of his van and fought back tears as it started to register that Mike, from whom he had been inseparable for those wonderful years and with whom he had been through so much, had been dead since March and neither Liam, nor Andy had been at the funeral because neither of them had the slightest idea it had happened.

The fact that Mike had married Becky didn't sink in until later.

Chapter Two

"Hey, Andy."

"Hey, Liam. How are you doing?"

"Not so bad, mate. Can't complain. You?"

"Same as ever, really. Plodding on. Like my old granddad used to say, every day's a bonus."

"Did he really say that? He never!"

"He probably did. He used to say all kinds of shit. How's business? You must be able to retire soon."

"Cheeky bastard. I'm still younger than you. Yeah, business is okay. I think a lot of guys' wives had too much time to look at the house during lockdown and found plenty of work for me. Just as well, really, because I earned next to nothing at the time. What about you?"

"Still living the dream. People need insurance, so there'll always be something to do."

"You back in the office now?"

"Part time. I do two or three days there and two or three days at home. It's a bit of a mixed blessing, really. I think Alison and the kids quite like having me around, but I just wish they'd realise that just because I'm there, it doesn't mean I'm not working. The kids especially. Jesus, I was glad when they went back to school."

"Are they still at school? I thought..."

"Stevie's on his A Levels at the moment and then off to uni, God willing. Then we do it all again next year with Amy."

"Bloody hell. Where has the time gone?"

"I know. I swear the years are getting shorter."

"You still there?"

"Yeah, sorry. I was just thinking. Fucking Michael, hey? Didn't see that coming."

"I know. Bit of a shocker. I couldn't quite believe it was him at first. Hardly recognised his picture."

"What was it? Do we know?"

"Cancer from the look of it."

"Shit."

"There was nothing on his Facebook. The only thing you could tell from his page was that he didn't do social media much, but he certainly loved his dog. That's all that's there. Even Christmas pictures are the bloody dog in a hat. I had to look on Becky's timeline to find out. She didn't post much either, but there were a few fundraising things for cancer, so I guess that must have been it."

"Poor Michael, though."

"I know. First of the gang to die."

"Hey! We're not supposed to quote Mozza anymore."

"Yeah, I know he's turned out to be a bit of an arse, but old habits die hard."

"Know what you mean there. Morrissey and Rocky Horror. Even after all this time, if anyone says 'So...' I want to say 'Come up to the lab...'"

"'...And see what's on the slab.' I remember. You used to do that all the time. It was really fucking irritating, you know?"

"Sorry. You should have said something."

"I did. Often. You still did it. Anyway, Michael's not the first to go. There was Spanner."

"Spanner? Is he dead? Jesus."

"Didn't you know? I thought I told you."

"No. I had no idea."

"It was a while ago now. Sorry, I thought you knew."

"Nope. Mind you, I'm not surprised. With his lifestyle, he was always a prime candidate. I'm surprised he made it to his twenties. What was it? Overdose?"

"No, it was really weird, actually. Are you sure I haven't told you this?"

"I think I'd remember."

"Okay. So what would be the last job you'd expect Spanner to go into?"

"I don't know. The police?"

"Haha. No. Worse than that. He went into investment banking."

"What, Spanner? *The* Spanner? Banking? No. Really?"

"I know. That's what I thought when I heard. I just can't picture old Spanner in a suit, you know? But he did. Did really well in it, from all accounts. Made a load of money. In the old days, he would have spent it all on weed, but it seems like he cleaned himself up and went straighter than all of us, probably. That's the weird thing. If he hadn't, he might still be alive now, like Keith Richards. It was the job that killed him."

"What? Stress?"

"No, it wasn't. Turns out part of his job involved flitting backwards and forwards between here and the States. So, yeah, guess who was in the World Trade Centre on 9/11?"

"Oh bloody hell. That's typical Spanner, that is. He probably tried to punch the plane."

"He tried to punch pretty much everything else. Remember that hole he punched in the wall in that house in Victoria Street?"

"And hid it behind a Jesus and Mary Chain poster? Then moved out without cracking on and left the poster there?"

"It's probably still there."

"Nah, it'll be Ed bloody Sheeran or Stormzy or one of them whoever the kids are into now. All sounds like shit to me."

"It's funny that. I still can't listen to REM without thinking about Michael. He was the first one who bought *Reckoning*, wasn't he?"

"Yes, and that other one. Who was it? Guadalcanal Diary? I never got into that one but he used to play them all the time. Still like a bit of REM, though."

"Do you know what's bizarre? I've never really thought about this, but whenever I play REM, it's Michael who pops into my head, but I've not properly thought about him for years. Maybe if I'd thought about him a bit more, I'd have got in touch. I wish I'd known."

"You can't think like that, mate. It cuts both ways. We all lost touch. It's not like these days with all your Facebooks and WhatsApps and shit. Those days, if you wanted to speak to someone, you called round or picked up the phone and when we left, we just kind of *didn't*. We're fucking dinosaurs, man."

"Tell me about it. I don't know when I turned into my dad, but I have. I'm at the age now where if I drop something, I have to make a conscious decision about whether to try and pick it up or just go *fuck it* and leave it there."

"Me too. You know what I was wondering the other day? If you fall over, what age do you have to be before you can say you 'had a fall'?"

"Bloody hell, Andy, we're not that old! You make us sound like that old one in the adverts who's always hitting the deck but 'knows help is coming' because she's got one of those emergency call buttons round her neck. I reckon she's just a pisshead. Mind you, we've done a bit of that in our time, haven't we?"

"We certainly have. They were good times, though, weren't they?"

"They were that, mate. Bloody good times."

Chapter Three
1985

Liam put his bag down and fumbled with the key to open his room. He was more than aware that his father was lurking restlessly behind him, laden down by the box containing all the kitchen utensils and crockery he was probably not going to use and the tins of food his mum had insisted he took 'just in case.' Stan Rawlinson was not a patient or sentimental man at the best of times, and Liam knew he couldn't wait to dump the box down, grab the rest of the stuff from the car and get off. It wasn't like his mum, who was so upset about her only child leaving home that she couldn't bear to come. Liz Rawlinson had seen Liam off on the doorstep of the family home with a somewhat moist hug, then he and Stan had driven from Liverpool to Bangor mostly in silence apart from the car radio, whose signal kept disappearing, and Stan's muttered curses at other drivers.

Eventually, Liam discovered that, of course, the key turned in the opposite direction to the one you expected and opened the door to the room that was going to be his home for at least the next year.

"Bloody hell," Stan said. "It's like a cell."

At first sight, the rectangular room did indeed look a bit like the prison cells he had seen on the telly, equipped as it was with a single bed against one wall and some shelves on the opposite wall. What made it substantially different, however, was the presence of a large window which took up the whole wall at the head of the bed and gave the room views of the trees and the grassy areas of the site on which Emrys Evans Hall stood. The hall of residence was, according to the sign outside, actually called Neuadd Emrys Evans, but Liam didn't really trust himself to try and pronounce that first word yet. Maybe soon, once he'd had a chance to immerse himself in the Welsh language and culture.

The hall was a large, four-block building, with, as they had discovered, four floors on each block. Liam was quite glad he was only on the second floor because his dad had muttered enough about the stairs as it was. He'd have probably exploded if he'd had to go up three flights of stairs instead of just the one.

Liam stood in the middle of the room, *his* room, imagining its potential, until Stan coughed noisily and reminded him that he still had loads of stuff in the car. The way he said 'loads' implied a 'God knows why you brought it all' that didn't really need to be said. It had already been said several times when they were loading the car back in Liverpool.

In the end, it only took two more trips, but all the same, by the time they had finished, they were both hot and sweating, despite the fact that outside, the day was overcast with a distinct hint of autumn about it. Stan looked at the sky through the window and grunted.

"Better be getting back, then," he said. "Might just beat the rain."

"Yes," Liam replied because he couldn't think of anything better to say. "So, thanks, Dad. For the lift."

"At least you'll be able to get the train home," Stan said, and Liam thought he could detect a slight note of emotion in his voice, though it was hard to tell. "You know, whenever you want. When you're not busy."

"I will, Dad."

"Oh," Stan said, reaching into his pocket and pulling out an envelope, "there's this. Your mother wanted you to have it. Just 'til your grant cheque clears. Make it last, though. I don't trust these councils. Cheque might not come at all."

For a second, Liam was tempted to hug his father but thought better of it and held out his hand instead. Stan paused, then awkwardly shook his son's hand. There was a tricky silence for a moment, then Stan cleared his throat.

"Best be off then," he said.

"Yes. Thanks, Dad."

Stan nodded, turned and walked out of the room. Liam was alone and free and had no idea what to do about it.

16

This wasn't the first time he'd been away from home. He'd been on a couple of camping trips with the Scouts and only last year he'd spent a fortnight in Toulouse on a school exchange trip, but he had never been on his own before. He might as well have been on his own in France for all the notice his host family took of him because he was not confident in speaking French and so did it as little as possible. The fact that the three kids in the family laughed every time he tried didn't help much, either. While he felt isolated and lonely in the Bertillon household, at least he got to see his friends just about every day.

Here, he knew no one. A small part of him wanted to run after his father and go straight back to Liverpool with him, but he shook it off and decided that the best thing to do was to get a brew on. Luckily, he had packed his brand-new kettle at the top of one of the boxes, a jar of coffee too. All he had to do was fill it, but first, he had to find the sink. Surely, the room had one.

On either side of the door was what looked like a double fronted cupboard. He opened the one on the left and found quite a spacious wardrobe with a small shelf unit to one side. He was glad that his mother had insisted he bring some coat hangers, despite his protestations, because there were none in the wardrobe. He left the wardrobe door open and investigated the right-hand side, which revealed a sink with a mirror over it. The mirror, he was oddly pleased to note, even had a light with a shaver socket. The most important thing, though, was that he could now fill the kettle, which he did. Then, as an afterthought and just because he could, he balanced the kettle at the side of the sink and used his cupped hands to splash some water on his face. It was only after he had done so that it occurred to him that he hadn't yet unpacked a towel. He used his T-shirt to dry his face, reasoning that he could always change his shirt once he had unpacked and before he encountered anyone else.

The plug socket was next to the window frame, allowing him to situate the kettle on the desktop, which ran the full width of the room under the window. It was the perfect place to have it because as long as he kept the kettle filled, he could make plenty of coffee while he worked without getting up.

While the water boiled, he retrieved a mug from the box (it was brand-new as his mother wouldn't let him bring his mug from home) and shook some coffee powder into it. Some of the coffee went onto the desk, but he would clean that up in a minute, he decided. And find a teaspoon.

He sat on the edge of the bed and looked around the room. It was very bare at the moment but wouldn't be once he had put some books and his collection of cassettes on the shelves. Some of the cassettes might have to stay in the box, at least until he found out the musical tastes of any new friends he made and invited back to his room. He wasn't ashamed of his tape collection exactly, but there were some bands who probably weren't cool to like as a student, not even in an ironic way. This was a strange new world and Liam wasn't sure what the rules were yet. He finished his coffee and started to unpack.

It took him nearly an hour to empty the boxes and bags, but he was quite happy with the result. The room had gone from being a generic, characterless shell to looking like something that belonged to Liam Rawlinson. It needed a few posters on the bare walls, but the ones on his bedroom wall at home were tatty and well out of fashion, so he would see what he could find when he got around to investigating the town. He'd need some Blu-Tac, too, because he had noted the hall's strict anti-Sellotape policy. He didn't know if anyone ever inspected but thought it safer not to risk it. Otherwise, he was pleased with himself.

Outside his door, he could hear voices and footsteps as other students arrived. He wasn't sure whether he was ready to meet them yet, though he knew he would have to sooner or later. Emrys Evans was a self-catering hall, which was one of the reasons he had chosen it. He was a fair cook, having spent quite a lot of time over the years watching his mum cook and then helping. He liked cooking, so feeding himself wasn't going to be a problem. It did mean, however, sharing a kitchen with the other residents on his floor and a doubt niggled at the back of his mind – *what if they don't like me?*

He had never found it easy to make a large circle of friends and had gone through school with only two really close mates. Colin had gone to Newcastle, and Johnny had failed to get into university, but they had promised to write and meet up in the holidays. Moving to Bangor meant making new friends and Liam was anxious about whether he could.

The other factor that separated Emrys Evans from the rest of the halls was that students had an automatic right to retain their room for each of the three years of their degree, whereas the other halls didn't. This worried Liam a little because there were probably already established friendship groups on his floor - students in their second or third years. What if he was the only first year?

He debated whether to risk going to see if there was anywhere in the kitchen to put his pans and plates and also see if there was anyone else around. He would have to do it sooner or later, but he wasn't sure whether it was ruder to barge in now or hide in his room and emerge later.

He was still wondering what to do when there was a knock at the door. For a second, he froze. He suddenly realised that he hadn't got around to changing his shirt and the one he was wearing was still slightly damp. While he was dithering about whether he had time to change, the knock came again and settled the issue.

He opened the door and was greeted by the sight of a lad about his own age, dressed in an army surplus jacket and a 'Frankie Says Relax' T-shirt. His blond hair was gelled up in impressive spikes, making him look a bit like the guy out of a Flock of Seagulls, a style Liam knew he could never achieve himself, even if he had the nerve to try.

"All right?" the newcomer said. "Just moved in?"

"Yes," Liam replied. "About an hour ago. My dad dropped me off. He's gone now." Mentally, he kicked himself for adding this last, rather unnecessary detail.

"I should hope so," the blond lad replied and smiled. "I'm Michael. I'm next door."

"Liam."

"You a Scouser?"

"Yeah, I am. Where are you—"

"Preston. But I escaped. Come on then, Scouse Liam. Come and meet the other inmates."

Chapter Four

Andy was quite glad he was working from home when he learned about Michael. For a start, if he had been in the office, he might never have found out at all. He was by no means a slave to social media, but he did enjoy the occasional browse. There were too many distractions in the office, but at home, he allowed himself more breaks from his desk, probably too many, but he was pretty much his own boss, so who was going to tell him otherwise?

It was while he was having a coffee, sitting outside so he could grab what he could of the sunshine, that he happened to come across the post. He wasn't sure why it popped up, but then he'd never understood the algorithms of a site that suddenly threw up posts from months ago but on which he sometimes missed posts from that day. He supposed he must have connected with Michael at some point and forgotten about it because his old friend posted so rarely and never interacted with Andy's own posts. The post drew him up short and he read it several times before texting Liam. He had been about to call, figuring that it was really something that needed a conversation, not a string of texts, when Liam beat him to it and called him.

Now, he was at a loss as to what to do. Stevie and Amy would be home from school in maybe an hour or so unless they had gone somewhere with their friends, which they often did on a Friday. Alison got in from work around six, so he still had a couple of hours before he needed to get the dinner going. Because the kids sometimes didn't get home on time, he usually knocked together a Bolognese or a chilli on a Friday, something that could stay in the pan and be eaten by whoever, whenever. He and Alison opened a bottle or two of wine on a Friday to celebrate the end of the working week and he was half tempted to get started on that now, but much as he felt like doing so, he hadn't quite clocked out of work yet. He finished his coffee and went back inside to finish up and get cracking on the meal.

Work took his mind off Michael for a bit, but once he moved into the kitchen to start chopping and cooking, it came flooding back, and it did so, as memories often tend to, through music. Andy always liked to have a few tunes going while he cooked. He and Alison had rather different tastes and this was the time when he could happily have his own music on, not just because he was on his own but because being the one doing all the work gave him the right. He had a long, rambling playlist of all his favourite music on Spotify, and while he cooked, he allowed the shuffle feature to surprise him with the selection of songs. It was perhaps inevitable that REM would come on and it just had to be 'The One I Love', didn't it? The memories it brought back, of that summer they all stayed in Bangor, were so vivid that Andy nearly skipped the track, but instead, he stood leaning against the kitchen counter and let the song play. He could picture Michael sitting in an armchair, one leg over its arm, a beer in his hand and one of those foul French cigarettes he thought were so cool in his mouth.

He tried to shake the memory away by focusing on the cooking, though chopping onions was not the best of ideas under the circumstances. He wiped his eyes on a piece of kitchen towel, threw the onions into the pan and, as they cooked down, thought again about what he was supposed to do with the information he had found.

He had tracked Becky down on Facebook quite easily, once he had realised that he was supposed to be looking for her under her married name rather than searching for the Becky Dee ('Look at me!') he was used to. But having done so, it presented him with the dilemma of what to do next. What, exactly, was the correct thing to do? He was tempted to send her a friend request and leave it up to her, but that seemed a bit impersonal. On the other hand, they had been out of touch for so long and Michael had been gone for six months. He couldn't say what effect it would have if he contacted her out of the blue to offer his condolences. Would it all still be too raw for her? Or, if she was trying to get her life back to some kind of normal, might reminding her set her back? Considering that a large part of his job involved settling life insurance claims, he should have known what to do, but the claims and, therefore, the bereavements he dealt with were strangers, names on a computer, not someone he had once known so well.

He had known bereavement himself, of course. There weren't a great many people who got to his age with both parents still alive and kicking. His father had died seven years earlier and he had helped his mother through it, but his dad had been in his eighties and the fact that Michael was Andy's own age felt different. It was too soon, and he was too young.

The truth was that inside, Andy still felt like the same person he was when they had all been friends. He still listened to much the same music and kept going back to watch the same old films. His body tried to tell him differently, reminding him that he was pushing sixty by introducing inexplicable aches and pains, but he tried to ignore it. The fact that he would rather be in bed reading by ten instead of that being the time the night was just getting started was another reminder, but he didn't mind that. He was well out of the habit of late-night drinking sessions and didn't miss them at all. He liked being comfortable in bed with Alison while they both read their books and wound down. But the Andy inside, the Andy who used to think nothing of being out all night and then sleeping in and missing early lectures, wasn't ready to think about retirement and he certainly wasn't ready to think about death.

By the time the dinner was ready and Alison came home, he was feeling melancholic and strangely cross, and his wife noticed it straight away.

"Are you okay?" she asked as he took her in his arms for their usual kiss hello and held on tighter and longer than usual. "Has something happened?"

"I'm okay," he replied, his standard response to that question. "I'll tell you later. Let me just get the dinner sorted."

Alison frowned but didn't press it. He might have got away with it, too, had it not been for the spoon. He always stirred with a wooden spoon. It was how his mother had taught him back when non-stick pans were a relatively new thing and came with dire warnings about not using metal utensils because they could damage the surface. Tonight, however, he had not only used a metal spoon but had left it in the pan of bubbling sauce while he greeted Alison. When he took hold of it, it was so hot that he dropped it straight away. It landed on the floor, spraying orange Bolognese sauce all over the quarry tiles.

"Shit! Fuck!" he shouted and immediately bent down to retrieve the spoon.

"Leave it," Alison said. "Get that hand under cold water. I'll clean up."

"I'm fine," Andy snapped. "I'll sort it. Just leave me alone."

"Bollocks to that," Alison replied. "You bathe that bloody hand; I'll clear up and then we're going to have a glass of wine while you tell me exactly what the hell is wrong."

Andy started to protest but then caught a look in his wife's eye that had become very familiar over the past twenty-six years. He called it her 'hard stare' after Paddington Bear, and it meant that resistance was utterly futile.

***

A little later, as they finished the first bottle of wine and Andy finally finished serving the meal, Alison surprised him by raising her glass.

"To Michael," she said.

"To Michael," Andy replied, raising his own glass. "Thank you. That was nice, considering that you didn't know him."

"No, but you did, and that's what counts."

Andy was glad that Stevie had elected to stay out for a bit with his mates and Amy had taken her dinner up to her room so that she could urgently message the friends she had only just left. He hadn't felt like talking to them about Michael, but Alison seemed to understand.

"I don't know what to do about it," Andy said. "I feel like I need to do something, but I don't know what."

"Well, you need to get in touch with his widow – Becky, is it? Both of you - you and Liam."

"I know. It's difficult."

"No, it's not. I'm sure she'll be glad to hear from you."

"It's been so long."

"Yes, but underneath it all, you're still the same people. Does she live round here?"

"I'm not sure. Her Facebook doesn't say."

"Then ask her and see if you and Liam can go and see her. I think you have to."

"I suppose. No, you're right. I'll message her over the weekend. Probably best not doing it when I've had a drink."

"True. The last thing she needs is you pissed-texting her out of nowhere. Do it tomorrow."

"I will."

"Good. And then you, me and Liam will have a sit-down and decide what you're going to do to commemorate Michael."

Chapter Five

"Liam."

"All right, Andy? How's things? How was your weekend?"

"Okay, apart from...well, you know."

"I hear you. Gave me a lot to think about."

"Me too. I was quite glad to get back into the office today. Or at least I was until lunchtime and bloody Duncan. Have I ever told you about Duncan?"

"Doesn't ring a bell."

"You'd know if I had. Don't get me wrong, he's all right mostly. Works hard, gets the job done, like, but sometimes he...well, probably the best way of saying it is that sometimes he doesn't make the best decisions. To give you some context, he always has his lunch at his desk, which is very dedicated and that, but his choice of lunch can be a bit odd. Today it went disastrously wrong, and he managed to fuck up a perfectly good laptop with a melon."

"Sorry, he did what with a *what*?"

"I know! So there he was, beavering away and at the same time tucking into a watermelon. And I mean, a whole half of a watermelon, which he was eating with a teaspoon and putting the seeds in a Tupperware box. Knowing him, he was probably going to take the bloody things home and plant them. Anyway, I was on the phone to a client, and I heard a splat and Duncan had only dropped the whole bloody melon on his laptop."

"Jesus."

"It gets better. He was just sitting looking at it like he didn't believe what had happened and smoke started to come out of his laptop. I dumped my client and pulled the plug before he set the sprinklers off. Duncan looked up from the smouldering ruin of the computer and had to acknowledge that the melon was no longer fit for consumption."

"Is that what he said?"

"No, he couldn't actually speak, but that's what his face said. How's your day been?"

"Okay, really. I went over to Chapel Bay to price up a job on a school. Could be a big one, but then they're all working to budgets, these schools, so they'll probably try and screw me on price."

"Weren't you at Chapel Bay last week?"

"Yeah. Only good thing to come out of that one was the headteacher got my number off the van. It's a bit of a trek, but it could be worse. There's a boss café right by the beach, so my lunch is sorted."

"As long as they don't do watermelon."

"True."

"Anyway, I didn't just call you to chat about melons. Ali and I had a good talk over the weekend about Michael. Just so's you know, I've sent Becky a friend request. She may not respond, but..."

"So did I. I was going to text you later. She's not got back to me yet, either."

"She may not want reminding. I don't blame her, really. I'm sure she's been up the wall since...you know."

"It's probably okay to say it, mate. Since Michael died."

"I know. Saying it makes it real, though, doesn't it?"

"It *is* real. Nothing we can do to change that."

"No. Wish there was. But Ali did suggest that maybe we could do something to, I guess, commemorate Michael."

"Like what? A service or something? I'm sure they've already done that."

"No, I mean like something for charity, maybe. People do all sorts of stuff."

"What, like a fun run, that sort of thing? I mean, I'm not being funny or anything, mate, but have you seen the state of me lately?"

"Oh God, no! I'm sure we can come up with something a bit less physical. I'm not exactly in great shape myself. It wouldn't do any good if we killed ourselves doing it. Last time I did any exercise was that football game at Bangor, remember? Went over on my ankle and spent a couple of weeks in plaster? I took that as a sign."

"I thought that was an excuse to do your exams in the sick bay. So a five-a-side match is out, then."

"Definitely. I've not played footie since. We'll have a think. There must be loads we could do."

"Only if Becky gets in touch. I wouldn't want to do anything in Mike's name without telling her."

"Fair point. Okay, we'll think about it in the meantime, but see what happens, yeah?"

"Sounds good. Andy..."

"What?"

"Do you...do you, you know, check?"

"What, for lumps and that? I didn't. I'm going to start, though. I've got no idea what I'm looking for. I might have to look on bloody YouTube or something. Do you?"

"I did last night in the shower. It's been a long time since my bollocks had that sort of attention. They thought it was Christmas. It's a bit fucking embarrassing, really. Might have to look it up myself. God know what my search history will look like!"

"Bet there's worse than that on there. A single bloke like you."

"You think you're dead funny, you."

"I know. That's because I am."

"Woah! Shit!"

"What's up?"

"Just felt like someone walked over my grave. You know that was the first thing you ever said to me, don't you?"

Chapter Six
1985

Liam was relieved to see there was no one else in the kitchen when he and Michael entered. It was a big room, bigger than he had expected, though if truth be told, he wasn't really sure what to expect. There were three large cookers against one wall with cupboards above them and more cupboards along the next wall. In one corner was a large fridge/freezer; opposite, a row of padded easy chairs had been placed under the window. In the middle of the room were several large, round, Formica-covered tables, around each of which were plastic chairs. There was plenty of room for most of the floor's occupants to cook and eat at the same time, and it was obvious that the room also served as a communal meeting area.

"Bloody hell," Michael said, opening one of the large windows. "Smells like Adrian's been burning one of his curries again. Word of advice—if Adrian offers you a taste of one of his curries, make your excuses. They're rank."

"Are you a second-year, then?" Liam asked.

"Yeah. History. You're a Fresher, aren't you?"

"Can you tell?"

"A mile off. It's the look of wide-eyed wonder. Don't worry. Give it a week and you'll be just like the rest of us." Michael flopped down on one of the easy chairs. "What are you doing?"

"Degree? English mainly."

"English in Wales. Makes sense, I suppose. Why here?"

"It was the only offer I got. But I liked the look of it anyway."

Michael stared at him.

"What, you *wanted* to come here? Bloody hell, mate. That's going to make you a bit of a novelty. Most people come here through Clearing, unless you're doing Marine Biology; it's supposed to be good for that. They've got their own boat or something. Don't know how they make it go round all those students. 'You're gonna need a bigger boat.' *Jaws*?"

"Loved that film! No, we used to go to Anglesey when we were kids and we always stopped off in Bangor on the way, so I sort of know it. Just as well, really. My other four choices rejected me."

"Bangor doesn't reject anyone, from what I hear. I got talking to a lad last year and he just walked into a place on the Linguistics course. Some girl at his school had been offered a place but got better grades and went somewhere else. So he rang up the Linguistics Department and said, 'I know you've got a place going because so-and-so turned it down. Can I have it?' They asked what his grades were, he told them, and they went, 'Okay, no problem.' So he said anyway."

"Is it that bad?" Liam asked, wondering now if he'd made a terrible mistake.

"No, it's all right, really. Nightlife's sound and this hall's a good crack. Good bunch of lads. Well, they were last year. I think about half of them said they were coming back. Guys like Adrian will probably be here forever. He's a post-grad, but I reckon he'll be a student 'til he dies. Him and Wingnut."

"Wingnut?"

"His name's Dave, really, but you'll know when you see him."

At that moment, the door opened, and a lanky, dark-haired lad looked in.

"Is this the...?" he began, then stopped. "Oh, yeah, it is."

"Come on in," Michael said. "Come and join the party."

"Oh, nice one," the newcomer said. "Ta."

"You sound like a fellow Scouser," Liam said.

"I know. That's because I am."

"Whereabouts?"

"Well, I live on the Wirral now. Prenton?"

"Oh, you're a plazzy Scouser."

"You think you're dead funny, you."

"I know. That's because I am."

"I was born in Mossley Hill, if that helps," Andy said. "We only moved over to the dark side a couple of years back. You?"

"Bootle born and bred, me."

"Fucking hell," Michael said. "I'm going to have to start locking my door. I'm Michael. He's Liam."

"Andy. You both Freshers?"

***

It was a good half hour or more before anyone else made an appearance. During that time, Liam had gone back to his room briefly to collect his jar of coffee and some mugs (his room was the nearest, plus Michael had run out of coffee) and boiled the communal kettle (which was made of white plastic but had a number of smudged fingerprints on it that Liam didn't quite like the look of).

While they drank their coffee, they chatted some more, and Liam felt his earlier anxiety begin to dissipate. He had worried that he would be out of his depth, especially with students who were already established there. When he was younger, he'd been called 'shy' or 'quiet', usually in a patronising way and was never able to explain why he felt so awkward in company and went red any time anyone spoke to him. That was why he'd only had a few good mates back home; most of the other kids in his school were louder, more confident, and had no time for someone who didn't speak very much. But talking to Michael and Andy, he felt so much more relaxed. They were funny and laughed at the jokes he cracked. More than that, they seemed to be interested in what he had to say. After only a couple of hours, he thought he was going to like it here.

Gradually, more and more of the floor's residents dropped by the kitchen. Some were passing through, but others stopped and chatted for a bit. Liam tried to remember the names but soon began to lose track. He wouldn't forget Simon because he was the longest-serving resident of the floor and was treated like some kind of elder statesman and certainly acted the part. Adrian was obvious, because he was a good ten years or so older than Liam and with his long hair, beard, John Lennon glasses and tie-dyed T-shirt, he looked like he had just walked in from Woodstock. The lingering aroma of patchouli when he went back to his room only reinforced the image. There was Rob, who was dressed in a moth-eaten Aran sweater that looked three sizes too big for him and who seemed to have only just woken up (Liam would later find out that this was his permanent state), and Nils, an overseas student from Holland, whose English was excellent, if loud. Chris was overweight and very studious and took being the butt of a number of jokes remarkably well, and Carlos, from Columbia, smiled a lot but said little.

The time passed and Liam was quite surprised to see that the sun had come out but was now dropping behind the roof of the block next door. Michael noticed this, too, and got up.

"Best get myself sorted. Said I'd meet some people down the Union in a bit. Who's coming? I don't think there's anything much on tonight, but at least we can have a pint."

"I'm up for that," Andy replied.

"I don't know..." Liam said though he wasn't quite sure why.

"Come on, lad," Andy said. "Let's show them how the Scousers do it."

"Yeah, okay."

"About eight, then?" Michael asked. "Not much point in going before that."

They were just about to return to their rooms when one of the strangest figures Liam had ever seen came into the kitchen. Had he not been wearing a sweatshirt that was so tatty that it appeared to be more hole than shirt, and a pair of patchwork flares, Liam would have sworn that he had escaped from Middle-Earth. He was short, only coming to somewhere around Liam's shoulder, had ginger hair that stuck out at a variety of angles and a face that was covered in ginger stubble that was either a bad attempt to grow a beard or a bad attempt to shave. Probably his most remarkable feature, though, was that he was possessed of the most impressive, protruding ears Liam had seen outside Knowsley Safari Park. This peculiar little hobbit walked into the middle of the kitchen, looked around, crossly said, "Bollocks," and walked out again.

Liam looked at Michael, who grinned and nodded.

"Yeah," he said, "that's Wingnut."

***

The homesickness didn't hit Liam until later, when he sat on an unfamiliar bed in an unfamiliar room, and it really sank in that this was his life now. The fact that he was more than half-pissed didn't help. It had been a busy day and a good evening, so he didn't really have time to think about it, but now, as he contemplated getting ready to turn in, the massive change in his life washed over him in horrible, what-the-hell-have-I-done waves of misery. It seemed like he might have made some new friends, but they weren't his old friends. In-jokes that would have creased Colin and Johnny up only got blank looks. Even his duvet cover was brand new and had that stiffness that takes a while to settle in and he hated it. Most of all, though, he missed saying goodnight to his mum and dad. Stan was distant and often humourless, and Liz fussed too much and smothered him, but right now, they seemed so far away that it felt like he would never see them again.

He went over to the wardrobe and dug out a Marvel comics T-shirt that his mum had bought him, which he'd had no intention of wearing. She thought it was a treat; he thought it was childish. Now, there was nothing else he would rather wear to bed. He put it on, cleaned his teeth, turned off the light and climbed under the hated new duvet. Only then did he allow himself to cry.

Chapter Seven

Liam didn't hear anything more about Michael for nearly two weeks, and during that time, he was able to file it away at the back of his mind under 'Things to Worry About Later'. In the meantime, life and work carried on. He spent a day in Beaumaris replacing some halogen bulbs in a gift shop, whose owner suffered from vertigo, so wouldn't go up a ladder to do it herself. Liam had heard similar stories many times before and suspected that she simply didn't know how to do it. As it turned out, what should have been a very straightforward job took longer than expected because whoever had installed the lamps in the first place hadn't done it right and even Liam struggled to get the blown bulbs out. By then, Liam had quoted for the length of time it *should* have taken and couldn't go back on his word. Luckily, the school who wanted a quote had phoned him and asked for his visit to be put back to later in the week, which suited him fine because he didn't have much else booked in.

When he went to the school, he was provided with a potent reminder of Michael and not in a way he would ever have expected. He had spent a while looking around the school premises in the company of Ruth, the attractive, bubbly, but somewhat harassed headteacher.

When he first arrived, she didn't seem to be expecting him. That was mainly because she wasn't altogether sure what day it was, or it was a bit early in the day for her. He had arranged to be there before school started to avoid being in the way. Once she had adjusted to his sudden arrival, however, she was altogether more professional and showed him all the work she wanted doing. He duly made notes on his iPad and the occasional suggestion. The school building was quite old and, in places, poorly maintained, but the electrics were plainly more recent than some things in the school, such as the plumbing and the paintwork. He only found one socket that was actively dangerous (in Ruth's office, though fortunately, it was hidden behind a filing cabinet and never used), three more that looked a bit iffy, and a couple of light fittings that needed renewing.

"It's quite good news," he told Ruth as she walked him back into the playground. "I'll need to price up materials and labour, but it's not going to be too bad. I won't need to bring anyone else in, so that'll cut down the labour costs."

"What does that mean?" Ruth asked cautiously. "Only I've had enough trades in here to know that what you call 'not too bad' and what I call 'not too bad' might not be the same thing."

"I can't say exactly. Well under a grand, though. I'll try and get the quote over to you by the end of the day."

"What, really? Wow! That *is* good news. I'll be straight with you, though. I've had a couple of other guys in to quote and they all did that head-shaking-tutting thing that you just know is going to push the quote up. I think they're under the impression it's government money, so it's more or less a blank cheque."

"No, there are still plenty of us good guys around. Most of your electrics are in good shape. Have you had work done recently?"

"A couple of years ago, I think. We've just tended to do what needs doing as and when."

"It's not always the best idea, but you've been lucky."

"Thanks again, Liam, isn't it? Look, I've got a few minutes before it all kicks off here. Do you want a coffee before you go?"

Liam glanced towards the gate and could see that the school's pupils were starting to straggle in or saying goodbye to parents at the gate.

"No, I'm fine, honestly. It looks like you're about to get busy."

As he said that, a young mother approached, holding one little girl by her hand and wheeling a pushchair that contained an even smaller girl, who looked fast asleep. When they drew level, Liam could see that the older girl, who must

35

have been five or six, was wearing a tiara and carrying a plastic unicorn, which she held out to Liam.

"This is my unicorn," she said.

"It's okay, Evelyn," the mother said. "I'm sure the man doesn't want to see your unicorn." She looked at Liam, gave a faint smile and said, "Sorry."

"It's fine," Liam replied. "You've got an awesome unicorn there, Princess Evelyn."

"He talks," Evelyn said.

"Come on," Evelyn's mother said, "we'd better go in before Eleanor wakes up and wants to run around. Mrs Evans will be waiting for you."

"If I know Paula," Ruth said, "she'll still be finishing her coffee, so you're okay. How are they, Jenny?"

"They're...they're fine. They run us ragged, but they're fine. John's off work next week, so he'll bring Evelyn if that's all right."

"No problem," Ruth replied. "I've got a note and I've told Paula, so it's all sorted."

"Thanks, Ruth. Let's get you in then, Evelyn."

"'Bye, Princess," Liam said. "Have a good day."

Evelyn, however, seemed to have forgotten all about him and chatted happily with her mum as they disappeared into the school. Ruth watched them go and Liam could see a frown of concern on her face.

"Poor girl," she said, though Liam wasn't sure she had intended to say it out loud.

"How so?" he asked.

Ruth mouthed the word *cancer* and pointed in the direction of her breast.

"You can say the word," Liam said and realised he sounded harsher than he had meant it to.

"Sorry," Ruth said. "Only it's just so unfair. She's so young. She's got surgery next week and then chemo."

"That's rough," Liam said. "I'm sorry to hear it."

"The thing is, she's so positive about it. It might be an act for the girls, but it just doesn't seem to get her down. I don't

36

know how she does it. I'd be in bits. I mean, I know they say it's treatable, but all the same..."

"I'm sure if she stays positive, she'll be fine," Liam said, but it sounded hollow even to him. "And I'm sorry if I snapped. I've just heard that an old mate of mine has died. He had cancer."

"Oh, how awful. Were you close?"

"Once. To be honest, I haven't seen him since we left uni, but yes, we were very close once. Me and another mate are thinking of doing something for him."

"What, like a fundraiser? What are you going to do? An abseil or something?"

"No chance!" Liam said and laughed. "I mean, look at me! Anyway, sorry. I've taken your time up. I'll get that quote over to you."

"Thanks, Liam. And good luck with your whatever-it-is."

On his way back to the industrial estate, where he rented a small unit that served as an office and storeroom, Liam thought about the young mother and her children. He couldn't imagine how they would have coped if anything had happened to Nic when the girls were that age. The mother, Jenny, was probably only ten years or so older than Delyth, his oldest and the idea that something like this could happen to her was just inconceivable. He suddenly felt very old.

While driving, he felt his phone buzz a couple of times in his pocket but thought nothing of it. It was probably spam emails, offering him a great deal on his electricity or phone or card payments, none of which interested him in the slightest. He was of the opinion that he was okay as he was, and while he could afford his bills, it was better to leave well enough alone. It was only when he pulled up outside the unit that he checked his phone and saw that the buzz had been a Facebook notification. When he saw what it said, he felt a sudden wave of shock that made him go light-headed for a second.

Becky Smart has accepted your friend request.

It invited him to send Becky Smart a message to say hello, but as he stared at her profile picture and studied her face, the face that once filled his thoughts but now carried the lines of her years (though not that many), he hesitated. He had once been able to talk to that woman for hours. There was nothing he liked more if he were honest. But there was her picture, her once raven-black hair now threaded with a hint of grey, and somewhere out there, she had been reminded he still existed and didn't mind him getting in touch. For the first time since they had become friends, Liam hadn't a clue what to say.

Chapter Eight

"You all right, Andy?"

"Bloody hell, Liam. I think we've spoken more in the last week than we have in the last year!"

"Sorry. Are you busy?"

"No, mate. Ali's out with a friend, and the kids are...well, they're somewhere. I'm just catching up on a bit of the telly they won't let me watch."

"EastEnders marathon?"

"As if. No, they're showing the whole of *Star Trek: The Next Generation* on that Forces TV and I've been secretly recording them."

"Don't you think it's time you told Alison? You've been married long enough, and I think she has a right to know."

"What, that I'm a middle-aged Trekkie? No, I don't think she's ready to hear that yet."

"Middle-aged. Fuck. I hate that expression. When we were young, middle-aged meant old. I didn't think it would ever mean *me*."

"Does, though. At least you're not old."

"Thanks. That's not what the mirror tells me. Anyway, speaking of which, Becky accepted my friend request."

"Yeah, mine too. Have you replied?"

"Not yet. That's sort of why I'm ringing. I mean, what the hell do you say?"

"I know. That's why I haven't replied yet, either. It seems...I don't know...*wrong* to go, 'Remember me? Sorry I never got in touch with Mike, but it's too late now.' Do you know what I mean?"

"No, that's probably not the best way to put it."

"But it sort of *is* what we're saying, though, isn't it? We just need to put it better. Something like, 'Really sorry to hear the sad news about Mike. I've got so many happy memories of—'"

"Hang on! Slow down!"

"What are you doing?"

"I'm writing it down."

"Don't do that! It'll look really stupid if we say the exact same thing. I just said something like."

"It's not a fucking exam, Andy. No one's going to take marks off for copying. I'll have a think."

"We don't want to leave it too long, though. It'll seem a bit weird if we both send her a friend request and then don't say anything. Anyway, we need to get in touch with her soon to see if she's okay with us doing something for Mike."

"Even though we haven't got a bloody clue what we're doing. Have you had any thoughts about that?"

"I've had plenty of thoughts, but they're all crap. I had a look at the sort of things people do, and most of them scared the shit out of me. People jump out of planes and climb down Liverpool Cathedral and all sorts. Some guy did a bungee jump off the Forth Bridge."

"No chance. I mean, I'm sorry about Mike and all that, but I'm not in a hurry to join him. I'm not doing a run, either. I couldn't even run for a bus these days."

"It's a good way to get fit, though."

"It's a good way for me to end up in intensive care. It's all right for you, you've always been a skinny bastard, but I'm built for comfort, not speed these days."

"These days?"

"Shut it, you. What about a walk? Lots of people do those."

"Are you sure you could manage it? They're long walks, you know, not just down to the shops. I've had a look at some and they're all like 10k or more. Some of them are a lot more. Would you really be up for climbing Snowdon?"

"Put like that..."

"They're old hat, though. Everyone does them. I fancy doing something a bit different."

"Something a bit different that's not going to kill us. Is there anything?"

"Don't know. We'll keep looking. Anyway, we still need to get in touch with Becks first. She might say no."

"Do you think she will?"

"Don't get your hopes up, mate. We just need to talk to her. Tell her how we feel. It's Becky, remember? We've known her for years. She was our friend, Liam. It can't be that hard to send her a quick message. If she doesn't reply, she doesn't reply."

"It's probably harder for you. You were dead close, weren't you?"

"Oh, fuck off! We weren't that close."

"You know what I mean."

"I doubt she even remembers that. I'm certainly not going to remind her. Anyway, you met her first. Wasn't she in your tutorial group?"

"Yeah, with Doctor...what the hell was his name? Jesus, my memory. I can picture him and everything. Scottish guy. Russell! That's it. Doctor Russell. How did I forget that?"

Chapter Nine
1985

Liam was quite surprised to find that his new routine was taking a bit of getting used to. He had thought that university life would be so much easier than the rigid school timetable. At home, he got up at the same time every morning (generally when he was told to), got to school at the same time and left at the same time at the end of the day. Here, every day was different, and he had to keep a close eye on where he was supposed to be and when. Most of his lectures for English and media studies were in the arts building, but drama had its own building with a studio theatre and it wouldn't do to find himself in the wrong place and have to sprint across the campus from one to the other.

He was definitely not used to taking responsibility for what time he got up in the morning. It hadn't mattered much during Freshers' Week because lectures and tutorials didn't start until the following week. This was probably just as well; with the social whirl of Freshers' Week, he wasn't really in any fit state to get up much before midday.

Once the academic timetable started, his body seemed to remember what it was supposed to do in term-time, and he started to wake up at the same time each morning as he used to when he was at school. This was fine on the days when he had an early lecture, but there were a couple of days when he had nothing until late morning and those were the days when he had to be careful. Getting up too early meant hanging around and waiting to go; staying in bed and there was a danger of going back to sleep and not getting up in time. In a few weeks, it would most likely be second nature, but for the time being, he had to keep one eye on the clock.

The whole way of learning was also strange and bewildering. In lectures, you had to listen, pay attention and make notes. The trouble was that you couldn't write everything down; it wasn't like the lecturer ever stopped to let you catch up and they certainly didn't often tell you which were the important bits, so you had to decide for yourself. Some of the other students seemed to have no problem keeping up and kept their heads down and scribbled frantically. Liam struggled to listen and write at the same time and sometimes found that by the time he had finished writing one thing down, he had missed the next bit of what the lecturer was saying. He didn't want to write too quickly because he had terrible handwriting (as teacher after teacher had pointed out over the years) and knew that if he tried to get everything down, the chances of being able to read his notes afterwards were virtually nil. He hoped that if he became friends with other students on the course, there might be opportunities to share notes, not that he would particularly want anyone to see how embarrassing *his* notes were.

The seminars in tutorial groups were a different matter but came with their own set of problems. They were held in the office of whichever lecturer was taking that module of the course and involved half a dozen or more students, most of whom didn't yet know each other. They were crammed into a small room, all trying hard not to make eye contact with each other or the lecturer. For these seminars, you weren't just supposed to have read the text under discussion but come along equipped with opinions on it. There were a number of authors about whom Liam was looking forward to offering his opinion, but none of them would come up just yet and some were not on the syllabus for this year at all. The course was, perhaps sensibly, arranged chronologically and the seminars at this stage all concerned early and middle-English writing, which Liam could barely read, let alone understand and certainly didn't know enough about to have any kind of informed opinion about. He spent the first couple of seminars with his head firmly buried in his copy of the text and his notepad, living in as much fear of being asked what he thought as someone who has accidentally ended up on the front row of a stand-up comedy show and desperately doesn't want to be picked on by the comedian.

His tutor for poetry was Dr Russell, a genial Scottish man who read the poems in a beautiful, lilting accent. Liam wasn't sure where in Scotland Dr Russell came from, but he suspected it might be Troon (wherever that was) because the tutor stirred his coffee with a small spoon with the word 'Troon' enamelled on the handle. It was either a reminder of his home, a souvenir, or possibly some kind of hilarious academic joke about the rhyming of Troon and spoon.

Irrespective of his taste in cutlery, Dr Russell's accent was perfect for reading poetry and it was a revelation to Liam that the words of Geoffrey Chaucer, which appeared to be impenetrable on the page, came to life and were full of meaning when read aloud. Liam could quite happily have listened to him for hours. It also gave him a break from making notes and a chance to sneak glances at the other students in the group.

One lad, who Liam thought was called Ashok, seemed to be very serious. He was dressed smartly in a neatly pressed jacket and a shirt buttoned up to the neck. From where he was sitting, Liam could see that he was filling page after page of his notebook with very thorough notes in small but immaculate writing. He made a mental note that this could be someone worth knowing because anything he might have missed, Ashok was extremely likely to have written it down.

By contrast, Rod sat in the corner, slouched in his chair and, as far as Liam could see, made virtually no notes at all. His hair was bleached white and cropped close to his scalp, and his lower lip was pierced, which Liam, who had rarely encountered such things in real life, thought couldn't possibly be comfortable. He looked like the sort of person who would wear sunglasses at night (in fact, it turned out later that he did). He only appeared to have two facial expressions, bored or slightly mocking, but when he spoke, in an accent Liam found out was from Northern Ireland, his observations, although presented in a rather argumentative way, were acute and gained Dr Russell's approval.

Of the two girls in the group, Christine was the more talkative, although most of her thoughts seemed to be simply agreeing with everything the tutor had just said. She had a tendency to wear embroidered linen tops and long, flower-pattern skirts. Liam was fairly sure he had seen her at the Freshers' Fair enthusiastically signing up for the Folk Music Society.

The other girl had introduced herself in the first seminar as Becky, but Dr Russell preferred to call her by her full name, almost certainly so that he could roll the r at the start of Rrrebecca. She was quieter than Christine, but when she spoke, she clearly knew what she was talking about. She favoured a faded denim jacket, T-shirt and jeans and loosely tied her long, dark hair with a patterned scarf. She smiled easily and even laughed once or twice at things Liam said. He was, of course, immediately smitten.

The trouble was that even if he had the courage to ask her out, which he very definitely didn't, there was no time. Dr Russell's office was only a short distance from the stairs which led to the arts building's entrance, so there was only time for a brief conversation before they all went their separate ways. Any conversation tended to relate to the seminar they had just had and was usually dominated by Rod, who took the opportunity to sneer.

"Christ, that man likes the sound of his own voice, doesn't he?" he said after one session. "I thought it was supposed to be a seminar, not a lecture."

"You managed to say plenty," Christine said, though she had said a fair bit herself.

"It's meant to be English literature anyway, not Scottish," Rod argued. "But he's all 'Och, not the Loch, Doc.' Gets on my tits."

"That didn't sound a bit like him," Becky said.

"Yeah, well, that's because I'm a Mick, not a Jock."

Liam was about to say something witty about an Irishman doing a Scottish accent in Wales, but before he had a chance, they reached the main door.

"See yez," Rod said. "I'm off to the bar. Anyone coming?"

Nobody was. Liam had to get to a drama lecture, and when he looked around, Becky was already heading off up the road. *Next time*, he thought as he watched her until she had turned the corner and disappeared from view, knowing full well that next time, exactly the same thing would happen again and, in all likelihood, every time after that.

He had spent too much of his teenage years concentrating on his studies to get to uni and far too little time on his social life. He barely knew how to talk to girls, let alone ask one out. It was obvious that the deeper meaning of *The Pardoner's Tale* wasn't the only thing he had to learn.

Chapter Ten

Andy was working from home and had just signed off from one of those interminable Zoom meetings that could have been dealt with in one very short email, when his mobile started ringing. At least, he thought it was his mobile, even though it wasn't his usual ringtone. Normally, his phone rang with the intro to *Sweet Child of Mine* and had done ever since he found out (probably years after everyone else did) that you could set it to anything you wanted. Despite the fact that he could have changed it to a different song every week if he wanted, he'd never bothered. It was yet another thing he was happy to leave to the young ones.

He would have preferred to leave Zoom calls to the younger generation, but it was just one more thing that Covid had altered, probably forever.

Before the lockdown, he would never have considered doing a day's work in anything other than a suit and tie. Every morning's routine consisted of a shower and a shave before anything else (Sundays were the exception) and being able to work while dressed in a T-shirt and jogging trousers was a bit of a shock to the system. To go without shaving for several days until Alison made remarks about how scratchy his face was felt rebellious and wrong, but he was managing to adjust to it just the same.

He carried on his business through phone calls and emails, and nobody had the faintest idea what he looked like on the other end. Then somebody somewhere decided that video calling was the way to go, and everything changed again. He had to go back to shaving every day and dressing in a clean, pressed shirt (he drew the line at a tie) because although most matters could have been settled in easier ways, it was now vital that clients and colleagues alike could see his face and he needed to look presentable. This practice had continued after the lockdowns ended and he had to get used to dressing for the office whether he was in it or not.

The biggest problem with video calling was that some of the clients who insisted on them had no idea how to do it properly, so far too much of Andy's day was wasted either talking to a blank screen or watching someone mouth words while making no sound. The meeting he had just finished was one such meeting with an elderly client with the wonderful name of Enid Plantagenet, who had achieved the combination of sound and vision perfectly, provided that perfectly meant a view of her ceiling for some reason. Andy spent the meeting trying to decide whether the stain on the artex was a map of Guernsey or a very bad picture of John Major. He had explained to Mrs Plantagenet three times that her claim couldn't be processed until she had filled the whole form in, not just the bits she liked, and the meeting had over-run considerably.

His next one was due and somewhere his mobile rang like a robot gargling and he didn't know where it was. He searched for it in the way that Alison always called 'typical man', which involved standing in the middle of the room and looking right and left, waiting until he remembered where he had left the phone or the damn thing made itself visible. On this occasion, it actually worked. He remembered the invoices he was looking at the last time he used his phone and sure enough, the noise was coming from underneath the stack of paperwork.

Predictably, by the time he retrieved it, the ringing had stopped. He looked at the screen and saw that someone had been trying to call him via Messenger, which was unusual because hardly anyone ever did that. What was even more unusual was that the person who called him was Becky Smart. He sat back in the office chair he had ordered at the start of lockdown and spent two full days translating the instructions and assembling.

He stared at the screen of his phone. His finger hovered over the 'call back' icon twice before he had the courage to tap it. The image on the screen flashed for what seemed like minutes but was really only seconds, and then a very familiar voice said, "Hello?"

"Becky? It's Andy." There was a pause, so Andy filled it. "Andy McGovern?"

"Who? Oh. Oh God, *Andy*! Wow!"

"You sound surprised."

"I am. I mean...I saw the name but didn't click."

"But you rang me."

"No, I didn't. I was going to message you, but I didn't...Oh, wait. That wasn't me."

"Sorry. What?"

"I had my phone in my back pocket. My bum rang you."

Andy breathed out and then took a swig from the water bottle on his desk.

"Well, I wasn't really expecting to hear that after all this time," he said. Becky laughed on the other end of the phone, and it was as if the years had fallen away.

"Okay. I'm a bit embarrassed now," Becky said. "Seriously though, I was thinking of messaging you. That's why the page was open, but the cat needed to be let out. How are you? It's been a long time. I couldn't believe it when I got a friend request from you. I didn't even know you were on Facebook."

"I'm not much. Just now and again."

"Me too. Hey, you'll never guess what. I got a friend request from Liam Rawlinson, too. Do you remember him?"

"Liam who? No, I'm kidding. We're mates. I see a fair bit of him. To be honest, Becks, we both wanted to try and get in touch with you because of...well, you know..."

"Mike?"

"Yes, Mike."

Alison chose just that moment to open the door, peer in and, seeing that Andy was on the phone, offer him a cup of coffee through the medium of mime. Andy mimed back that a cup of coffee would be lovely by blowing her a kiss, and she withdrew.

49

"We were really sorry to hear about Mike," he said. "I'm sorry we didn't know."

"Thanks, Andy. I nearly tried to get in touch with you, but I just got busy with everything, and time went and it just got a bit harder to know what to say. Sorry, I should have tried harder."

"I should have tried to stay in touch. It's just...life and shit. You know?"

"Okay, let's stop apologising. It's no one's fault."

"I'll go for that."

Alison returned with a mug of coffee and put it on the desk. She caught something on his face, frowned and mouthed *You okay?* He smiled and nodded, then mouthed *Thank you* in return. Satisfied, Alison left the room again, quietly closing the door behind her.

"So what happened?" he asked. "I mean, you don't have to tell me if you don't want to."

"It's all right. I did all my screaming six months ago. There's not loads to tell. He got cancer and he died. I went to pieces for a bit, but only a bit, then came back again." Even over the phone, Andy could hear a sadness in her voice that said she hadn't come back, not fully.

"I'm so sorry," he said. "We should have been there for you."

"How could you if you didn't know? It was a really shit time, but life goes on. It's got to. So anyway, what about you? How are you?"

"I'm good, thanks. Working in insurance of all things."

"That's very respectable for you."

"Yes, it's not exactly rock'n'roll, is it?"

"You never were. Married? Kids?"

"Yes and two. Seventeen-year-old son and sixteen-year-old daughter. Stevie and Amy."

"They're *how* old? Shit, where's that gone?"

"I know! What about you? Did you and Mike...?"

"No. We didn't. Never seemed to happen and I'm quite glad now. We've had a succession of cats, though. And a dog, but the dog was more Mike's than mine. He died a month before Mike, which was sad. I don't think it helped, either. But I've always been a mad cat lady. Marvin is the third. So how's Liam? What's he up to?"

"He's fine. He's divorced. He's got two daughters and they're older than mine, in their twenties somewhere. He's got his own business on Anglesey. He's an electrician."

"An electrician? How did that happen?"

"There's a story there. I'm sure he'll tell you all about it."

Andy suddenly noticed that a Zoom call was calling him on his laptop. He had forgotten all about it.

"I'm sorry, Becks. I've got to go. It's work. Can we keep in touch, though? There's something Liam and I were thinking about."

"You think I'm going to let you go now? No chance. I'll message you my number. Now go on, back to work. Tell Liam I said hi and give him my number, too."

Before he had a chance to reply, she had gone. He drank some of his coffee and then dragged himself back into the real world to join the Zoom call, but his head was still full of Becky's words.

You think I'm going to let you go now?

Chapter Eleven

"Liam? Hi. Have you got a minute?"

"Yes, just a sec...Right. With you now. I was just parking up."

"Sorry, are you on a job?"

"No, it's fine. I've just been out to get some lunch. I'm at my unit. I'm supposed to be doing paperwork today, but I keep looking at it and thinking 'fuck it'."

"Are you okay? You sound out of breath."

"Just walking to the unit."

"It can't be that far."

"It is when you're as fit as me."

"Get your lunch from somewhere other than Maccies, then."

"I don't go there all the time!"

"You go there so often they're going to invite you to the staff Christmas party one year."

"Cheers, mate. As it happens, I haven't been there today. I've been to the Spar and bought some proper food."

"Such as?"

"A Pot Noodle and a bag of Space Raiders."

"Pot Noodles aren't proper food!"

"You've got to cook them. Sort of."

"Just as well you're on your own in the unit today and not mixing with people."

"Look, was there a reason you rang, Andy? Apart from slagging off my lunch?"

"Yes, there was as it goes. Guess who rang me yesterday?"

"No idea."

"Guess."

"I don't know. Paul Daniels?"

"Paul Daniels? I thought he was dead."

"Oh, yeah, he is. Who was I thinking of then?"

"Of all the random people you could think of, you come up with Paul Daniels?"

"I was looking at my Space Raiders. It's something about the face."

"It's not Paul Daniels."

"You're going to have to tell me then."

"Becky."

"You still there, Liam?"

"Yes, just needed to sit down. Becky rang you?"

"Well, she sort of didn't mean to. Her arse rang me."

"Sorry, what? I thought you said..."

"She did that phone in the pocket thing. I thought I should tell you, though, because you always liked—"

"Yes, okay, Andy. That's enough of that. How is she? What did she say? Did she sound different?"

"She sounded exactly the same. It was weird, really. She's okay under the circumstances, I think. She sounds like she's had a bit of a rough time."

"I think your husband dying qualifies as a rough time."

"That came out wrong. I think she's doing all right, but she's hardly going to tell me everything when I've only just got in touch out of nowhere, is she?"

"Point. I didn't really think she would, you know?"

"I don't think I did either. She asked after you."

"Did she? What did you say?"

"I told her that you were a sad divorcee and a diet of shit food has meant that you can hardly get out of your van without help and you can't do any jobs that need you to squeeze into tight spaces."

"Bastard. Just because you've always been able to eat what you want and look like a good meal would kill you. I've got a slow metabolism, that's all. Anyway, you didn't tell her that, did you?"

"No, of course I didn't bloody tell her that. If she meets you, she'll be able to see it for herself. I said you were fine. I've got her mobile number. I'll text it to you—she said I could."

"Thanks, mate. I might give her a ring."

"I think she'd appreciate it."

"Did you ask her about the challenge thing?"

"Didn't get a chance. It was only a short call. Why don't we see if we can all meet up? I don't even know where she lives now."

"I suppose we could ask. She can only say no."

"Oh, she's got a cat. She always did love cats, didn't she? Remember Raymond?"

"Oh bloody hell. Raymond! I'd forgotten about him!"

Chapter Twelve
1985

Raymond shot out of the door as soon as Becky opened it and nearly collided with Liam's leg. Raymond was a large ginger and white cat who lived with Becky and Jo sometimes. He also lived in several other houses. He didn't seem to be owned by anyone in particular but had a tendency to move in and stay for a bit if you fed him. He looked and moved like a bruiser but was one of the daftest cats Liam had ever come across. Apparently, he slept on a blanket on top of Becky's wardrobe when he felt like it, and she said that sometimes, when she turned the light off, she could feel his weight land on the end of the bed, but he was never there in the morning.

Liam thought sometimes that he might like a pet, but they weren't allowed in halls, of course. Becky was unusual for a first-year in that she lived in a house rather than halls. Jo's dad was loaded and had bought a house for his daughter as an investment so she wouldn't have to live in halls while she was in Bangor. Becky, who had left it too late to get a place in halls, had answered an advert and now she and Jo were best friends. Because it was a house and so not bound by the rules and regulations of halls, it had become the place where they all dropped around and often went back to for chips and coffee after a night at the Students' Union.

"Come in," Becky said. "I'll get the kettle on. It looks freezing out there."

"It is," Liam agreed. "Look like it might snow."

"Ooh. A white Christmas. That would be lovely."

"I don't fancy getting stranded here, though. I'm supposed to be going home on Tuesday."

"I'm going Monday. My mum's coming to pick me up. I've told her I could get the train, but she still thinks I'm bloody twelve or something." She spooned coffee into a mug and opened the fridge. "You do take milk, don't you?"

"Every time, Becks! You ask me every time. No, thanks. Just black."

Becky laughed, but Liam felt secretly slightly hurt. He'd been calling around for months now, sometimes with Andy or Mike, sometimes on his own, and still, Becky didn't know how he took his coffee. It was like she didn't notice him at all, and he wondered if she minded him calling unannounced.

"You guys going down the Union tonight?" Becky asked.

"I don't know. Anything on?"

"Don't think so. Not with the Christmas party tomorrow."

"I'll probably save myself for that. I've got an essay to finish for history anyway."

"When's it due?"

"January, but I don't want to be doing it over Christmas. So who's going? Tonight, I mean."

"Not sure. Mike, I think."

"Andy?"

"Don't think so. He said he'd think about it, but that usually means no."

"I'll see. I don't know what Jo's doing and I really do need to get that essay done."

Liam finished his coffee and left soon after. Outside, the sky was grey and heavy, though there was still no sign of the snow. He buttoned his army greatcoat (an absolute bargain in the Oxfam shop) and headed back up Glanrafon Hill to his hall.

All the way there he wondered whether Becky would have changed her mind about going to the Union that night if Andy had been going. Not that Andy was interested. He kept going on about Angela off his course and was hoping the Christmas party might be a good time to make a move.

Liam didn't bother going to the Students Union that night. He stayed in and listened to The Smiths instead. There were some nights that called for 'How Soon Is Now'.

**

"Have you seen Andy?" Mike had to shout above the noise of the disco. 'Love and Pride' was blasting out and the crowd of drunken revellers kept shouting 'Get your boots on!' at the wrong time.

"Not for a bit," Liam shouted back. "He was in the Refectory for Mud, but I haven't seen him since." He gestured with his empty pint glass. "Having one?"

"Thanks, Wack. I'll try and find a seat."

Liam laughed and tried to pick his way through the throng to the bar. Mike must be pissed. He only ever called Liam 'Wack' when he was half-cut. He'd done it once, ages ago, and even though Liam had pointed out that nobody in Liverpool had called anyone Wack since 1964, and they probably didn't then, it had stuck, but only after a few pints. Liam sort of liked it, though. He'd never had a nickname before, apart from a few mean ones at school, and it felt like he really had friends now.

He wasn't really looking forward to going back home next week. He'd rather have stayed here, but the halls were only booked on a termly basis. Tomorrow or Monday, he'd have to put everything he wasn't taking with him in the cupboards because the rooms were sometimes used for conferences and the like during the holidays. It was a pain in the arse, but the rules were the rules.

He eventually managed to get served and went to look for Mike, carrying the pints precariously through the crowd. He spotted his friend in a corner of the raised seating area talking to Rod, who had a couple of the local goth girls in tow. Liam wasn't sure of their names but thought one might be called Rhian. At the next table and deep in conversation were Claire and the two Donnas, a trio who had met in Freshers' Week and went everywhere together like conjoined triplets if you could get such a thing. Rod had once tried to give Claire the nickname of 'Batman' ("You know, like Donna Donna Donna Donna Batman!"), but it hadn't stuck. Liam quite liked Claire and the Donnas, but even after a term, he wasn't sure what he thought about Rod. He was a smartarse in seminars and always turned up to the Union drunk or high and took great delight in putting as many people down as he possibly could. He did it with great wit and could be really funny if it wasn't you on the other end of it, but his presence tended to dominate, and Liam didn't find that comfortable. He squeezed past Rod, who didn't seem to notice him until he put the pint down in front of Mike.

"Where's mine?" he demanded.

"Sorry, Rod. Didn't know you were here," Liam said, though he wasn't really sure why he was apologising. Rod laughed and turned back to the goth girls. Mike pushed a stool he had been guarding toward Liam.

"Andy's up on the third floor," Mike said. "Claire saw him up there."

"What's on up there?"

"Some band. Perfect Crime, I think they're called."

While Liam and Mike preferred to see bands they knew or had at least heard of, Andy tried to get to see pretty much every band that came to the Union, even the ones who played in the small bar on the third floor who nobody had ever heard of and who, in all likelihood, would never be heard of again. He was, by his own admission, paranoid about missing the next big thing and had been ever since some third year he'd got talking to told him that a couple of years earlier, this band he'd vaguely heard of were playing on the third floor. He couldn't be bothered going up there and had missed the only chance he was likely to get to see The Smiths play live. It was a bit unlikely that the meteoric success of Morrissey and the lads would happen again, but it wasn't impossible, and Andy didn't want to miss it.

The music from the disco was too loud to hold a normal conversation (not that it stopped Rod trying), so Liam sipped his pint and looked around the sea of faces to see if he could see Becky and Jo. Jo was usually easier to spot in a crowd because she was tall and red-haired, but at the moment, Liam couldn't see either of them and felt a pang of disappointment.

Everyone went to the Christmas party, so they must be here somewhere. He decided to have this pint and then go and look for them. Before he had a chance to, Andy appeared, looking flushed, with sweat plastering his dark hair to his forehead, raving about the band he'd just seen. He was also able to supply the essential information that while he was up there, he'd seen Becky and Jo. Liam didn't want to seem too keen, so he waited a few minutes, then drained his pint and said he had to go to the toilet.

When he left the bar, he bypassed the toilets and went up the two flights of stairs to the third floor. He was about the only person going up because now the band had finished, most people were coming down and he kept having to stop to let them go by. By the time he got to the third-floor bar, it had mostly emptied out apart from a few stragglers, and a couple of members of the stage crew, who were helping the band sort their equipment out. Jo was at the bar with Becky. She was sitting in the corner, staring at the floor. Even in the semi-darkness of the bar, Liam could see she was crying.

"Are you okay, Becks?" he asked, going over and sitting next to her. "What's up?"

"Fucking Paul!" Becky wailed and Liam's heart sank.

"Who's Paul?" he asked.

"Paul on my course. You know—*Paul*!"

"What's he done?"

"I saw him. He was right over there," she waved a hand vaguely towards the stage, "and I saw him. He was sticking his tongue down some girl's throat. Bastard." She sniffed long and loud. Liam put his arm around her, something he would have preferred to have done under other circumstances. She buried her face in his shoulder and snuffled wetly.

"He's a dickhead," he said.

"I thought he liked me," Becky replied, her voice muffled by Liam's jacket.

"He doesn't deserve you."

Becky lifted her head and had a go at a smile. "I must look a right state."

"You look like a panda. You don't really. You look fine."

"Thanks, Liam. You're a good friend. Wish I could fancy someone nice like you."

You could, Liam thought, but said nothing. Just then, Jo came over from the bar, bearing two elaborate-looking cocktails, one of which she put down in front of Becky.

"It's another tequila sunrise," she said. "I think you need it."

Becky moved away from Liam, pulled the straw out of her cocktail and drank greedily from the glass.

"You go back down, Liam," she said. "I'll just have some of this and sort my face out, and we'll be down."

"If you're sure."

Reluctantly, Liam left them and made his way back down to the bar. Everywhere he looked, there were couples snogging as the Christmas spirit smashed down barriers of inhibition. Liam couldn't help but wonder if this Paul was one of them and wished he knew what the wanker looked like so he could...do nothing, probably.

Down in the main bar, the festivities had been cranked up a notch. The DJ had put on 'I'm Your Man' by Wham, and Mike was down on the dancefloor with at least one of the Donnas and possibly Claire too. On the raised area, Rod was standing on a stool, beating a tin ashtray like it was a tambourine.

"Look at her!" he shouted to no one in particular, pointing to some girl on the dancefloor below. "She's a fucking spanner. My nuts are tightening looking at her!" Then he fell off the stool and dragged a table full of glasses over as he went.

For many years, Liam would remember his first Christmas party as a student. It was the night Rod acquired the nickname of Spanner that would follow him for the rest of his student days and beyond. And it was the night Becky broke Liam's heart for the first, but not the last time.

Chapter Thirteen

Liam dried himself after his shower and decided he was probably due a shave. He was booked in to install a ceiling light fitting in Benllech that morning, and if the address was where he thought it was, it was quite a nice area, so he didn't want to turn up looking like a scruff.

He wiped the steam off the bathroom mirror, took a new razor out of the packet and lathered his face. As he shaved, he examined his face, something he usually preferred not to do. He was sure there were more lines on it than the last time he looked. He wasn't perhaps as lined as some guys his age, but all the same, his face was starting to show its age. Inevitable really.

At least he was lucky still to have his hair. He'd always had thick hair, got it from his mother, and he remembered how annoying it had been when he left home and wanted to do the student thing of letting his hair grow long, but couldn't because his hair just seemed to grow outwards instead and looked like a mop. These days, his once thick hair was considerably thinner on top, and he wished he had appreciated it when he could.

His only other act of rebellion was to grow a beard and moustache for a bit, but it got itchy, so he shaved the beard off. The first time he went into the communal kitchen with just the moustache, someone had shouted, "Christ, it's Ian Botham!" so the moustache went too. While he was married to Nic, he shaved every day because she would remark upon it if he didn't. It was usually subtle, but a remark was a remark and made its point. Now, he shaved when he felt like it. Did that qualify as 'letting himself go'? He wasn't sure and didn't really care.

As he shaved his neck, he felt a sudden sting and blood started to mix with the soap suds, first turning them pink, then red. He swore and rinsed the soap off to see what he had done. He had somehow nicked a mole on the side of his neck and a thin rivulet of blood was trickling down onto his collarbone. He grabbed a handful of toilet paper and pressed it to the cut, which generally did the trick, while he finished shaving the rest of his face. When he took the paper away and looked at it, there was a deep red stain, and the cut was still bleeding. He disposed of the paper, got some more, held it tight against his neck, and went into the bedroom to consider getting dressed. He sat on the end of his bed for a bit to give the cut a chance to stop bleeding so he wouldn't get blood on his shirt collar and as he did so, a thought made his stomach turn over. Had that mole always been there? He'd certainly never cut it before as far as he knew, but if it had always been there, why was this the first time he had caught it? It could simply be luck, of course, or...

It had been quite a decent summer this year and he'd picked up a few outside jobs while people took advantage of the good weather to have patio lighting fitted or, in one case, a socket in the garage so they could plug in the pump for a water feature. Although Liam had never really been one for sunbathing (he tended to go from white to red and back again without the attractive brown in between), this work had meant he was out in the sun a bit more than usual. He hadn't bothered with sunscreen, hadn't even thought about it, and didn't really read the dire warnings in the newspapers because they were aimed at the real sun-worshippers, weren't they?

At any other time, he wouldn't have given it a second thought, but now, as he looked at the mole in the bedroom mirror, it made him nervous. It was red and inflamed, which you'd expect from being hacked with a Gillette twin-blade, but as he ran a finger over it, he wondered if it had always been slightly raised like that and he had never noticed or if this was something new.

He put his shirt on and then did something he very rarely did. He phoned his GP's surgery and made an appointment.

***

Liam rarely went to his GP. Considering his general fitness, he wasn't often ill, apart from the usual colds and the like, for which he took over-the-counter remedies and got on with his life. He didn't like going to the doctor's, mainly because he didn't like his GP much. Dr Ehlers was not well-liked in the area and most people preferred to see one of the other doctors in the practice, even if sometimes that meant seeing a locum. Dr Ehlers was a very large man, tall and broad and with a booming voice which was instantly recognisable when your name was called over the waiting room tannoy. Even if patients didn't recognise the volume of the voice, they would certainly have recognised the GP's German accent. It was not Dr Ehlers' size or his voice that Liam didn't like, and it certainly wasn't his nationality, but the fact that his manner could be both blunt and patronising at the same time, which was a very difficult trick to pull off. Liam knew, for example, that he needed to lose some weight, and he knew that smoking wasn't very good for him (although he had cut down over the years), so he didn't need telling every time he attended the surgery, regardless of his reason for being there. He thought that if he turned up to see Dr Ehlers with an axe embedded in his head, he'd be told it was because he was an overweight smoker. Predictably, when he sat down in Dr Ehlers' room, the first thing the good doctor said was that he needed to cut down on his eating and his smoking and that was even before he had asked what was wrong. When he finally got to the point of the visit, he pulled down his shirt collar to reveal the mole, which had now stopped bleeding but was sore where his collar had rubbed it.

"It's this, Doctor," he said. "It's probably nothing, but I just thought I'd get it checked out."

"I think I'll be the judge of that," Dr Ehlers said, sounding mildly affronted that Liam had dared to have an unqualified opinion. He hauled himself out of his chair and loomed over Liam in much the same way as the iceberg must have loomed over the Titanic.

"Is it new?" he asked.

"I'm not sure," Liam replied.

"But it is on *your* neck! Have you not noticed it before?"

"I really can't say. Sorry. I don't remember noticing it before, but then I don't remember not noticing it either." Aware that he had started to babble, Liam shut up and turned his head as the Doctor's huge face drew close to his neck. Whatever aftershave Dr Ehlers was wearing, it definitely wasn't going to be on Liam's Christmas list.

"It's sore, yes?"

"Only because I caught it with the razor. It wasn't before."

Dr Ehlers lumbered over to his desk, sat down and made some notes on his computer. Then he turned back to Liam and peered at him over his glasses. Liam braced himself.

"I don't think it is anything to worry about," he said. "It was as well to get it checked but it doesn't look like anything sinister. I can remove it if you wish, but that is up to you."

"Remove it? How?"

"I burn it off. Don't look so alarmed! It is a very simple procedure. It will take seconds and you won't feel a thing."

Liam thought for a second, but then remembered how he had felt when he saw the mole that morning and wanted rid.

"Please," he said. "Do I need to make another appointment?"

"No, I will do it now."

Dr Ehlers went over to a cabinet in the corner of the room and came back with a device that looked a bit like a disposable e-cigarette. He tilted Liam's head so that he was looking away, which he was glad about and then wiped something cold on Liam's neck. He was right; Liam felt absolutely nothing except something touching his neck. The only reason he knew anything had happened was the giveaway smell of burning hair, which he recognised from the occasions when he got a bit too close to a gas burner if he'd lost his lighter and needed to spark up a ciggie in a hurry.

"That's it," Dr Ehlers said, straightening up. He was holding a bunched-up tissue in his hand. "I'll send this off to the lab, just in case, but you shouldn't worry too much." He took a plastic envelope from his desk and pushed the tissue inside. "If there is anything, we will ring you, but I do not believe it is a malignant mole," he pronounced, giving Liam a vision of a somewhat dark *Wind in the Willows*.

"Thank you, Doctor," Liam said, standing up. "That makes me feel better."

"Good!" Dr Ehlers boomed. "And Mr Rawlinson, don't forget now. Get some of that weight off and give up the cigarettes if you want to live to be a hundred!"

Liam thanked the GP again and got out of the surgery as quickly as he could. Once he was safely back in his van, he took a battered packet of cigarettes out of the glove compartment, lit one and inhaled deeply. The relief he felt was profound. Ehlers had sounded very sure that there was nothing to worry about and Liam was determined that he wasn't going to dwell on the fact that the mole had gone off to a laboratory somewhere 'just in case', and he certainly wasn't going to live in fear of getting a phone call to tell him that Moley was malignant after all. He'd done the right thing and got it checked, and that was that.

He finished his cigarette and started the van up. It was only three o'clock and he had probably better catch up on some paperwork before he could legitimately claim to have done a day's work.

As he drove back to the unit, he mulled over the parting shot Dr Ehlers had fired at him. When he thought about it, which he didn't do very often, he wasn't entirely sure if he wanted to live to be a hundred at all. He was aware that he occasionally forgot things (but didn't everybody?) and that sometimes his body let him down when he didn't expect it. Did he really want another thirty-odd years of that and worse? On the other hand, both his parents had just about made it into their seventies before heart attacks got them—seven years apart. Liam was built like his dad, and Stan had been a smoker too. If Liam followed suit and only had another thirteen or so years left, he'd probably better have a think about what he wanted to achieve before he went. He had never even considered the idea of a bucket list, but the news about Mike had put everything into perspective. How many years did Mike think he had left before he was given the diagnosis that told him he had far less than that? What had he hoped to do with his life but never got around to? These thoughts were a bit too depressing for Liam's liking, so he decided that there was only one thing to do. He'd knock off early and go home and get something to eat. Then he'd nip down to the Red Lion for a couple of pints and a game of pool and forget all about it.

Chapter Fourteen

"Hi, Andy."

"Oh, all right, Liam?"

"Sorry. Is this a bad time? Can you talk?"

"Hang on. I'll go in the other room."

"Right. I'm here."

"I can call back if..."

"No, you're all right. I'm glad to be out of it if I'm honest."

"Trouble?"

"How did you do it, Liam? How did you manage to cope with two teenage girls?"

"I let Nic sort it out, mainly."

"Remind me why you're divorced again? Alison does the whole 'Tell her, Andy' thing and doesn't give me any choice."

"What's Amy done now?"

"Came home with her new boyfriend last night and wanted to take him up to her room. Alison said no, so she flounced out and didn't get back 'til gone one o'clock. I virtually had to physically restrain Ali from calling the police twice."

"Shit. Here we go, Andy. You've got lots more of this to look forward to. What's he like, this boyfriend?"

"He's called Jackson, which says it all. Luckily, it's spelt with a ck, not an x, or I'd have had to kill him on the spot. He's got that bloody hair like they've all got and dresses in The North Face and trainers I don't understand. Stinks of blueberry vape. He's a scrote, basically."

"He sounds lovely. When's the wedding?"

"It's no joke, mate. He's got one of those faces you'd never get tired of slapping and it makes me feel dead old. I don't get why these kids all go round looking exactly the same. Remember when we were kids, and it was all our mums could do to make us wear a coat and a scarf? Now, these kids all go out in what are basically anoraks and balaclavas. They look like our mums have dressed them and think they look hard. I don't get it."

"That's kids for you. If it helps, give it a month or two, and Amy will be crying in her room, and you can say, 'I told you so'."

"That's just it, though. I don't want to say, 'I told you so'. I don't want it to happen in the first place."

"Except it doesn't work like that. As far as I can see, the only way not to worry about your kids is not to have kids."

"I don't want to sound like all those old fellas, but I'm sure we weren't like that at Amy's age. It feels a lot more dangerous out there, like these kids don't have any fear or respect."

"It's not all of them, Andy. Same as any generation. It's always been like that. Teds, Mods, Punks, Skinheads..."

"I know that. We used to go round Bangor getting up to all sorts, pissed out of our heads a lot of the time, but I don't remember feeling unsafe. There were fights and that, especially if Spanner was around, but no one really got hurt. Nobody went out for the night tooled up like they do now."

"It wasn't all a laugh. Remember when Shaun Cripps got his head kicked in by the locals? They put him in intensive care."

"Yes, but to be fair, Shaun Cripps was a racist Tory dickhead who went round slagging the Welsh off in their own country. He kind of had it coming, really."

"There is that."

"It felt safer, though. We had a laugh. It was all harmless enough."

"I wonder if our parents thought that? Not sure mine did. There was one time...God, it sounds like so long ago, but you remember the pay phones in halls? You used to have to queue up to phone home, like they do in prison. I used to phone them once a week or so, and my dad would always pick up but then hand me straight over to my mum, apart from this one time. He answered the phone and when he heard it was me, he just went 'Oh' and then paused. Then he said, 'You know you forgot your mother's birthday?' I was fucking mortified. I mean, I knew when her birthday was, but I'd lost track of what date it was. Too busy having a good time, I guess. Took them a while to stop reminding me about that."

"That's what I mean, though. If that was the worst you did, they were lucky. I worry myself sick every time Amy goes out with her mates and she's a good kid, you know? She's sensible and so are her mates. They don't go to pubs or hang round in the park with a bottle of whatever they drink."

"Woodpecker cider in our day, wasn't it?"

"Or Kestrel lager. That was always what was left at parties, wasn't it? You'd bring the cheap stuff so you'd look like you'd brought something, then drink the better stuff. Amy doesn't do anything like that. Not yet anyway. Doesn't stop me worrying, though. You read so many stories in the papers about kids getting their drinks spiked or taking all kinds of shit and ending up in hospital."

"Mine turned out okay. They got pissed a couple of times, but nothing mad. The papers don't report on kids like them. Amy will be fine, mate. You and Ali have done a great job with her. You need to let her make a few mistakes, or she won't learn."

"I haven't ever worried like this about Stevie. And it's not just because he's a lad. So far, touch wood, he keeps his head down and gets on with his schoolwork. He's hell-bent on getting into uni and isn't really interested in much else. Nearest he gets to trouble is when him and his mates are shooting people on their computers."

"Tell you what, you couldn't have said things like that back at Bangor. You'd have been called a sexist and kicked out of the Union."

"I wouldn't have said anything like that then. We were all dead politically aware, weren't we? Boycotting Barclays Bank over apartheid, even though we didn't really know why. Remember that pathetic strike over student grants?"

"Oh bloody hell, yes! There was supposed to be a mass sit-in in the lecture theatres, but nobody bothered. Ended up as a handful of people on the picket line, you and -what was his name? -Tony Owen oh, and Irish Barney. And wasn't that girl there? Colette someone?"

"Hunt. She was at everything. You got your photograph on the front of the student newspaper, and they made it look like the demo was a massive success, even though they cut out all the students who were walking past and ignoring us. We thought we were great, like we were Arthur Scargill or something. Thought we were going to change the bloody world."

"We never did, though, did we?"

"Nah. The world changed all by itself."

Chapter Fifteen
1986

Liam gritted his teeth as the minibus hit another pothole and hoped that nothing would fall off before they got to Colwyn Bay. Not for the first time, he wondered if this maybe wasn't his brightest idea.

He had forgotten that he had signed up for the Anti-Bloodsports League at the Freshers' Fair. It was four months ago, after all, and he'd signed up for a lot of things that he hadn't bothered following up. He had never played squash or got involved in the try-outs for the University Challenge team (probably just as well because he would have been crap at both of them). When he had seen the ABL stand with its lurid photographs of foxes and hares, he had put his name down, partly because it seemed a very studenty thing to do and partly because he did love animals and was genuinely opposed to hunting for fun. The fact that a very pretty girl was also putting her name down might have had something to do with it. He hadn't seen the girl again and hadn't heard anything from the ABL until he'd been back for a few days after the Christmas holidays.

The Christmas break had been a strange few weeks. He was pleased to see his parents and hadn't realised how much he had missed them until he saw them. His mum had fussed over him and fed him enough to keep him going for the next term and his dad even managed to hold a few conversations with him. He met up with some of his school friends for a drink a couple of times, but somehow, it wasn't the same as the long, late-night conversations he had with his new friends at Bangor. He rang Mike twice and Andy once and it sounded like they were feeling much the same. They vaguely discussed meeting up in one of their hometowns, but it didn't happen. The holidays were quickly over and they were back in their adopted city again.

It might have been because he had missed student life, but when a member of the ABL knocked on the door of his room and invited him to come along to a demonstration in Colwyn Bay the following weekend, he agreed.

It was only as the day drew closer did he start to have reservations. He hadn't been involved in a demonstration of any kind before. Sure, he had strong political beliefs (left of centre, of course) and was happy to expand upon them at many a drinking session, but taking action was quite a different thing and he hoped there wasn't going to be any trouble. His parents had brought him up to be a law-abiding citizen and he had only ever been spoken to by a police officer once in his life and that was for cycling on the pavement. He had no intention of starting now, no matter how worthy the cause.

The sight that greeted him when he arrived at the meeting place in the Union car park did nothing to allay his fears. He spotted the lad who had knocked on his door straight away, but even if he hadn't, he would have recognised the ABL immediately. They looked like someone had gathered together a bunch of tramps and turned them into a paramilitary organisation. They all had semi-shaved heads or dreadlocks (even though they were all white) and seemed to have come in a uniform of combat jackets and camouflaged cargo pants. The only thing that wasn't uniform was the array of different hair colours, none of which, he guessed, the owners had been born with.

Liam was wearing his greatcoat, his favourite New Model Army T-shirt and jeans. He had thought he looked rebellious when he left his room but now felt rather overdressed.

They were all gathered around a battered, dark-blue minibus that looked like it should be on a scrapheap, not a road. Nobody seemed to notice him much, so he spoke to the nearest person—a woman with pale-blue hair that was severely shaved at the side. Her ears were pierced with more studs than Liam had seen on one person and her combat jacket was ripped in several places, though the rips looked far too neat to have been an accident.

"I'm here for the demo," he said, trying to sound as nonchalant as he could.

"So are we," was the rather curt reply. "We're going in a minute."

That was apparently as much conversation as he was going to get because she turned away to roll a cigarette. Nobody else seemed to be in any hurry to speak to him, and he wondered if he should walk away. Before he could, one of the men opened the back door of the minibus and everyone started to climb in. Liam hesitated but then followed and wasn't at all surprised to find that there were no seats inside and everyone was sitting on the floor. He found a space and did his best to make himself comfortable. It wasn't easy. A couple of latecomers arrived, and Liam tried to shift along a bit to make space. At least these two looked a bit less scary than the rest; one was a lad who looked the polar opposite of the other protestors. In a neat jacket and trousers and very tidily brushed hair, he looked like he had been dressed by his mum for his first job interview. He avoided everyone's eyes and sat hunched up with the appearance of someone who had got into the wrong bus and now couldn't get off without embarrassing himself. The other newcomer was a girl Liam vaguely recognised from somewhere. She was dressed in a duffel coat, had blonde hair tied back in a ponytail and the most arresting green eyes he had ever seen. She gave him a tight smile, the sort that you give someone you think you should know but can't quite place but didn't speak. Suddenly, with an alarming roar, the bus started up and they were on their way.

There was no conversation during the forty minutes or so it took to get to Colwyn Bay, apart from the occasional obscenity from one or other of the occupants when the bus went over a rough patch of road and juddered as if it were about to fall apart. Someone in one of the front seats was smoking, and a sweet, cloying aroma filled the bus, which Liam was pretty sure didn't come from anything manufactured by Lambert &

Butler. He wished there was a window in the back he could open or that someone in the front would open one, but he didn't dare say. Instead, he spent the rest of the journey trying not to cough and occasionally trying, but failing, to catch the blonde girl's eye.

By the time the minibus stopped, Liam's throat was sore, he was stiff and possibly slightly high. He got out as soon as he could and stretched. It had been overcast in Bangor, but it was drizzling in Colwyn Bay as a sea mist drifted in.

It was quite obvious that this wasn't going to be a pleasant day by the seaside. He wasn't sure what he was supposed to do, so he followed the others to the high street, where a few ABL members had arrived early and set out a trestle table with banners and leaflets. He still wasn't sure what was expected of him, so he hung around until the blue-haired woman thrust a pile of leaflets at him and said, "Hand these out." He took them and went to stand near the stall, but she gave a very dramatic sigh.

"Not here! Go up the road a bit."

He trudged up the street as far as WH Smiths, feeling like the stupidest person alive.

It rapidly became clear that, whatever the ABL thought, Colwyn Bay was not a hotbed of animal rights activism. For the first half hour, he tried to be polite and asked passers-by politely if they would like a leaflet. Most either refused, ignored him, or reluctantly took a leaflet and tucked it in their pocket or the nearest bin without looking at it. Very few seemed eager to engage in conversation but instead hurried past to get out of the rain that was now beginning to get heavier. In a way, Liam was quite glad about that because he didn't really know what he was talking about and couldn't read the leaflet to find out because he was trying to keep them as dry as he could. The few people who did stop did so to argue, not agree. One middle-aged woman, dressed in tweed and quite possibly wasn't averse to riding with the hounds herself, nearly poked Liam in the eye with her umbrella, then snatched a leaflet out of his hand.

"This is disgusting!" she said.

"I know," Liam replied. "The poor foxes."

"Poor foxes nothing!" the woman snapped, crumpling the leaflet into a tight ball and handing it back. "This rubbish is disgusting. Do you have any idea what damage these vermin cause farmers? Well, do you?"

"There are humane ways," Liam replied, confident that he had read it somewhere. "They don't have to kill them for sport."

"You're a student, aren't you?" she asked. Liam had to agree that he was. "Well then, you want to educate yourself in the real world and bloody grow up!"

With that, she walked away, leaving Liam wondering what to do with a soggy, balled-up leaflet. He didn't want to be seen putting it in the bin, so he put it in his coat pocket to get rid of later.

After that, he stopped asking people if they would like a leaflet and merely held them out for the public to take. He stood there for the best part of an hour, feeling his jeans getting wetter and wetter. When an elderly man accused him of being anti-vivisection and actively committing murder by trying to deny sick people the drugs they need and then called him a hypocrite for wearing leather shoes (they weren't), he decided that enough was enough. He couldn't face going back to the stall and being labelled a quitter, so he posted the remaining leaflets in a bin and made his way to the train station.

As he sat on the platform waiting for the Bangor train, he had to admit that his first attempt at political activism hadn't been what you would call a success. Maybe he wasn't cut out for it and should stick to what he was good at, whatever that was. Drinking too much and talking crap about things he knew too little about, mainly. His jeans were sticking to his legs, and his coat felt (and smelled) damp. He couldn't wait to get back to his room, get changed and put the whole day behind him.

The train was pulling into the station when, out of the corner of his eye, he spotted the blonde girl from the minibus coming down the steps onto the platform. He didn't recognise her at first because the rain had made her hair a couple of shades darker, but it was definitely the same duffel coat. As the train drew to a stop, he moved down that platform so that when the doors opened, he was able to get into the same carriage. There were plenty of people on the train already and few seats available, so when he sat down opposite her, it looked like a pure accident. He pretended not to notice her at first, and she was either doing the same or really hadn't noticed him. In the end, he decided to speak first.

"Weren't you at that ABL thing?"

She looked up and realisation dawned on her face. "Oh, hi," she said. "So were you, weren't you?"

"Yes, I was. I'd had enough, though. Thought I'd get home out of the rain."

"Me too. Waste of time, really. No one wanted the leaflets. I don't think the ABL lot will notice."

"Bit up themselves, aren't they?"

"I thought they were bloody rude."

It was while they were talking that Liam realised where he had seen her before. He was sure she had been going into the drama studio with a different tutorial group.

"You do drama, don't you?"

"Yes, with history and linguistics. It's the drama I want to do, though. I'll probably drop the other two after this year. You're in Pam's group, aren't you? I wish I'd had her. Gareth's okay, but everyone says Pam's great."

"She's all right. Very interesting."

"What else are you doing?"

"English and media studies. I haven't decided what to do next year yet. I was thinking about joint honours English and drama, but I don't think I'm good enough. It was English I came here to do. I only did drama because I was in some school plays."

"It's probably just as well neither of us is doing politics, isn't it?"

Liam laughed and was pleased when she did too. It made her eyes sparkle.

76

"We'd have failed today, that's for sure," he said, and she laughed again. "I'm Liam, by the way."

"Pleased to meet you, Liam," she replied, reaching out a cold, slightly damp hand. "I'm Nicki, but most people call me Nic."

Chapter Sixteen

"Are you sure this is a good idea?"

It wasn't the first time Liam had asked that and Andy was starting to get a bit fed up with it. They'd only just hit the M56 and there were still about thirty miles to Knutsford, which wasn't a song anyone was likely to write. He'd picked Liam up at Chester station and was already regretting suggesting that it would make more sense to travel together than making their own way.

"What did you tell Alison?"

Andy sighed. He still felt bad about lying to his wife and didn't really want to admit to it.

"I told her I was seeing a client."

"Why?"

"I don't know, Liam. It just sort of came out. Then it was too late to take it back."

"Doesn't she know about Becky?"

"You're full of questions today, aren't you? Yes, Ali knows about Becky. She knows I've spoken to her. The first time, I mean. It was her idea, in fact. Look, we've got Amy still acting up and everything, so when Becks rang last week and suggested meeting up, Ali and Amy weren't speaking, and it just didn't seem the right time to mention it. I'll tell her later. I'll tell her I bumped into Becks by chance or something."

They drove on without speaking for a while, accompanied by Greatest Hits Radio, which Andy liked because at least they played music he knew, even if the adverts got on his nerves and they played the same ones over and over again. He'd already heard 'Baker Street' twice that day and had never been a big fan of Gerry Rafferty in the first place. It was only when 'Sometimes' by Erasure came on that Liam spoke again.

"Do you remember Jacko?"

"Bloody hell. Jacko. Wonder what happened to him?"

Andy had never known what Jacko's real name was. None of them did. He was called Jacko, apparently because his hairstyle once reminded someone of Jack Nance in *Eraserhead* and the name stuck. Most of the time, Jacko was a quiet, almost invisible character who seemed content to hide in the shadows at the Students' Union, occasionally making doom-laden pronouncements to anyone who got close enough to listen. He told Andy once that he was inventing his own language, and Andy believed him without question or surprise. The most notable thing about Jacko was his dancing. As soon as anything electronic with a good beat came on, especially if Vince Clarke was on keyboards, Jacko hit the dancefloor like a thing possessed. His timing was immaculate as he spun like a top, this way and that, with a look of intense concentration on his face. Everyone else on the dancefloor was content to give him space because he was that good. Then, as soon as the song was finished, he would fade into the shadows again.

"I wonder if he still does it," Liam said.

"Bet he does. I bet he looks like us now, but if Depeche Mode or someone comes on in the pub, he's up and away. I hope so. The only time he looked happy was when he was dancing."

They lapsed into silence again and before too long, Andy saw the first signs to Knutsford.

"Do you think we should have worn name badges or something?" Liam asked finally. Andy laughed.

"I think Becky will recognise us," he said. "We look exactly like we did back then, only older. Well, I do anyway."

"Thanks for that. You had hair then."

"I've got hair now."

"That's not hair. It's stubble."

"At least I'm honest about going bald. You think that if you don't get your hair cut, no one will notice you haven't got much on top. You're like a hippy monk."

In one of those strange moments of synchronicity, the DJ on the radio chose that exact moment to play 'Suedehead' by Morrissey and they were still laughing about it as they turned off the motorway towards Knutsford.

Once they reached the town, Andy pulled over to check the map on his phone. Alison had once suggested getting a SatNav, but Andy said that having one person in the car to tell him it was the wrong road just after he'd taken it was quite enough. Even using the map function on the phone was a recent innovation. If he and Ali were going somewhere new, he preferred to print off the instructions from an internet route finder and give them to his wife to navigate so that he could snap at her when she didn't tell him to turn off in time (so Ali said). If he was alone, he tried to memorise the route before he went. He had developed a habit of leaving early wherever he went to factor in the fact that, at some point, he usually took a wrong turn and got lost.

"It's Oakbridge Road," he said. "Number one. There it is. It's not far. Do us a favour, Liam? Get it up on your phone too, just in case."

He started the car up and ten minutes later (it would have been five, but a roundabout confused him), they turned into Oakbridge Road. Andy drew up outside number one and texted Becky to let her know they had arrived. She had suggested they pick her up from her house because the pub she thought they could go to was easier to find if she showed them. She suggested texting her when they got there, and she would come out. Andy thought at the time that this was a strange way of going about things. Was there some reason Becky didn't want them to enter her house? Was it to cut down the time she spent with them? If that was the case, why had she suggested they meet up at all? He decided it was best to take it at face value and not overthink it. He felt nervous enough about seeing Becky as it was, which was ridiculous since they had all spent so much time together in Bangor. That was a long time ago, though; they were all so much younger then and Mike was still alive.

She didn't keep them waiting long. No sooner had Andy sent the text than the front door opened and a woman came out. She was dressed in a knee-length, red wool coat rather than a denim jacket and her hair was shorter now, just about reaching her shoulders, where it once tumbled down her back when she let it loose. She had abandoned her glasses (presumably in favour of contacts), but there was no mistaking her. Andy got out of the car to meet her.

There was an awkward moment when neither of them seemed certain about whether to hug, shake hands or neither, but Becky made the decision and gave Andy a quick hug, then pulled back to look at him.

"Andy," she said. "It's really you."

"It really is. You look great, Becks."

"No, I don't. I look awful, but it's nice of you to say so."

She looked past Andy to Liam, who had lowered the car window.

"And Liam, too. This is so weird!"

"Hey, Becks," Liam said. "How are you doing?"

"I'm okay. But come on. Let's go to the pub. I could do with a drink."

Andy opened the rear door of the car, and she got in, putting a hand on Liam's shoulder as she did so. She directed Andy down a few roads and then pointed out the entrance to a pub car park. Andy parked and got out. The pub looked nice, not too upmarket, just a comfortable, family pub. Becky led them inside, where there was low music playing and a friendly server led them to a table by the window.

"Can I get anyone drinks?"

"Just a lemonade for me," Andy said. "Becks?"

"Could I have a white wine, please? Dry if possible."

"And I'll have a pint of lager, please," Liam added. The server smiled and trotted away. Liam looked at Becky and raised an eyebrow.

"Dry white wine?" he asked.

"Listen, we're in Cheshire now," Becky said. "It's Footballers' Wives country, this."

"What did bring you here?" Andy asked.

"My job, mainly. We were in Manchester, but a post came up round here and it was too good to resist. I'm a Deputy Headteacher, can you believe it?"

The server brought their drinks and promised to come back in a few minutes when they were ready to order food.

"Deputy Head?" Liam said. "I didn't see that coming. I know you wanted to go into teaching, but..."

"It wasn't my original plan, no, but if you want the pay, you've got to move up and take on all the paperwork that comes with it. Now, come on, let's look at the menus."

Like most people do, they spent the next few minutes discussing what looked good on the menu and weighing up what they wanted to order. Becky had a seafood allergy, which Andy either never knew or had developed sometime in the last thirty years, and ordered pasta, while Liam went straight for a burger. Andy usually went for fish and chips when he was out, but just in case the smell of fish put Becky off, he ordered a steak.

While they waited for the food, they talked about their jobs. Liam explained how he had drifted from job to job until his Uncle Billy, who had his own business as an electrician, had taken him under his wing and trained him. He had surprised himself, and Billy too, by taking to it straight away and loving it. He learned so much so quickly that when Billy decided to retire to Majorca, he passed the business on to Liam. Andy said he was in insurance and there wasn't much else to say about that. It was only when Becky said more about her job that the name they had all been avoiding came up for the first time.

"I was offered a Head's job," she said. "It was in a great school, and I'd have taken it like a shot, but Mike..." she broke off and drank some of her wine while the server brought their food. Once the server had gone, she carried on. "I didn't have the headspace to start a new job and certainly not a promotion. And my school were very good about leave while Mike was ill. But the job offer came at exactly the wrong time, so I had to turn it down. There may be others; you never know."

Becky toyed with her food and there was silence for a while. Andy was glad he had his own food to distract him because he didn't really know what to say. He'd never been particularly good in situations like this and didn't want to say

82

the wrong thing, especially to Becky. Liam, who had always been better with words, spoke up.

"I'm so sorry you've had to go through all this Becks. I can't begin to imagine how bad things have been for you. How are you doing now? Is there anything we can do?"

"Thanks, Liam, but no, not really. It's done. Mike's gone and I have to get on with my life, not just for him, but for me. You know how everyone says, 'He'd have wanted you to be happy?' I'm lucky, I suppose, because I know he did. That's one advantage of knowing he was going to die. We had a very good three months after he was told there was nothing more to be done. Yes, he was in a lot of pain, but we talked a lot. I think we were closer in that time than we'd ever been. We could be completely honest, you know? There wasn't any point in hiding anything anymore. All those little lies couples tell, thinking they're protecting each other...there was none of that. He even did the thing of telling me to find someone else. How clichéd is that? He meant it, too, although it broke his heart. Like I'm going to find someone now, at my age! I'm definitely not going internet dating!"

"I don't know how you do it," Andy said.

"You go on a website and look at pictures, I think," Becky replied with a small smile.

"No, not that! How you keep going. If anything happened to Alison..." As he said it, Andy suddenly felt bad about not telling Ali the truth about where he was going today. *All those little lies.* He wasn't sure who he was supposed to be protecting. Himself, probably.

"You've got to," Becky said. "There's no choice. There are times when I don't want to go on anymore on my own. Of course, there are mornings when I wake up and he isn't there and I cry. Occasionally, I rage. I've got a lot less crockery than I used to have, but there's only one person using it. But the bills need paying, I've got a responsibility to the kids I teach and life just goes on. You get on with it. It's like they say – what doesn't kill you makes you stronger. It killed Mike and made me stronger."

83

"Fucking hell," Liam said. "How did we get so grown up?"

"How do you mean, 'rage'?" Andy asked. "I don't think I've ever seen you angry, not plate-smashing angry."

"It's not something you do in public. I get angry because Mike didn't have to leave me. Certainly not so soon. This is what I mean about the lies. He found a lump under his armpit, but he never told me. He said later he thought it was just a blocked hair follicle or something because he got those. He was quite hairy. But it didn't go away, and he never did anything about it. He hid it from me for months. He only got medical attention because he started coughing up blood and I had to take him to A&E. All the way there, he was telling me it was nothing to worry about and he'd be fine. He wasn't. The fucking cancer was in his lungs and his bones and there was nothing they could do. It had started in his breast and if he'd gone to get himself checked, they might have been able to do something about it. That's why I get angry. He could have got himself checked out and didn't. He was too proud or too scared or too *whatever* to go to the doctor and it killed him."

Andy saw that Becky was gripping her wine glass and gently took it off her.

"That isn't your glass, Becks," he said.

"Promise me something," Becky said. "Promise me that you will check yourselves. And if you find anything – *anything* – get it looked at."

"Of course," Liam said. There was something in the way he said it that made Andy wonder for a second if there had been something, but it wasn't for him to ask.

"No, don't just say that," Becky said and looked at them with a fierce look Andy had never seen before. "*Promise me.*"

"I promise," Andy said.

"Liam?"

"I promise."

"Good. I think I've had all the pasta I want. Anyone fancy a dessert?"

For some reason, nobody did. They talked about other things for a bit and then it was time to go. Becky declined a life back to her house, saying she had shopping to do, and they parted in the car park with hugs, genuine ones this time, and promised to keep in touch.

It was only when they were on their way back that it occurred to Andy that they hadn't mentioned the idea of doing something to remember Mike. Still, it was a good reason to speak to Becky again. There was the small matter of what he was going to tell Ali about today, but he would deal with that when he got home. In the meantime, he had to navigate his own way back to the motorway because Liam was staring out of the window, lost in his own thoughts. He turned on the radio and the Eagles sang 'Lyin' Eyes'. Of course, they bloody were.

Chapter Seventeen

"How did it go with your client today?"

"Yeah, fine."

"Shift over a bit. I think you're sitting on the remote."

"What's on?"

"Nothing much, I don't think."

"Let's not bother then. How's Amy?"

"She's up in her room. Came in with a face like thunder, so I think there's trouble in paradise."

"Good. Hope she dumps the little twat."

"Me too. So, your meeting today..."

"I don't really want to talk about work if that's okay. Let's just relax."

"We can't really talk about work, can we? You weren't there."

"How do you mean?"

"Andy, do you honestly think we haven't been married long enough for me to know you're lying? There's something you do that always gives it away."

"What?"

"I'm not telling you. You'll stop doing it. So where were you?"

"Liam and I went to see Becky. You know, Mike's..."

"Widow. Yes, I know. I wondered when you would. I thought it was funny that you'd said nothing about her since she rang you that time. So how was she?"

"Okay. Doing better than I thought."

"It can't be easy for her. God know how you cope with a thing like that. It doesn't bear thinking about."

"No, it doesn't."

"Are you going to tell me why you didn't say anything about it? Or do I have to guess?"

"I don't know. That's the honest answer. It didn't feel right."

"But it felt right to lie to me."

"I'm sorry. And no, that didn't feel right either. I didn't know what to do."

"Then you should have asked me."

"I know. I'm sorry."

"Okay. I suppose I did suggest it in the first place. But don't do that again, Andy. I've got two kids who are at a difficult age, one especially. I don't need a husband who's at a difficult age too."

"No. You don't. I don't deserve you."

"Damn right. So, I'm only going to ask this once and you'd better answer honestly. Don't forget, I'll know. Do I need to be worried about this Becky?"

"What? No! Of course not. She's a friend from a long time ago and she's lost her husband who was a good mate of mine. That's all."

"Okay."

"Did I do the thing?"

"No, you didn't. Speaking of things, did you and Becky have one back then?"

"No, we didn't. We were friends, that's all. Liam was the one who fancied her."

"I thought Liam got together with Nic back then."

"Not exactly. They didn't really get together for good until after."

"Except it wasn't for good, was it?"

"No. Not as it turned out."

"Not like us."

"No. Not like us. Thank God."

"That was the right answer. Now, stick the telly on. I think there's a repeat of DIY SOS we haven't seen."

Chapter Eighteen
1986

The Slum was in full swing, but Liam couldn't enjoy it. He was nursing a pint and staring towards the dancefloor, where Becky was dancing with Paul. It looked very much as though she had forgiven Paul for the snogging incident at the Christmas party and they were obviously on very good terms now. It might have been because the dancefloor was very small and full of goths swaying earnestly to The Sisters of Mercy, but Becky and Paul were very close indeed. The only consolation as far as Liam was concerned, was that 'This Corrosion' was about as far removed from a romantic slowy as you could get.

Liam and his friends had only discovered The Slum, Bangor's alternative disco, this term. It took place every other Thursday in the small bar at the bottom of the Students' Union and the music was great, a mix of goth, indie and punk, and the DJ, a tall, genial Irishman called Barney, played tracks you would never hear at the regular Union discos. There was no way the general student populace would tolerate 'Bela Lugosi's Dead', but here it was a staple.

Barney was a well-known, popular figure in Bangor. He was well over six feet, and his spiked and crimped hair made him taller. He had a penchant for dressing in paisley silk shirts, baggy black trousers (often with chains) and bright-blue suede winklepicker boots and could often be seen skateboarding down the steep Glanrafon Hill that separated Upper Bangor from the lower part of the town where the Students' Union was located. He often wore make-up and beads, and as far as anyone with any taste was concerned, he was the epitome of cool. That meant that the Slum discos at which he DJd were also cool, and, by extension, so were the attendees. It was a place where students and locals alike could dress how they wanted and listen to the music they liked without judgement or criticism.

Liam had never been cool. It didn't seem to be something he could pull off without either feeling or looking (to his mind at least) silly. Mike had his trademark hair and a taste in bands that rarely troubled the commercial charts. If they ever did, Mike would probably be mortified and stop listening to them. Even Andy had taken to wearing a battered leather jacket and T-shirts featuring the names of the minor bands he still went up to the third floor to see. They were the sort of bands you'd hear on John Peel's or Annie Nightingale's show but never on *Top of the Pops*. Liam liked some of the music his friends played, especially the indie bands who had emerged from Liverpool in recent years, but whenever he tried to decide what to wear, he could still feel his parents looking over his shoulder and disapproving. His dad particularly had a way of showing his disapproval and disappointment without ever saying anything; you could tell it by the shape of his mouth. Even though his parents were a hundred miles away and so extremely unlikely to walk into the Slum on a Thursday night, Liam still couldn't bring himself to dress in anything that might be considered even slightly outrageous. In any case, nothing like that really suited his shape. The goths and punks whose dress sense he aspired to usually looked like they spent their money on clothes rather than food. It was very rare to see an overweight punk. Liam preferred to wear baggy pullovers that went some way to concealing his figure but were not really conducive to keeping cool in a hot, sweaty bar like this one, especially not later on when Barney started playing the livelier stuff like the Pogues and The Cramps. He always finished his set with one of the more frantic Pogues tracks, usually 'Sally Maclennan' and the goths and punks went mad. The dancefloor was a morass of pogoing bodies and flaying arms and could get quite dangerous. It was brilliant. Sometimes, Liam even took his pullover off because it was dark enough for no one to see and everyone was far too concerned with their own moves to notice.

Mike had been away for a while, trying to get served at the bar, and eventually returned and sat down next to Liam.

"You all right?"

"Yeah, fine."

"Packed tonight, isn't it? Thought I'd never get served."

Liam didn't reply but kept his attention on the dancefloor. Mike followed his gaze.

"Looks like Becks has forgotten about Christmas, then."

"Yes, Mike. I know," Liam snapped, then said, "Sorry."

"He's all right, Paul. I thought he was a bit of a dickhead, but he's okay."

Liam had to admit that Mike was right. He really wanted to dislike Paul, but since he had been hanging around with their group, he had got to know him a bit better, and he was all right for a southerner. He came from Bath or somewhere like that and was studying agriculture. He was also a member of the Mountaineering Club, and none of these things should have made him a good fit for their little group, who were, by and large, art students from various places in the North of England. But he was friendly, funny, had good taste in music and always got his round in, so it was hard not to like him. Becky certainly seemed to like him and had even talked about possibly going on one of the mountaineering expeditions. This had made Liam feel sad when he heard it. He had no chance with Becky, he knew that, but if she started seeing Paul and got involved with the mountaineers, she would probably start hanging around them instead and he wouldn't see her apart from in tutorial groups. Even then, those groups would almost certainly change next year when they took different study modules. Liam had found a group of people he felt comfortable with and who seemed to like him, somewhere he felt he belonged, and he didn't want that to change.

But changing it was because now the small gap between Becky and Paul closed and they were in each other's arms. Any second now, they would be kissing, and Liam didn't want to see that. He got up without saying anything to Mike and fought his way to the bar, where, when he finally got served, he bought himself a pint of lager and a vodka and lime, which he poured into his pint.

He stood near the bar, where he couldn't see the dancefloor anymore and let the music wash over him while he drank his pint, and then, because it wasn't far off the carnage of last orders, bought the same again and a pint for Mike and made his way unsteadily back to his friend. By the time he got there, Becky and Paul had gone, but he didn't ask Mike where because he didn't want to know the answer. Andy had now appeared from somewhere and they sat and drank and didn't talk about Becky. When Barney cranked up the tempo of the music, Liam finished his drink, plunged onto the dancefloor and tried to dance his troubles away. It worked for a while.

It was only when he trudged back up the hill towards the halls that sadness overtook him. When he reached his room, he lay on the bed as the room spun around him, trying not to be sick or to cry. Before he finally went to sleep that night, he had done both.

Chapter Nineteen

"What are you doing?"

Liam looked up from the skirting board, from which he was trying to remove the front of a plug socket. The screws were well and truly rusted in and he had to lie down on the floor of the school corridor to try and get some traction. As he looked up, he saw the face of a small girl staring earnestly down at him.

"I'm fixing this," he said.

"Why are you lying down? Are you tired?"

He realised that he was being observed by the little girl he had seen the last time he came to the school, the one whose mum was ill.

"No," he said, "but I'm too big to see what I'm doing when I stand up."

"My mummy lies down when she's tired," the girl, Evelyn, said.

"I'm sure she'll feel better soon," Liam replied, unsure if it was the right thing to say. It was a long time since his girls had been that age and so full of questions about everything.

"There you are, Evelyn," a voice said, and an adult's hand reached down and took Evelyn's little one. Liam thought it was better manners to get up and did so, brushing dust off his work jeans. It made little difference to the jeans, but it made Liam very much aware of how much more of a challenge it was to get up off the floor these days.

The grown-up was a young woman, perhaps in her twenties, who was wearing a sweatshirt with the school logo on it and leggings.

"I'm sorry," she said. "She will go wandering off."

"It's fine," Liam said. "I've been looking for an apprentice and there aren't nearly enough female electricians these days."

The young woman smiled and led Evelyn away, presumably back to the classroom down the corridor, where someone was singing 'The Wheels on the Bus' badly. It wasn't the sort of music Liam usually liked while he worked, but it would have to do for now. Normally, he would put on one of his Spotify playlists to keep him company, but he had forgotten to charge his phone the previous night and his battery was quite low. Hopefully, they would sing one of the classics, like 'Old MacDonald' next, not some of this modern 'Baby Shark' rubbish.

When his girls were little, they liked the music he played, or rather, the more poppy Erasure and Depeche Mode-type tracks. They weren't that keen on Bauhaus or Siouxie and the Banshees. Just remembering that and the serious look on little Evelyn's face made him want to ring his girls up. It was probably their turn to ring him—it usually was—but he had a strong desire to hear their voices and get all their news. Time was passing and recent events had proved to him how short time can be.

It still surprised and pleased him that his daughters had turned out so well. Despite what he had said to Andy, there hadn't been much more trouble than most parents have during their teenage years. They had their heartaches caused by early forays into the world of relationships, and Delyth, in particular, had a tough time until she came out to Liam and Nic, who were happy to reassure her that they had known for quite some time and were just waiting for her to be comfortable enough to tell them. Both girls had clashed with their parents (Nic more than Liam) on occasions, but it was never very serious and never lasted long. They worked hard at school and made sensible choices at the end of it. Freya did a design course at college and was now doing nicely in the fashion industry (even if Liam didn't fully understand much of what she did) and Del had gone straight into work after leaving school, and she and her partner Rainie had recently opened their own café in Llandudno. They intended to do it a couple of years ago until Covid put all their plans on hold, but now it was full steam ahead, even though Liam thought that in the current uncertain economic climate, they must be insane. They seemed to know what they were doing and were very happy together. They had even apparently been looking into IVF, which was a completely alien world to him, but if it was right for them, then he'd have to swallow being a grandfather, a word he felt slightly sick even contemplating. He resolved to get his phone fully charged, finish up here, then get a takeaway and a few beers and give them both a ring that evening.

He had finally managed to get the cover off the socket and replaced it with a new one when he saw the headteacher coming down the corridor towards him.

"How are you getting on?" she asked.

"Okay. Should have the sockets done today and I'll get the lights done tomorrow, then I'll be out of your hair."

"No, it's fine. I'm glad to get it done. I only came to see if you wanted a coffee or anything."

Liam looked at his watch. It was coming up to midday.

"Thank you, but I might grab a quick lunch if that's okay."

"Of course. You're more than welcome to join us for lunch if you want. The school dinners here are better than many."

"That sounds very tempting, but I thought I might take a quick stroll down to that café on the beach. I won't be long."

"I'm not keeping tabs. You go and enjoy. It's a lovely little place. Tell Kate I said 'hi'. She's the owner and a good friend."

"I will."

The headteacher turned and started to move away, but then stopped.

"Did you decide what you're going to do for your friend? I know you were thinking about it last time I saw you."

"No, not yet. We've decided on plenty of things we're definitely *not* going to do, though."

"Well, have a look at the leaflets on Kate's counter while you're there. I saw something there yesterday that might just interest you." With that, she gave him a smile and disappeared into one of the classrooms, leaving Liam none the wiser.

He cleared up the mess he had made so far, packed his tools away out of sight of curious little eyes, and then let himself out of the school.

It was a pleasant day, sunny, if a bit chilly, so he walked briskly down the road to the café; it wasn't far enough to justify taking the van and in any case, he knew from past experience that places like that were sometimes a bit short on parking and the van could be a beast to manoeuvre in tight spaces. Nobody would notice if it picked up a few more dents, but he didn't particularly want to hit anyone else.

The café didn't look very busy when he got there. There was an old man who looked like he had emerged from a skip sitting by the window and a very attractive, dark-haired woman sitting near the counter, chatting to the owner, but apart from them, it was empty. Liam had no idea how places like this stayed in business when things were so quiet and felt a pang of worry for Del and Rainie but dismissed it. Their café was in the middle of the town, not tucked away on the coast. With luck, it wouldn't be dependent on the seasons for its trade.

As he approached the counter, the owner broke off from her conversation and greeted him with a warm smile.

"Hi," she said. "I'm Kate. Welcome to my little place. I haven't seen you around here before, have I?"

"No," Liam replied. "I'm not from round here."

"Oooh!" the dark-haired woman exclaimed. "A stranger! We don't get many strangers round here, do we, Kate?"

"Gemma, behave! You'll scare him off and I need all the trade I can get. What brings you to these parts, stranger?"

"It's Liam, and I'm doing some rewiring at the school. The head—Ruth, is it? —says 'hi'."

"She's lovely, Ruth," Kate said. "I'm sure she's looking after you."

"She is, apart from offering me a school dinner. I thought I'd come here instead."

"Good choice. It's spotted dick on Thursdays." Gemma sniggered at that, but Kate pretended to ignore her and she turned away to concentrate on something on her phone. "She's got a terrible mind, that one," Kate said. "So what can I get for you?"

"I'll have a bacon sandwich, please," Liam said. "And a flat white."

"No problem. Grab a seat and I'll bring it over to you. White bread for your butty? Don't say brown or I'll judge you."

"It's got to be white for a bacon butty, hasn't it?"

"Is the right answer. Just be a few minutes."

Liam was just about to sit down when he remembered what Ruth had said about there being something on the counter that might interest him. He couldn't see what she meant at first. There were fliers for local businesses, some handbills for a production of a play he'd never heard of, and some leaflets for some of Anglesey's tourist attractions, but nothing that looked relevant to him. Then he spotted it. Half concealed under the play handbills was a small pile of flyers. They were dominated by a photograph of a disco ball and the words *Dance For Cancer*. He laughed out loud, causing the dark-haired woman to look up from her phone, but picked one of the leaflets up and took it to a table as far away from skip-man as he could get.

Once settled in his seat, he took a proper look at the leaflet. From what he could gather, a hospice near Bangor was looking for entries into a charity ballroom dancing competition, a sort of *Strictly Come Dancing*, but with real people, rather than pampered celebrities, who would be paired up with local expert dancers. The event was due to take place in December. Liam tossed the leaflet down onto the table and nearly laughed out loud again. If Ruth seriously thought something like that would interest him, then he was starting to doubt her suitability to be allowed out on her own, let alone teach children.

Shortly after, Kate came over, bearing his sandwich and his coffee. The bacon sandwich, made with thick-cut, fresh bread, looked very appetising and the coffee was piping hot. As she put them down, she noticed the leaflet.

"That looks brilliant! I'd love to go in for something like that, except I'd be bloody useless. Two left feet doesn't come into it! My wife, Briony, wanted to do that dance from Dirty Dancing at our wedding. You know, the one with the lift, only I'd probably have killed her."

"Nobody puts Baby in the corner," Gemma piped up in a very bad American accent.

"Shut up, you," Kate said, not unpleasantly, "or I'll put you in the corner."

"I can't see me doing it either," Liam said, tucking into his sandwich. "The competition thing. I mean, look at me!"

"There's nothing wrong with you. I think you'd look great in sequins."

"That thought's enough to put me off for life! I'll give it a miss, thanks."

Kate grinned and went back to the counter, leaving him to finish his lunch.

***

Later, after he had finished his day at the school, Liam drove back to the unit to stow his tools away for the night. When he reached into his jacket pocket to take out the unit's keys, a crumpled-up piece of paper fell out and landed at his feet. He had almost forgotten picking up the flyer from the table when he left the café and stuffing it in his pocket. He wasn't even sure why he had done it. There was no way that he was anywhere near fit enough to do something as daft as dancing. Even when he was younger, he didn't dance much unless he'd had a skinful and didn't care what he looked like. He and Nic had the first dance at their wedding to Sinatra singing 'Someone to Watch Over Me', but it was more of a sway than a proper dance, and they had been too wrapped up in each other to care much what anybody thought. Those were the days before the arguments and the stupid mistakes and life in general made them drift apart.

He went into the unit, dumped his tools down, sat at his desk and plugged his phone into the charger he always kept there. Then he put the leaflet down on the desktop and smoothed it out with the palm of his hand. It was a ridiculous idea, wasn't it? But then, so were all the other ideas he and Andy had rejected, and he still wanted to do *something* for Mike. No one was going to sponsor him to sit on his arse or to change light fittings, and those were the only things he was any good at. Whatever they did was inevitably going to take him out of his comfort zone. That was surely the whole point of doing a challenge. But dancing? Really? He took a packet of cigarettes out of his jacket pocket, looked at it for a second, then took a cigarette out and lit it. There was an old McDonald's cup on his desk that would serve as an ashtray. He knew he wasn't supposed to smoke in the unit and never normally did, but how could the laws against smoking in the workplace apply when he was the only employee and didn't object? He waited until there was enough charge on his phone and then, leaving it still plugged in, made a call

Chapter Twenty

"Hi, Nic."

"Liam? What's up? Is everything okay?"

"Yeah, I just thought I'd call, that's all. Are you busy?"

"Not right now. And you never just call. What is it? Is it one of the girls? I only texted Freya yesterday."

"No, it's not the girls. I thought I might ring them later."

"Well, if you're ringing me *and* the girls, there must be something up. Are you ill?"

"What? No! I'm fine. Sorry, I should have told you this a couple of weeks ago..."

"Liam, you're worrying me now."

"It's not me, Nic. Do you remember Mike?"

"Mike from uni? That Mike? Of course, I remember him. Why?"

"I found out the other week that he's dead."

"Oh, shit."

"Yes, that's pretty much what I said. It was Andy who told me, and he only found out by accident."

"When?"

"Last March, apparently."

"What was it? An accident or something?"

"No, cancer. He had a lump and didn't do anything about it, and it was too late. It had spread."

"Poor Mike. And poor Becky. She must be in a state."

"She's...Hang on. How did you know Mike and Becky were married? I never knew."

"Yes, you did. I told you."

"No, you didn't. I'd definitely have remembered that."

"I'm sure I told you. I bumped into her at a conference about what...six, seven years ago. We had a good chat. She was a bit surprised we got married. Mind you, so was everyone, including me. I *told* you."

"No, Nic, you didn't. It wouldn't have been *that* conference, would it?"

"Oh. Oh, yes. I think it was."

"Well, there was quite a lot you didn't tell me about that conference, wasn't there?"

"Do we have to get into that again?"

"You brought the conference up."

"Anyway, it's not about us, is it? It's about poor Becky and Mike. Have you spoken to her? I think I might still have her number somewhere."

"Yes. Andy and I went to see her the other day. She's doing okay, she said. Under the circumstances."

"She would tell you that, though, wouldn't she?"

"How do you mean?"

"Two blokes she knew years ago show up after all this time. She's not exactly going to bare her soul, is she? She's bound to put a brave face on it."

"It didn't look like that's what she was doing. She genuinely seemed quite together. I mean, she said she'd had her moments, but..."

"'Had her moments?' Bloody hell, Liam, she's lost her husband, not a fingernail. You men haven't got a clue, have you? Of course, she's going to play it down. I'd better give her a call. I wouldn't be surprised if you've made it worse."

"Fucks sake, Nic! What do you think I am?"

"No, sorry. This must all have been a shock to you. I'm sure you did your best."

"Andy and I were thinking of doing some charity thing in Mike's memory."

"Charity thing? Like what?"

"Don't know yet. Something."

"If I see you doing a fun run in a giant chicken costume or something, I'll never speak to you again."

"No, it won't be anything like that. I'm not going to make myself look stupid or anything."

"Good, because the girls would be mortified. *I'd* be mortified. If you do it, and that's probably a very big *if* right now, have a think about what your message is."

"It's for Mike, isn't it? I don't know what..."

"It's not going to do him any good, though, is it? Not now. If I were you, I'd be trying to think of a way of turning this into something positive."

"Positive? My mate's dead and Becky's a widow. What's positive about that?"

"You said Mike found a lump and didn't do anything about it. Maybe you should think about getting the message out that people need to check themselves. Women *and* men. If anybody listens to that and finds something in time, isn't that something positive that can come out of this?"

"You're right. I hadn't thought of it like that. I'll talk to Andy about it, but that's a really good idea."

"I know. I'm full of them."

"Nic..."

"What?"

"Do you? Check yourself, I mean."

"Yes, Liam. I'm pretty obsessive about it. I go to my mammograms and smears, ever since..."

"Since what?"

"Nothing."

"Since what, Nic?"

"I...I had a bit of a scare a few years back. Something showed up when I had my smear. They called it 'abnormal'. I needed a little procedure to sort it out."

"A procedure? What? An operation?"

"No, a laser, actually."

"What? A laser? Up...? Fucking hell, Nic!"

"I wish I could see your face! It wasn't like, 'No, Mr. Bond, I expect you to die!' It was a bit uncomfortable, but all sorted, and everything's been fine since."

"You didn't tell me."

"No, Liam. I didn't. It was about eighteen months after you left, and we weren't exactly on speaking terms and definitely not about something like that."

"You could have told me."

"No, I couldn't. It was none of your business."

"Did the girls know?"

"No. They still don't. They were going through enough upheaval at the time. It's no big deal. It was over and done. I even had it done in the holidays, so I didn't have a day off work. Stop it, Liam."

"Stop what?"

"Worrying. I only mentioned it because you asked."

"I do care about you, Nic."

"I know. And it's sweet, but you don't need to worry. I'm not your responsibility anymore."

"You're the girls' mum. And you're still my friend. I hope you know that."

"We were always good at being friends. It was just everything else that we were shit at."

"You think so? Look at the girls. I think we did pretty well there."

"No, that's true. Look, I've got to go. Let me know if you and Andy do something. I might just throw you a tenner."

"Will do. You take care, Nic."

"I do. You too."

Chapter Twenty-One
1986

Liam felt weird being back in his room. He hadn't thought he would miss it quite as much as he did, but the summer break had dragged on and as the time to return drew nearer, he couldn't wait to get back.

But here he was, now a second-year, doing single honours English. Somehow, he had done well enough in the exams at the end of his first year to take single or joint honours in any combination of the three subjects, and he had debated long and hard whether to carry on with drama. He liked the course and many of the plays he had read but didn't think he was very good at the practical stuff. Nic had tried to persuade him, of course, but in the end, he decided that as there would be an element of drama on the English course, he would stick to that. He had come to uni to study English in the first place and, after talking it over with his parents, thought it best to stick to the course that really interested him.

He had spent the summer trying to avoid his parents and the feeling that he had outgrown his old home. His mother was made up to have him back, even if it was just for a while. She had left his old room exactly as it was when he left and it felt odd to be surrounded by the books and posters that belonged to a different, much younger version of him. There were even a couple of his old teddy bears that he'd had since he was little, and his mum had left them on the bed. They were the first things to be hidden away in a cupboard, along with embarrassing cassettes he hadn't taken away with him and a very dog-eared Bananarama poster that he had carefully removed from the centre pages of *Smash Hits*. It had the lyrics for 'Cruel Summer' printed on it, which, considering he was so far from all his new friends (especially Nic), seemed rather ironic. He didn't really know why he was putting these things out of sight; it wasn't as if anyone was going to see them apart from him, but if he was going to have to spend the summer sleeping in his old bed, then at least he wouldn't have to do it surrounded by things that made him cringe.

He spent quite a lot of time in that room over the summer, listening to the selected music he had brought back with him and trying to get ahead with some of the reading for the next year. He could have done that downstairs in the living room if he had wanted to, but with his mother fussing around and his father watching the cricket (which he somehow managed to do by closing his eyes and snoring), it was easier to concentrate in his room. None of his old mates from school were around, so he was on his own for most of the time, which wasn't something he was used to. In Bangor, he was used to spending his time with his social circle, either in each other's rooms or houses or hanging out at the Union or in town. Even when he went to the library to work, there was usually someone he knew that he could sit with. He had lost the knack of being on his own.

He escaped from Liverpool once when Mike invited him to stay in Preston for a week. He felt the same sense of dislocation and was only too pleased to have someone to show around his old haunts. He got to meet Mike's parents, too, which was an experience. He'd heard a lot about them from Mike, but meeting them was something else. Jack Smart was a large, loud Lancastrian who declared more often than strictly necessary that, in his opinion, someone should put a fence around Liverpool to stop the scallies getting out and that if Wales wanted to be its own country, it should be cut off from the rest of Britain and sent out to sea. Having a Scouser who now lived in Wales in the house was a heaven-sent opportunity to expound on his theories, but Liam laughed politely and let him get on with it. Mike's mum Sandra was out a lot. She was a nurse and worked shifts, but when she was around, she treated Mike like he was twelve, which annoyed him but amused Liam no end. At least it wasn't just his mother who behaved like that. The Smarts also owned a beautiful dog called Maggie, a golden cocker spaniel, who took to Liam straight away and liked to sit with her head on his knee, having her ears stroked. Liam joked that he was going to kidnap her when he left, which sent Jack Smart off on another 'robbing Scousers' tirade. Although he enjoyed his week in Preston, it made Liam miss the friendships he had made in Bangor all the more and made the prospect of the rest of the summer seem even longer.

Liam also spent hours at the old desk in his room writing letters, mostly to Nic, most of which went in the bin without being sent. He had to keep reminding himself that they were just friends, and even though she had given him her address in Hereford, it was way too soon to be saying some of the things he put in the letters. It made him feel better to get his thoughts on paper, even if nobody would ever read them.

Nic was one of the main reasons he was so restless that summer. Since that first meeting on the train after the abortive demo in Colwyn Bay, he had seen her in passing in the Drama Department building and they exchanged smiles but no conversation. He didn't even think about her very often; she was just someone he recognised in passing, someone he had shared a train with once. It was Becky who took up most of his thoughts, even though since she had started going out with Paul, it was obvious that she would only ever be a friend. Of course, there was always a possibility that this thing with Paul wouldn't last, which made Liam watch them closely for any sign of arguments. He hated himself for doing it because he liked Becky a lot and Paul was okay too, really, so he didn't wish the upset of a break-up on either of them, especially Becks, but if it happened, she might need comforting, and Liam would be only too happy to oblige.

It was only towards the end of the last term that Nic came onto Liam's radar again. She came along with Claire and the Donnas to the Union one night and it turned out that she was in the same history tutorial group as Claire and one of the Donnas. Why they'd never brought her along before, Liam didn't know, but then his own circle of friends had changed a bit since the first term. Spanner didn't hang out with them much these days, preferring to go around with some of the local punks and Becky's housemate, Jo, was seeing a lad called Rich and spent most of her time with him. Paul had come onto the scene, but only because of Becky, so still felt like an outsider. He wasn't much of a replacement for Spanner, either, because he wasn't anywhere near as funny.

Because Liam hadn't expected to see Nic that night and because she was out of context, he didn't immediately register who it was when she arrived. The fact that she was wearing a dress rather than sweatshirt and leggings and her hair was down instead of tied back might also have had something to do with it, as did the two pints of strong lager Liam had already consumed. Whatever it was, it caused Liam to gape like a myopic carp until Andy elbowed him sharply in the ribs.

Claire and one of the Donnas went to the bar, while the other Donna and Nic sat down. It was still quite early for a Saturday evening, but Liam, Andy and often Mike liked to get there handy before the bar got busy and get a few drinks down them before the regular Saturday night disco got going. Many students liked to go to one of the town's pubs first before coming down, so it was unusual for Claire and her friends to get there so early.

Liam stole glances across the table at Nic and was very glad they had. When the girls' drinks arrived, there was a bit of rearranging of the seating, which resulted in Nic moving her stool around the table and next to Liam. For ten minutes or so, he was struck dumb while everyone else chatted about their days. Once he had unglued his tongue from the roof of his mouth, he turned to Nic, trying to be casual and give the impression that he had only just noticed she was there.

"So," he said, with the air of one about to impart something of critical importance, "been on any good demos lately?"

Nic fixed her startling green eyes on him and a small frown furrowed her brow. *Shit*, Liam thought, *she doesn't know who I am*, but then she smiled.

"Never again," she said. "What a waste of time that was."

"I know. I've started deliberately wearing leather in protest."

"I don't think..." she began but then stopped and narrowed her eyes. "That was a joke, wasn't it?" Liam nodded. "Is this that famous Liverpool sense of humour everyone goes on about?"

"That's it."

"It's shit."

For some reason, probably the lager again, Liam found this far funnier than he normally would and laughed so hard that everyone else stopped talking and stared at him. He apologised, but out of the corner of his eye, he could see that Nic was still smiling, and it felt like they had shared something secret. After that, they chatted easily and comfortably for the rest of the night about their courses and their hometowns. They even danced a couple of times (admittedly, it was at the same time as everyone else did, but it still counted). And that was where it began.

That was also where it stayed, more or less. Liam eagerly awaited the following Saturday when he turned up at the Union in his cleanest shirt and freshly showered and shaved, only to spend the night staring with increasing despair at the door through which the Donnas, Claire and Nic resolutely didn't come. He went home and played quite a lot of The Smiths that night.

Nic did come to the last disco of the term and Liam wasted far too much of the night trying to muster up the courage to talk to her again and feeling like an idiot because she had been so easy to talk to last time. By the time he did, the volume of the music had risen and conversation was difficult. Before they all parted for the summer, however, he did manage to find the nerve to ask if she'd mind him writing to her over the summer. She looked surprised but still tore the front off a beer mat and scribbled her address on it. Liam went back to his room that night and played some Marvin Gaye and imagined what it would be like if Nic was there listening to it with him.

Then term finished, and they all went back to the lives they had spent the year trying to forget about. In the end, Liam only wrote to Nic twice. The first time was a fairly dull letter about fairly dull things he had been getting up to and didn't receive a reply for more than a fortnight because, as she explained at great length, she had been away in Spain with her family. His second letter, the one in which he wanted to say profound, important things that would set things up for the next term, was perhaps even duller than the first because he hadn't done anything worth mentioning while she was away. He tried to sound interested in all she had done and not convey his irrational jealousy about who she might have met in Spain, what she had done, and all the other things she wasn't telling him. It was a short letter.

Now he was back in Bangor and a whole new year stretched out in front of him, a year full of opportunities to build on what they had started before the summer. This was going to be their year.

Part Two
Beginners

Chapter Twenty-Two

"Dancing? Are you off your bloody head?"

Andy was tempted to laugh and put the phone down. Instead, he had pointed out all the potential problems: the event was in Bangor and he wasn't, it would inevitably involve a lot of practice sessions, he didn't know if he had the time, and the small matter of them both being crap dancers even when they were younger and fitter. Liam made the observation that at least it didn't involve throwing themselves out of a plane or off a cliff or running in a stupid costume and asked that Andy at least thought about it. Andy said he would give it very serious consideration. *Then* he laughed and put the phone down.

"Liam?" Alison asked, looking up from the newspaper she was reading while keeping an eye on *MasterChef* at the same time.

"He's an idiot," Andy replied. "He's come up with this bright idea that we should enter some charity ballroom dancing bollocks."

"So I gathered. Don't you think you were a bit mean laughing like that?"

"Couldn't help myself. Can you imagine it? Me?"

"I don't know. You were quite a mover in your day."

"I wasn't, but thank you. That was then, though. Nowadays, I'd look like an embarrassing uncle at a wedding. I'd make a complete fool of myself."

"Nothing wrong with that every now and then, not if it's for charity."

Andy sat and pretended to watch some amateur chef cock up the buttery biscuit base to his cheesecake while Ali went back to her paper.

There was everything wrong with making a fool of himself. It was something he had always hated and hated even more now he was older. Ever since his teens, when he had a growth spurt and became what could only be described as gangly, he had been conscious of how he looked and moved. Acquiring the nickname 'Stick Insect' at school hadn't helped much and the lack of control he had over his long limbs made him clumsy at times, which was often the cause of even more hilarity. He was lucky that Ali was tall, too, so his height hadn't mattered when they started seeing each other. Even the wedding photographs made them look in proportion and not like a nightmare version of Gulliver's Travels. In company, he had developed a tendency to try and keep as still as possible so that glasses, tables and sometimes people wouldn't go flying if his movements became too animated. At the uni discos of his youth, his dancing style involved keeping his hands in his pockets and moving his feet and shoulders a bit. If he let his hands go free, it could be dangerous. It had happened once, at a party in someone's house, when he'd had a bit too much to drink and got carried away. The room wasn't very big and much too enclosed a space for it to have been wise for the host to put 'Into the Valley' on. As everyone flailed around to the Skids, Andy forgot his inhibitions and joined in. Halfway through the song, he caught Mike on the chin and put him through a glass door. The trip to A&E was a sobering one for both of them, and although Mike only needed a couple of stitches in his back, despite the amount of blood, Andy vowed there and then that in future, if he got involved in any dancing, he would keep his hands very much to himself. He'd never told Ali that story and had no intention of doing so now. Some memories were best left alone.

Any further discussion of Liam's hare-brained scheme was abruptly curtailed by the sound of the front door as Amy returned from an evening out at the cinema with the lovely Jackson. He had come to pick her up earlier, and Andy and Alison had been pleasant enough to him, but Andy had given him enough serious looks to leave him in no doubt as to what fate would befall him should he misbehave. *Just you try it*, the looks said. *Even your mother won't be able to identify your body.* The sound of the door slamming, which was even louder than the sound Mike made when he took his Skids-induced trip into the glass door, suggested to Andy that the looks might have been ignored.

When he went into the hall to see what was going on, his daughter's back was turned to him as she tried to retreat up the stairs.

"Amy?" he said. "What's all the noise...?"

Amy turned to look at him and he saw the tears streaming down her face and forgot all about his joke about asking her if she had any idea how much a new front door would cost. Instead, he opened his arms to her.

"Hey hey hey, baby," he said. "Come here. What is it? What's he done?"

Amy rushed to him and let him put his arms around her. Whatever the little shit had done must be serious because she hadn't done that in a while.

"Come on," he said, leading her into the living room, "tell us all about it."

He sat down with her on the settee and let her sob while Alison abandoned her newspaper and suggested making a cup of tea.

"Fucking Jackson!" she managed to say through her tears and for once Andy didn't say anything about her language.

"It's okay, baby. What's fucking Jackson done?"

She sobbed some more, so Andy reached out and grabbed a box of tissues from a side table. She snatched a handful, blew her nose noisily and dropped the soggy clump of tissue on the floor.

"I've broken up with him," she said without looking up. Andy resisted the urge to say, "Good," and instead asked, "Why?" As he did so, he felt a tide of anger building up inside him. "Did he try something? Did he...?"

"No!" she exclaimed, sounding shocked at the very thought of it. "Dad!"

"Sorry. What then?"

"He...he said we were going out and made it sound like it was just us, you know? But it wasn't. Josh was there, and

Priya and bloody Jessica. He knows I know he used to fancy Jessica because he told me."

"Which one's Jessica?"

"You don't know her. She's blonde and thin—not thin like you, but *thin,* though. But he didn't tell me she was coming. Well, he wouldn't."

Alison brought three mugs of tea through and set them down on the coffee table. Andy gave her a *help me* look, and she sat down on the other side of Amy and took her hand.

"Amy was just saying she's broken up with Jackson," he explained. He wasn't sure he could explain the rest, not until Amy had elaborated a bit more.

"Oh, I'm sorry," Alison said. "I know how much you liked him."

"He didn't like me," Amy said, her eyes filling up again. "If he had, he wouldn't have spent all night looking at bloody Jessica!" That started the tears again, so Andy pulled some more tissues out of the box.

"You're worth more than that," Alison said. "You're worth ten of this Jessica."

"I'm not thin like her!" Amy wailed.

"There's nothing wrong with you," Andy said, hugging her tight to his side. "You're beautiful. Like your mum."

"Eww! Dad!" Amy nearly managed a laugh.

"Well, you are. If Jackson the Jerk can't see that, then he's even thicker than I thought." He took her other hand in his. "Look at me, Ames," he said. She lifted her head and looked at him with crimson eyes. "Now listen. You're sixteen. You've got the whole of your life in front of you and one day you're going to meet someone who will value you like you deserve. It took me a long time to meet your mum and I had a few heartaches along the way. But when you know, you *know.* Just be who you are, Amy, because that's a beautiful thing. If people like you, then good. If they don't, they've got no taste, and you're well rid." He was suddenly aware of the silence in the room and stopped speaking. His wife and his daughter were both staring at him.

"Wow," Amy said. "Dad made a speech."

"Wow is right," Ali agreed. "Good speech, Dad."

"I'm not doing it again," Andy said. "So you go and wash your face, try and get a good night's sleep, and when you wake up, you'll have forgotten about that little scruff. You can do anything you want to, baby. Never forget that."

He kissed Amy on the cheek, and she rewarded him with the first proper smile he had seen from her for a while. She stood up and went towards the door, then stopped and turned back.

"Love you," she said.

"Love you too, baby girl. Now go and get cleaned up. You look a mess."

She grinned and left the room and Andy listened to her footsteps as she climbed the stairs.

"Bloody hell, Andy," Alison said. "Where did that come from?"

"Here," Andy replied and tapped his chest. "Now, can I go and track that little bastard down and kick his nuts in?"

"No, you can't!" Alison slid over to close the gap Amy had left and rested her head on his shoulder. "She'll be all right, though, won't she?"

"She's a good kid. She'll have moved onto someone else by next week."

"Oh God, I hope not. So, all that stuff you were saying, you know, about how you can do whatever you want to? Is that true?"

"I suppose it is, yes."

"Like maybe learning how to dance?"

"I don't like where this is going."

"If they really wanted to, someone could learn to dance to remember their friend and maybe raise some money for charity?"

"It'll mean driving over to Wales a couple of times a week to practice."

"Probably."

"I'll look like a dickhead."

115

"Probably."

"I won't win."

"Probably not. I'll tell you what, though."

"What?"

"Once the kids have gone to bed, you can show me what moves you've got. Now, drink your tea before it gets cold."

Chapter Twenty-Three

"Hi, Becky?"

"Hey, Andy. How are you?"

"I'm fine, thanks. You okay?"

"Running around like a mad thing. Term starts next week, so loads to do, not enough time, that sort of thing."

"It's good to keep busy, I guess."

"Well, it depends on what you mean by busy. I could do without some of this. I've got loads of washing to do, all the work stuff I meant to do and put away at the end of last term and didn't and hey, guess what? The washing machine's bloody died."

"Give Liam a call."

"Liam? Why?"

"He's an electrician. He might be able to fix it."

"I don't think so. I think it's about ready to go to the great Currys showroom in the sky. I think he'd be wasting his time."

"Sorry, I've phoned at a bad time."

"No, it's okay. I could do with stopping for a moment. Catch my breath. What can I do for you?"

"It's just a quick one. We – me and Liam – we meant to mention this when we saw you, but we're planning on doing a thing."

"A thing? Nope. You might have to be a bit more specific there, Andy."

"A charity thing. We're going to do a charity thing in Mike's name. If that's okay."

"Andy! That's really sweet. You don't have to do that."

"I know, but we wanted to. We didn't know, Becks. We weren't even at the funeral."

"You didn't miss much. Just a quick thing at the crem and that was it. We didn't even have a wake. Mike didn't want a fuss. Oh, there was one thing. You'll like this. Mike insisted that the last song in the service was 'Always Look on the Bright Side of Life' and wanted me to stipulate on the service sheet that everyone had to sing along. Mike's dad was fuming! Did you ever meet him?"

"No, I didn't. Liam did once, I think."

"If anyone isn't the Monty Python type, it's Jack. He hated it. I think that's why Mike did it, just to piss him off."

"Sounds like Mike."

"So what is it that you're doing?"

"Dancing."

"Sorry. I didn't quite catch that. I thought for a minute you said..."

"Dancing. We've entered a charity ballroom dancing thing for a hospice near Bangor. Stop laughing, Becks. It's serious!"

"I...oh no!... I can't picture you and Liam in sequins and those tight trousers. Oh my God!"

"All Liam's clothes are tight."

"That's not nice, Andy. Are you serious? That's the funniest thing I've heard in...well, forever, probably."

"Don't, Becks. I'm nervous enough as it is. There's eight people taking part and we're all meeting up next week when we'll get introduced to our partners. I'm shitting myself."

"I wouldn't do that in those trousers. No, seriously, Andy, I think it's a lovely thing to do. When's the big night?"

"December sometime. Liam's got the date."

"You'll have to let me know. I'll be there. I haven't been back to Bangor since we left. I bet it's changed a bit."

"I believe so. Liam says they've knocked the halls down and built new ones. Even the Union's gone now. Sounds like everything's changed."

"It's been a long time. It was bound to."

"I know, but it doesn't seem that long sometimes. Other times, it feels like a lifetime ago. I don't know where the time's gone. Listen, Becks, there was something else I was going to ask

118

you. I never thought I'd say this, but my daughter is going to get me on social media to publicise this thing."

"Welcome to the 21st century, Andy. You'll be doing your banking on your watch next."

"No chance. That's too Star Trek for me. I mean, obviously the idea is to raise as much money for this hospice as we can, so I've got to shout about it. What I wanted to ask, is it okay with you if we use Mike's name? He's the reason we're doing it."

"I think he'd be made up, Andy. He'd be really pleased to know you remembered him."

"Shame we couldn't have done that when he was still alive. We could have been there for you both."

"Don't think like that, Andy. Please. Mike mightn't even have told you. He didn't tell many people until they had to know. I think he was a bit scared that too many people would have opinions about what he should and shouldn't have done. Like it would change anything. He got involved in a few online forums for a bit but packed it in because some of them were almost like a competition, you know, who had it worst, that sort of thing. I told him often enough about the things he should have done. I think that was probably enough for him."

"If anyone had the right to do that, you did."

"But I didn't really. I only did it occasionally when things got on top of me. So, could you do something for me?"

"Of course."

"When you do the publicity for this mad dance thing, could you shout over and over again how important it is that people check themselves? That was Mike's mistake and it's about the only real mistake he made all our married life. Raising money is great, but if you can save a few lives while you're at it, then maybe some good can come out of this."

"Nic said the same thing to Liam. Yes, of course we will."

"Are Liam and Nic still talking? I thought..."

"They're divorced, yes, but I think they're on quite good terms. To be honest, I think Liam's sorry they split."

"Why did they split then?"

"It's a long story and it's not mine to tell. I reckon Liam wants her back, but you know Liam. He'd never say."

"That's the Liam I remember. There was quite a lot he didn't say back then."

"I know. And it didn't do any of us much good, did it?"

Chapter Twenty-Four
1986

Liam woke up with a banging headache and a mouth like an ashtray soaked in beer. He thought he'd probably give his lecture a miss this morning. It was on a bit of the Literature of Ideas module that didn't really interest him and he had worked out from the format of the exams at the end of the first year that you could miss the occasional lecture and still have plenty to write about. Missing one lecture wouldn't be a problem.

Everyone had gone back to Becky and Jo's house after the Union the previous night. He and Mike had gone halves on a couple of packs of Kestrel lager. They wouldn't normally buy the cheap stuff, but Liam was all too aware that the possibility of his grant lasting to the end of the year was looking dodgy, to say the least and couldn't face the idea of calling his parents for a top-up this early in the academic year. It wouldn't take a psychic to predict what Stan would have to say about that. Mike always seemed to have plenty of money, but it wasn't something they ever talked about, and Liam didn't want to look like a charity case. He had enough cigarettes to get him through the next couple of days if he was careful and they had only bought the lager because you didn't go to a party empty-handed. There was often plenty of good stuff at Becky and Jo's, another advantage of Becky having a housemate whose father was minted. Parties at their house were always worth going to.

Liam lit a cigarette as he and Mike walked up the hill. Andy was up ahead talking to a couple of girls from his course, one of whom he definitely fancied, though he hadn't said so. Liam offered Mike a ciggie, but he declined. He smoked occasionally but often went for long periods without.

"I don't know how you can smoke and walk up this hill," he told Liam. "The bloody hill's going to kill me one day anyway."

Liam couldn't quite pinpoint when he had started smoking properly. He had never been tempted when he lived at home. His parents, like many of their generation, both smoked, although these days Stan favoured a pipe, which he seemed to chew more than smoke. The ashtrays at home were often full of his mum's butts and the viscous tar from his dad's pipe. Because of the smoke which permeated the house and the gunk in the ashtrays, Liam had always hated the idea of smoking. Yet here he was. He had started taking the occasional ciggie to be sociable in his first year, but during the long summer break, when there was no one else around, he had started buying his own. He only smoked outside and when his parents weren't around. Even though they were both smokers, his parents had always lectured him about the evils of tobacco and he knew they'd go mad if they ever found out. If they knew how often he rolled back to his room pissed, they would be horrified and probably drag him back to Liverpool by his hair. When he talked to them on the phone, which he still did every week, he edited everything he said before he said it, just in case he gave something away about what they would doubtlessly consider his debauched life. He wasn't as bad as some, though. Spanner never appeared to be sober and often bore the scars of the fight he'd had with someone over something stupid, and if you ever smelled weed being smoked in the Union bar or at a party, you could guarantee that the trail would lead to Spanner and his mates. Liam had tried weed once at a party one night that was being thrown by people he didn't know. He'd taken the joint when offered and had tried to imitate the way the others drew on it, but it had done nothing for him, and he was in no hurry to try again. He enjoyed himself enough without.

The party was in full swing when they arrived. Becks and Jo had left the Union early to get things ready and, seeing as it was December, already had a Christmas tree and decorations up. The glass-topped coffee table in the living room had a plastic ornament encased in a globe of a snowy-encrusted village scene which twinkled with glitter. Liam wondered how sensible that was because if things really got going, it wasn't likely to survive the night.

Claire and one of the Donnas were already there, though Liam wasn't sure how since they had still been in the Union when they left. Liam opened a can and went over to sit near them. It was always a good idea to get a chair while you could, and in any case, he wanted a word.

"Donna not coming?" he asked.

"She got off with Jez from the stage crew," Claire replied. "She's been after him for ages. She said she'd come on later, but she'll probably go back to his. You know what Jez is like."

Liam didn't but agreed anyway. He looked around the room. Jo was snogging the face off her boyfriend, whose name he couldn't remember, and Becky and Paul were deep in conversation in the doorway to the kitchen. There were several other faces Liam vaguely knew from Jo's course. Mike and Andy emerged from the kitchen with cans and had found cardboard hats from somewhere, which they found hilariously funny. There was one face he couldn't see, though, and it was the one he most wanted to see.

"Did – er – did Nic say she was coming?" he asked.

"I don't know," Claire said. "Did you see her, Don?"

"She's coming with some of the drama lot," Donna said. "She said she was, anyway."

"I think Liam likes her," Claire said. The two girls collapsed into giggles and Liam could feel his face burning.

"She's a mate, that's all," he protested, which set the girls off again. He wanted to get away from them but didn't want to lose his seat, so he turned away. Those wankers from the drama department were the last thing he needed, especially if bloody Geoff came with them. He was from London (as he never stopped reminding everyone) and, as well as being quite good-looking (if you went for that sort of thing, and plenty did), was also one of the best actors in the department. He was very funny, a natural comic, and always dominated any room he was in. Nic and the rest of the drama crowd hung on his every word.

Liam hated him. If he was coming, then there wasn't going to be much point sticking around. He'd never get to talk to Nic.

Sure enough, shortly after, there was a knock at the door and Nic and her friends arrived. Liam didn't need to look to know that Geoff was with them because he would know that stupid cockney accent (which he was sure Geoff put on) anywhere. He tried to catch Nic's eye as she passed, but she vanished into the kitchen in Geoff's wake.

Liam finished his beer, lit a cigarette and seethed. He could hear roars of laughter from the kitchen, and as much as he wanted another can, he had no intention of going in there while that cockney prick was entertaining his fans. He listened to a conversation Mike and Andy were having with the girls from Andy's course about some film they had seen.

"I still don't get why it was called that," one of the girls said. Liam thought her name might be Lyn.

"Because the boy saw the murder. He was the witness," Andy explained.

"Oh," Lyn said. "Oh. *Witness!*"

"Yes," Andy said. "He witnessed the murder. What don't you understand?"

"I thought it was called Witless. I couldn't work out why."

Andy and Mike cracked up at this, and Liam smiled despite himself. The conversation moved onto other films, some of which Liam had seen and some he hadn't, and he tried to join in where he could, until the drama lot came out from the kitchen and took over. Liam could see that Nic was near the kitchen door, so he took the opportunity to go and get another beer and maybe say hello. It nearly worked. She gave him a wave in passing but then followed her friends into the living room and stole Liam's seat.

By the time he had fought his way through the throng in the kitchen and found the beer (opening one can and putting another in his coat pocket to save him from going back again), Geoff had taken his traditional role of entertaining the party. He was lying under the coffee table, apparently pretending to be a giant threatening the model village on top of it. Of course, everyone found this to be the funniest thing they had ever seen. Liam lurked in a corner and concentrated on getting pissed.

Now he lay in his bed, contemplating getting a shower and some aspirin to get rid of his headache. It was getting on for eleven o'clock and the lecture was already nearly over. The party had been a complete waste of time, and he even recalled, to his horror, that at some point, he'd had a go at chatting Claire up. He didn't even fancy her and figured he might have to apologise for that one at some point, though she hadn't seemed to mind very much. He had hardly said two words to Nic and that was the main reason he'd gone in the first place. Never mind, the Students Union Christmas Party was coming up in a couple of weeks and there would be plenty of time to talk to her then. In the meantime, he had work he supposed he had better get one with, including one essay that was already late. He decided he would rest for a bit longer and then get on with it. He might even stay in for a few nights and save himself for the end of term celebrations.

Chapter Twenty-Five

When they pulled into the car park, Liam thought they had come to the wrong place. It seemed a bit ungracious to point it out, seeing as Andy had given him a lift. It was hardly his fault that roadworks had given them so little time to spare, but if they had to go driving around trying to find the right place, they were definitely going to be late. The directions they had been given had led them to a tiny church hall about a mile from the middle of Bangor. There were other cars in the car park and on the road outside and a van with the logo of something called Care Focus Ltd, so it looked like something was going on. He looked at Andy and the expression on his friend's face indicated that he was having similar reservations.

"It's like someone's shed," he said.

There was a sign above the door and Liam leaned out of the car window to get a better look.

"St. David's Church Hall. This is it, all right."

"Or," Andy said, "we could just turn round and drive away and pretend we couldn't find it. It's quite easy to miss."

"What, and tell Alison you brought her all the way to Bangor for nothing?"

"She's getting a night away out of it that she wasn't expecting and I'd be surprised if she doesn't find something in whatever shops they have in Bangor these days."

"Your bottle's gone, hasn't it?"

"Hasn't yours?"

"Yes. But let's do it anyway. What's the worst that can happen? If we decide it's not for us, at least we can say we tried."

It all seemed so simple a couple of weeks ago when they filled in the online application, comparing notes over the phone as they did so. Most of the form was fairly straightforward. It asked for names, addresses and so on, and also height and if the applicant had any medical conditions they should know about.

"Does being a lazy bastard count as a medical condition?" Liam had asked.

It was the last section that took the longest. It asked them to give their reasons for wanting to take part in the Larks House Hospice Strictly Amateurs Dancing Competition. They debated long and hard about the answer to this one, trying to make their answers different enough but still getting their reasons across clearly. In the end, Andy wrote an answer and Liam copied it and changed a few sentences around. They got their applications in with only a matter of hours to go before the deadline.

Neither of them really expected to be accepted, especially not Andy, who didn't even live in the area. Perhaps the Bangor University connection swung it for them because a few days after they applied, they each received an email saying they had been accepted, pending a brief telephone interview. The interview, with Lisa, a very pleasant lady from the hospice, went into greater depth about their reasons for applying, as well as explaining the process. When they discussed it later, it seemed they had given very similar answers. And that was it. They were in.

Today, they would meet the organisers, the other competitors and most importantly, the poor, unsuspecting individuals who were to be their dance partners.

Andy and Alison had driven over and booked into a hotel in Bangor for the night. Alison had stayed in the city to have a look around while Andy collected Liam from his house in Caernarfon. Liam had initially suggested meeting Andy there, but on balance, they agreed that it was better to arrive together.

Andy tried the church hall door, which opened with a push and went in. Liam put out the cigarette he had only just started and followed.

It reminded Liam a bit of the first time he had gone to join the Scouts. He hadn't really wanted to, but his parents thought it would do him good and enrolled him in the nearest troop. They met in a church hall just around the corner from where they lived. Liam had never forgotten the smell of wood and polish and the sight of a hall full of people he didn't know but who all seemed to know each other. He had lasted a couple of months before giving up. The rituals, uniform, church parades, flags and knots weren't for him. His parents weren't very pleased, particularly Stan, who had not long paid for the uniform but grudgingly understood. Now, walking into another church hall filled with another group of strangers, he was taken right back. It wasn't a feeling he relished.

Several rows of folding chairs had been laid out facing a small stage, and there were people of all ages milling about, some in ordinary clothes, some in sweatshirts which bore a logo, presumably that of the hospice. One middle-aged, rather harassed-looking woman was wandering about with a clipboard. When she saw Liam and Andy enter, she went over. Liam could see that the logo on her top did indeed say The Larks House Hospice.

"Hello," she said. "I'm Carol Rees, deputy manager of Larks House and the organiser of this whole thing. And you are...?"

"Liam. Liam Rawlinson."

Carol checked her list and put an enthusiastic tick next to Liam's name.

"And I'm guessing you must be Andy," she said. She wasn't especially tall, so practically had to stand on tiptoe to look into Andy's face.

"Yes. Yes, I am."

"You're a tall one, aren't you? That's why we ask for heights on the application form. We don't want to pair you with a five-foot dancer, now do we?"

"No, we certainly don't," Andy said. Liam had to turn a laugh into a cough in an effort to stifle it.

"Right, so welcome! If you'd like to come on over, I'll introduce you to the rest of our victims – sorry, competitors."

She laughed merrily and headed over to the throng that had gathered around the chairs. She rattled through the list of names, waving her hand around so vaguely that Liam couldn't

128

say whose name belonged to whom. There was a Jason, a Kelly, a Pete, a Jade, and Emma or Emily (Liam didn't quite catch it) and possibly someone called Estelle, though again, Carol was rushing so much that Liam wasn't quite sure if he'd heard correctly. He thought he'd probably know, though. It seemed likely that you'd know an Estelle if you saw one.

Carol trotted up a small set of wooden steps and clapped her hands together.

"Right, everyone!" she called and clapped again because some people were still chatting. Eventually, the hall fell silent.

"So, welcome everyone. Now that Andy and Liam have arrived, I think we're all here." She did a quick head count and consulted her clipboard again. "Oh, hang on. Where's Keith? Has anyone seen Keith?"

"He's gone to the loo!" someone shouted.

"Well, of course he has. We'd better crack on anyway. So, first of all, thank you all so much for volunteering for this. It's the third year we've done the Larks House Strictly Amateur Dance Competition, and in each of the past two years, we've raised over £8,000, which has been a massive boost to our funds. As you can imagine, it's not cheap to provide the level of care we do, so these events are a real help. But of course, we all know how costs have gone up over the past few years, so we're hoping that this year will be bigger and better than ever. So give yourselves a big round of applause for signing up!"

This speech was greeted not just with applause but with wolf-whistles and whoops, and Liam surprised himself by getting carried away and joining in.

"Now, the first thing I've got to say is that although this is a competition and there is a trophy for the winner, it really is the taking part that counts. We will have our expert judges on the night but don't worry, we couldn't afford Craig, so nobody is going to be judging you too harshly. We know that none of you have danced before and that you're giving up your time freely. Just do your best, have fun and let's see how much money we can raise."

There was more spontaneous applause, but Carol held up a hand to silence it.

"Let's get on to the important business of the day, shall we? Now, we're delighted to be joined by eight expert dancers. They're all either dance teachers, amateur competitors, or dancers who have won awards at festivals, and they will be training you in your dance. We've tried to match you in height or age as much as possible or as near as we can. So let me introduce you to..." she waved a hand towards a queue of people lined up by the steps, "...Andrea, Hayley, Julia, Lesley, Matthew, Johnny and Bill, oh, and Keith, who's just back from the loo now."

As she called their names, the dancers came up onto the stage and lined up. They all moved with a grace and fluidity that made Liam want to turn around and run.

"And now for the pairings," Carol announced. Once again, Liam was transported back to his childhood, to the football games he occasionally got involved in during school lunch-breaks. They all started the same way, with everyone lined up while the team captains (usually whoever owned the ball and his best mate) picked teams. Liam was picked last so often that for a while, he wondered if his name actually was 'You can have Liam'. He wasn't all that remarkable; he was terrible at most sports. Because he was expecting to have to wait until last, he nearly missed hearing his name.

"Julia will be paired with...Liam!"

Two pairs had already been announced, and just as they had done, he came up onto the stage to meet his beaming dance partner. Julia was possibly ten years or so younger than him, shorter by perhaps six inches, and unlike Liam, was slim and looked like she took plenty of exercise. She had dark-auburn, wavy hair cut to her jaw-line and was dressed in a hospice sweatshirt and neon green leggings. If she was horrified to see the state of her dance partner, she hid it well, greeting him with a friendly hug. They waited while the other couples were announced. Andy was paired up with a blonde woman called Lesley, who was nearly, but not quite, as tall as he was then Carol sent them all off to find a space in the hall and get acquainted.

"I'm sorry," Liam said as he and Julia carried a couple of chairs over to the side of the hall under a large window. "I'm afraid you've drawn the short straw."

"Don't be silly," Julia replied. "There aren't any short straws in this. None of you have any experience, as far as I know, so everyone's starting from scratch. It's fine."

"So they say, but I'm hardly a prime physical specimen, am I?"

"Don't put yourself down. The gentleman I had last year had just had a knee replacement and we did just fine. You work with what you've got. Besides, by the time I've finished with you, you won't recognise yourself. The main thing is that you're doing this for a reason, aren't you?"

"Yes, I am."

"Can I ask?"

"A mate of ours died earlier this year from cancer."

"I'm sorry. Were you very close?"

Liam thought for a second. He felt closer to Mike now than he had for a very long time, but the irony was that it was almost certainly only because he was dead. If Mike hadn't died, they would have carried on, thinking about each other occasionally but never doing anything about it.

"We hadn't seen each other in a long time," he said. "Not since we were students. I still think he looks like that."

"It doesn't matter," Julia replied. "You're here because you care. That's why we're all here. Everyone has a story. I've been free of breast cancer for three years."

"You? But you look..."

"If you say I look well, I'll probably smack you. You should have seen me when I came out of the hospital minus one boob and carrying a drain that was like a handbag full of Ribena. It wasn't a good look. I've worked bloody hard to look like this, but it isn't what I see in the mirror. Anyway, let's talk about dancing. Be honest now; what *can* you do? Are you married?"

"I was."

"Okay, what did you do at your wedding?"

"I got pissed, mainly. We sort of danced, but it was more like just moving, really. You couldn't call it dancing."

"What song? Or would you rather forget about it?"

When she asked that, a sudden realisation struck Liam. No, he didn't want to forget it. What he wanted was to take Nic in his arms, somewhere, sometime and do it right.

"Someone to Watch Over Me," he said. "It was sort of our song, but I'm not sure why."

Julia hummed a few bars.

"Good song," she said. "Bit of Sinatra always goes down well. How do you fancy learning the foxtrot?"

"I don't know what that is, I don't think."

"Good. Do *not* go away and look it up. Let me have a think about it, but we might just have found our song."

They exchanged phone numbers and Julia said she would be in touch very soon to arrange a time and place for their first proper meeting. Over the other side of the room, he could see that Andy and his partner seemed to be doing much the same thing. Before too long, Clipboard Carol started walking around the groups, suggesting that it was about time to wrap things up.

"I'll speak to you soon, Liam," Julia said. "It looks like your friend has had enough for one day. I think this is going to be fun." She must have caught a look on Liam's face and laughed. "It *will* be fun, Liam, I promise."

Back in the car, Andy looked as shell-shocked as Liam felt. He put his hands on the steering wheel and breathed deeply.

"Bloody hell," he said. "What have we got ourselves into?"

"Julia says it's going to be fun," Liam told him.

"Yes, Lesley said that too. I'm just not sure her idea of fun is the same as my idea of fun. It sounds like it's going to be bloody hard work to me."

"Any idea what a foxtrot is? That's what I'm doing, apparently."

"That's one of those slow ones, isn't it? You lucky bastard."

"Why? What are you doing?"

"You'll laugh."

"I won't."

"You will. I was telling Lesley how we want to try and get people to check themselves and you could practically hear the cogs going round in her head. So, get this. We're going to do a Charleston."

"Isn't that the one...?"

"Yes, it is. And that's not the best bit. She's got this bright idea of doing it to the bloody 'The Rockafeller Skank'. You know, 'Check it out now...'"

Liam didn't laugh. He sat back in his seat and looked at Andy.

"Fuck," he said.

"Yep," Andy agreed. "Fuck."

Chapter Twenty-Six

"Hey, Pops!"

"Freya, don't call me Pops. It makes me sound like a breakfast cereal."

"Sorry, Daddy. So, how's things?"

"Yes, okay, thanks. Keeping busy like you do. Sorry, I meant to ring you and Del the other week, but..."

"I know. Stuff happened. It's fine, don't worry."

"I should ring you more."

"It cuts both ways, Dad. It's okay. I know where you are if I need you."

"Always, baby. I mean that."

"Are you all right? You sound a bit, I don't know..."

"I'm fine. Bit tired, but fine. How are you?"

"Busy busy, like always. We've got that show coming up in Barcelona next March, so lots to do."

"Barcelona? Wow!"

"I told you about it, Dad. Remember?"

"Yes, of course you did. Sorry. It's my age. What did I say?"

"You said 'Barcelona? Wow!'"

"Oh, well, at least I'm consistent. How's it all going?"

"Very well. There's still loads to do, but it's getting there. I've got a really good feeling about it, actually. It could really put us on the map."

"That's amazing Frey. You really deserve it. You've worked so hard. I'm really proud of you."

"Aww, Dad! Stop it, or I'll cry, and it's not a good look. So what's going on with you?"

"Oh, nothing much. The usual, you know?"

"Really?"

"What does that mean?"

"It means it's not what I've heard."

"And what, exactly, have you heard?"

"Keeeep dancing!"

"Oh. That."

"Yes, that. Mum told me."

"I'll kill her."

"Don't be like that. I think it's an amazing thing to be doing. She told me about your friend, too. I'm sorry. But seriously, I think what you and Andy are doing is brilliant! Especially when..."

"When what?"

"Nothing. Forget it."

"Especially when we're so old. That's what you were going to say, isn't it?"

"No! I was going to say especially when you're so out of condition."

"Great. That's worse if anything. I'll have you know that I have the body of a man half my age! Admittedly, he's a seriously overweight man who has never done a day's exercise in his life, but all the same."

"Just you be careful, Dad. I mean it. It's an amazing thing to do, but it's not worth putting yourself in hospital for."

"I will, baby. I promise. I'm working very closely with my dance partner, Julia, and she's really switched on. She's got a pretty good idea of what I can and can't do. The things I can't do far outnumber the things I can do at the moment."

"Oooh, your dance partner, eh? Get you! And what's she like, this Julia? Is she nice? Is she pretty?"

"She's very nice. And I suppose she is pretty, yes."

"Well, just you behave yourself. I've heard what goes on in these dance shows. It's always in the news. Don't want you falling victim to the Strictly Curse."

"I don't think there's much to worry about there."

"Good. We wouldn't want Mum jumping up on the stage to batter her, do we?"

"Like that's going to happen! Your mother's more likely to send her a sympathy card. Nothing's going to happen like that. Julia will probably want to kill me by the time we've finished."

"Good. So anyway, I was thinking. If you're going to raise loads of money, you're going to need a marketing campaign, aren't you?"

"I don't know. Am I?"

"Dad! Of course, you are. How else are people going to hear about it? Have they shown you how to set up a fundraising page?"

"Yes, I think so. They sent me an information pack and there was something in there about it."

"Haven't you done it yet?"

"No. The event isn't 'til December."

"You haven't got a clue, have you? If you want to raise lots of cash, you're going to have to start now and keep battering it right up 'til the night and probably a bit afterwards too. Now you've got Facebook, haven't you? You'll definitely need Instagram as well."

"What for? Isn't that all pictures and stuff?"

"Well, exactly. People are going to want to see pictures of you and pretty Julia in training."

"Why would anyone want to see pictures of some sweaty, fat, middle-aged bloke who can't dance? Are they mad?"

"No, but if you want your audience to be invested in what you're doing, you've got to show them the whole story. That's how it works. And just think how inspiring it will be. If you can do it, anyone can!"

"I'm not sure how to take that."

"And TikTok! You've got to have TikTok. There's always people dancing on TikTok."

"No. Just slow down a minute, Freya. I think you've forgotten who you're speaking to. I can just about take photos on my phone and I hardly ever put anything on Facebook. I hate all that. All those people who put every second of their lives on the internet for everyone to see…it's like their life only exists if they put it online for likes and then get upset when it doesn't happen. That's not me. It's never been me and I'm not going to start now."

"You won't have to do anything. Just set your account up, give me the details, film stuff and send it to me. I'll do everything else."

"No. I don't think so."

"Why? What's the matter? Don't you trust me? I won't make you look stupid; I promise."

"It's not that. I *do* trust you. I just don't think anyone is going to want to see it. *I* don't want anyone to see it. It's...it's embarrassing."

"Well, tough. Because you're not doing this for you, Dad. You're doing it for your friend and for all the people it could help. There are people out there who let everyone see them going through chemo because they think it might help. I don't think you doing a bit of dad-dancing compares, really."

"Bloody hell, Freya. When did you get to be so grown up?"

"Probably round the time Mum had her scare. Did you know about that?"

"Not until the other week. She said you didn't know, either."

"Del was in her house when she got the call from the hospital saying everything was fine. Mum took the call in the kitchen and kept the door shut, but Del heard her say, 'So I haven't got cancer' and then had to wait outside the kitchen door until she stopped crying. We had to grow up, Dad, to stop you two treating us like kids."

"I'm sorry we did that. When you've got kids of your own, you'll understand."

"Maybe. But in the meantime, it's time for you to put your big-boy pants on and raise a shed-load of money, agreed?"

"Agreed."

"You know what?"

"No, what?"

"I'm really proud of you, too."

"Thank you, baby. That means a lot."

"Oh, yes! Just remembered. Mum told me you're dancing to a bit of Frankie, is that right? She said it was your song at one time."

"Mine and your mum's, yes."

"I think that's dead romantic."

"No. It really isn't."

"Maybe it would be if you did it with Mum."

"I think that is a very good place to end this call. Goodbye, Freya."

"'Bye, Dad. Speak soon. And get your TikTok set up. Love you lots."

"Love you too."

Chapter Twenty-Seven
1987

Liam should have seen it coming but didn't. The first indication he had that there was any kind of a problem was at the end of the Andrew Marvell tutorial with Dr Meadows, who wasn't Liam's favourite member of the English department at the best of times. Dr Meadows was a tall man who dressed sharply, although there was some debate amongst his students about whether his hair was real or synthetic. Unlike some of the other tutors, who at least attempted to speak to their students on their level, Meadows, who had several authoritative books on Metaphysical Poetry published (and on the syllabus), had a tendency to talk down in an almost sneering way. He could be extremely witty and charming, as long as you kept on the right side of him, but cutting if you did not. Becky had made no secret of the fact that she idolised him until she got an essay back once, which destroyed that. Written in the margin, in Dr Meadows' elegant hand, was the comment, 'Even if this word were spelled correctly, it is wholly inappropriate in this context' and the essay, in which there seemed to be little else wrong, was marked down. Becky hadn't liked Dr Meadows, or indeed the poetry of George Herbert, since.

The tutorial had wrapped up, and the students were either gathering their things together and getting ready to leave or, in Spanner's case, already halfway along the corridor. Liam was about to suggest going for a coffee to Becky when Meadows stopped him.

"Liam," he said, "I wonder if I could prevail upon you to remain for a few minutes."

"Yes, sure," Liam replied and gave Becky a quick shrug. Once the room had cleared, Meadows took a buff envelope file from his filing cabinet and sat down at his desk.

"Please, take a seat," he said. Liam sat on the chair nearest the desk and waited expectantly while Meadows opened the file and took out some papers. His heart sank when he saw that the papers were A4 sheets with what was unmistakably his handwriting on them. Meadows scrutinised them briefly as if he needed to remind himself of their contents, then laid them on the desk and regarded Liam over his glasses.

"Do you know why I have asked you to stay behind, Liam?"

"No, sir."

"I'm not sure if you are aware, and many aren't, that every student in this department is assigned a personal tutor for their time here. That tutor is someone to whom students can go if they have any academic or personal problems, though..." he laughed in a way that didn't sound very convincing, "we do tend to be better with the academic problems. For my sins, I am your personal tutor and so it is my duty to have this little chat with you. Is everything all right, Liam?"

"Yes, sir. Everything's fine."

"That is usually the answer that question receives. The problem is, Liam, that your work says otherwise. Now, it is not unusual, in itself, if a student doesn't take to a particular module. We can't, after all, like the same things, no matter what that says about personal tastes. It may well be that you simply either don't like or don't get the Metaphysical Poets. That's fine – they're not for everyone. But your last essay was, I'm afraid to say, poor. Where I could actually read it without giving myself a migraine, it was badly written and badly researched. The only thing that stopped the few good bits from being condemned as outright plagiarism was the slight rewording of some sentences. I feel I must point out that I worked very hard to phrase those words in the most apposite way, and I believe my version is rather better than yours."

He paused, perhaps expecting Liam to reply, but no answer came.

"Like I said, not everyone takes to every module, but I have spoken to your other tutors and both Dr Russell and Professor Wilton raised exactly the same concerns. The quality of your work has declined noticeably, which is why I have just asked you if everything is all right. Do you want to change your answer?"

"No, sir. Everything is fine."

"In that case, Liam, I must give you a friendly warning. Your first-year work was good. Most of it was worthy of a good 2:1 and occasionally even merited a first. At the moment, your work will get you a low 2:2. I don't want to see it decline any further, or you will find yourself in a lot of trouble when it comes to the end of year exams. Please don't forget that your paper on Shakespeare this year goes towards your final degree results. From your previous work, Liam, I fully predict that you will be able to pull this back, but it is entirely in your hands. If there is nothing else I should know about, I shall expect to see a marked improvement in your next essays. Is that clear?"

"Yes, sir."

"Excellent! Because I really hate having these conversations. The only thing I hate more is when students tell me there *is* something wrong and expect my advice on what to do about it. Right, off you go. If I were you, I would head straight to the library and not to the bar."

Liam waited momentarily in case there was more, but there clearly wasn't. Feeling utterly humiliated and demoralised, he stood up, mumbled his thanks to Dr Meadows and quickly left the office. He hoped he would be able to scuttle back to his room to think about this without having to talk to anyone. He didn't expect to find Becky waiting for him in the corridor.

"Is everything okay?" she asked.

"Fine," Liam replied, not meeting her eye. "He just wanted to give me my essay back. Go to go."

He tried to go past her but she stopped him by putting a hand on his chest.

"Oh, no, you don't. I've waited for you to come out. The least you can do is talk to me."

"I didn't ask you to," Liam snapped. Then he saw the shocked look on Becky's face and backed down. "Sorry. Sorry, Becks. Come on. I'll buy you a coffee and tell you about it."

Rather than going down the hill to the Union, they went to the small coffee bar in the arts building. The coffee wasn't as good, and it was served in those thin, white plastic cups that burnt your hands if you held them too long. Fortunately, the coffee here was never hot enough for that to be a problem. Liam paid for their coffees, and they sat down at a table as far away from everyone else as possible. Liam lit a cigarette and offered one to Becky, but she shook her head.

"So go on," she said. "What did he have to say?"

"Apparently, my work's shit."

"Did he say that?"

"Not like that. He used much bigger words, but that's what he meant."

"So, what then? He isn't going to fail you, is he?"

"No. He didn't say so. Just told me to do better. So I will."

"Is that it? You'll do better?"

"It's not a problem, Becks. I'll start my essays a bit sooner. I've been a bit busy, that's all."

"Busy? Busy with what? Drinking?"

"What's that supposed to mean?"

Becky drank some of her coffee and nursed the cup for a minute or two without speaking.

"Come on, Becks. What did you mean?"

"I didn't want to say this, but...well, you're drinking a lot these days. Everyone's noticed, but nobody wanted to say."

"I'm just having a good time. That's what we're here for, isn't it?"

"That and getting a degree."

Liam finished his cigarette and dropped the butt into the dregs of his coffee, where it extinguished with a hiss.

"If everyone's noticed," he said, "it's a pity nobody said anything before I got a bollocking off Meadows. Thanks a lot."

"You're the one doing it, Liam," Becky replied, standing up. "Grow up and take a bit of responsibility. Thanks for the coffee."

Without waiting for a reply, she turned and walked out of the coffee bar. Liam watched her go, then lit another cigarette. The packet was nearly empty, and he'd have to buy some more before he went to the Union that night. He'd just have to limit himself to a couple of pints.

He looked at his watch and saw that it was nearly three o'clock. If he was lucky, he might get an hour or two's work in before he got ready to go out. At least if he saw Becky later, he'd be able to say he had started doing something about it. He'd probably better apologise as well. He thought about Becky waiting for him while he was in with Meadows and wondered what it meant if anything. Probably best not to read too much into it.

He'd lied to her, of course. The reason he hadn't been doing as much work as he should was because he was spending a lot of time at the house Nic shared with a couple of postgrad students. They'd started seeing each other a month or so ago, though, for some reason, Nic wasn't ready to go public with it yet. That meant Liam spent what time he could with her and the rest of the time with his friends, trying to be as normal as he could. Maybe he over-compensated sometimes by drinking a bit much, but he didn't drink that much more than Mike or Andy, or at least he didn't think he did. He felt bad about not telling them the truth, too, but that was how Nic wanted it and he didn't want to put her off. It was too good to ruin.

He hadn't been expecting it. It had happened one Saturday night when they'd all been at the Union watching some fringe comedian and when they all left, Liam suddenly found himself walking with Nic. He wasn't sure where everyone else had gone, but he wasn't going to argue with it. He walked her back to her house, and she invited him in for a drink. The housemates were out and before Liam knew what was happening, they were in each other's arms on the rather threadbare sofa, kissing. Liam hadn't kissed many girls before and certainly not like this. He was very self-conscious about it, but something about Nic made him relax and it began to feel natural and good. They didn't sleep together that night, but when they were interrupted by one of the housemates coming back, they arranged to meet the next day. It was then that Nic asked him not to tell anyone just yet. He was too dazed to argue. The next day, when they met for coffee in a café in town, away from the prying eyes at the Union, Liam asked her out, though he stumbled over his words so much, it was a wonder she understood him at all.

"I'd like that," she said, taking his hand across the table. "Only...do you think we could keep it to ourselves, just for a bit?"

"You're not ashamed of me, are you?" Liam asked, feeling defensive and slightly hurt.

"No! Of course not. Why would I? You're lovely. I just don't want to jinx it. Everyone always sticks their noses in and I want to keep you to myself for a bit. Is that okay?"

"So we *are* going out?"

"Yes, we are, but it's our business. No one else's." Liam was quite happy with that and had managed to keep the secret since then.

They had been to bed together a few times when they could, and it was okay. Liam was pretty sure it would get better with practice, but it was complicated, trying to find times when they were both free and Nic's housemates were out. There was no way they could risk Nic coming to Liam's room in halls, not with Mike and Andy on the same floor, so they had to grab what time they could. He'd never been that good at lying, especially to his friends, but he was getting plenty of practice and getting better at that, too. It was difficult to maintain a distance when they were both at the Union, but for the most part, they moved in slightly different circles and could avoid any public displays of affection while still snatching moments together when no one else was looking.

The meeting with Meadows and what Becky had said had now complicated things further. Liam resolved to get himself sorted out, watch how much he was drinking and spend a bit more time working. In some ways, the more he thought about what Becky knew about his meeting with Meadows, worked in his favour. At least he had a ready-made excuse if anyone asked where he was when he was spending time with Nic. He could always say he had to work. Sometimes, it would even be true. He was fairly confident that it wouldn't be forever, anyway. Very soon, Nic would feel happy enough for them to tell everyone and he could stop sneaking around. He couldn't wait.

Chapter Twenty-Eight

"Okay, Andy. I think we should take a break there."

"But I've nearly got that bit."

"I wouldn't go that far, but you definitely need a break and some water."

Lesley ended any possible debate by walking off the studio floor and over to the seating area, where she picked her towel up from a chair and put it around her neck. Andy followed her over and sat down, looking at the floor. This wasn't going quite as well as he hoped.

"Cheer up," Lesley said, sitting down next to him. "You're doing great."

Andy looked up and gave her a wry smile.

"No, I'm not," he said. "I'm crap and we both know it."

"Andy, listen to me. You've never danced before and you're not used to this kind of physical exercise. Tell me something. If you put your car into storage for twenty years, would you expect to be able to take it out and go for a long, fast drive without giving it some attention?"

"No, but—"

"But nothing. That's what you're trying to do to your body. You're trying to push it harder than you've pushed it for a long time. You're trying to get it to do things it's never done before *and* you're trying to do that to music. If you could do all that straight away, you'd be better than anyone I've ever taught, and I've taught some very good dancers."

Andy stood up and went to get a bottle of water out of his bag. He was very much aware of how much his legs ached when he did so. The muscles in his calves and thighs felt taut as guitar strings and he wasn't sure if he would ever be able to bend them again.

"It's not just that," he said. "I always thought I could control my arms and legs, but it turns out I can't."

"Has that always been a problem for you?" Lesley asked, taking a drink from her own water bottle. She had a proper one with the name of her dance school on the side. Andy brought in bottles that he bought in a big pack from Asda.

"For a bit. I was never that tall as a kid, but I shot up. My mum said it happened overnight. As soon as I did, I had all the co-ordination of a pissed giraffe. I knocked so many things over that Mum started hiding all the ornaments away. She was made up when I went to uni and she could get them all out again. She used to say that when I came home, she was going to tie my arms to my sides, just in case."

"I was the same. It's no fun being a tall girl, I can tell you. The boys didn't want anything to do with me. It's all very well for the Jerry Halls of this world, but we can't all find a man who compensates for being a short-arse by having a large wallet."

"I take it you didn't."

"No. I found a lovely man who was secure in himself not to care. I might have found the only one, so I'm keeping him."

Andy laughed. He had hit it off with Lesley from the first minute he had met her on the introduction day. She had taken one look at him and said, "Finally. I can pick on someone my own size," and won him over.

She had gone easy on him in their first training session, showing him on her phone videos of different variations of the Charleston. He had been surprised when she suggested the music because, from what little he knew, he thought it was just an old dance. He associated with the 1920s and flappers, but she showed him that contemporary music could be used just as effectively. There seemed to be a nearly infinite variety of ways the dance could be performed, but he couldn't see how he could ever do any of them. Lesley had faith in him, she said, or at least faith in her ability to teach him. It was good that one of them did.

They spent the remainder of the first session with her showing him some basic steps and making him try them to see what he could do, which, as far as Andy could see, was absolutely nothing. When their time in the studio was up, Lesley assured him that she could see potential in him, but he drove home convinced she was just saying that. He didn't have any ability whatsoever and it must have been patently obvious. He imagined that Lesley went home that night in despair, but she came back the following week just as bright and optimistic. This time, she brought a young dancer called Gareth with her. She and Gareth had, she said, choreographed the routine and she wanted to show him.

Andy sat open-mouthed as Lesley started the music, and she and Gareth started to dance. As well as what looked like an impossible sequence of steps, the routine included two lifts that were, at best, very impressive and, at worst, highly irresponsible, even dangerous. When they reached the end, Andy applauded warmly.

"That was amazing," he said. "You're incredible."

"Thank you," Lesley replied, giving a small curtsey.

"Now, are you going to show me what we're really doing?"

"That *is* what we're really doing."

"No, seriously. I can't do that!"

"You can, Andy. And you're going to."

"But those lifts...no way! I can't do that."

"You can. I'm going to let you into a little secret. Gareth, can we do the run into the second lift, please? Now watch closely, Andy. I want you to watch Gareth and see what he does."

Andy watched in bewilderment while they performed the lift again, Lesley executing a perfect cartwheel and landing in Gareth's arms, from where he raised her into the air. She landed on cat feet and looked at him.

"Did you see it?"

"I don't know," Andy said honestly. "I don't know what I was supposed to be looking for."

"Good," Lesley said, towelling herself off. "That's the point and here's the secret. The audience won't know what

148

they're looking for either, apart from the dancers and the judges. The reason I asked you to watch Gareth is because he didn't actually do anything. I did all the work and he just caught me, but it looked like *we* did a lift."

"But I couldn't even do that."

Instead of answering, Lesley threw her towel at him. Instinctively, he reached out and plucked it out of the air before it hit him in the face.

"Nice reflexes," Lesley said. "So you *can* catch."

"I can catch a towel, yes. But a person? I don't think so."

"It's the same principle, just a bit bigger."

"No, it isn't. A towel doesn't get hurt if you drop it."

Lesley and Gareth laughed, and Andy suddenly felt left out of a private joke.

"I've been dancing for a long time, Andy. Have you any idea how many times I've been dropped? I've bruised pretty much everywhere you can bruise and I'm still here. Once it's happened a few times, you learn how to land. But that's my problem. I'll teach you how to catch in time. First, we've got to teach you how to move."

That was where they were at this, the third session. Andy had always thought that moving was something you did naturally, like breathing, but learned very quickly that this only applies when you're not thinking about it. As soon as Lesley asked him to do something as simple as walk across the studio from one side to another, he suddenly became so self-conscious that he lost the ability to do it altogether. Just the most basic technique of swinging an arm while moving the opposite leg abandoned him and he walked across the studio like a malfunctioning robot. It was even worse when she told him to watch himself in the wall-length mirror while he did it. It was like he was aware of every movement he made and every movement was ridiculous.

"What have you done to me?" he demanded. "I can't even walk now!"

"That's a start," Lesley said. "Now, I'll teach you how to walk properly."

And that is what they did for the next half hour. They walked backwards and forwards across the studio, with Lesley correcting Andy's every movement, encouraging him to keep his arms under control and even dictating the length of his stride. By the time they took a break, Andy was starting to feel a change in the way he moved. Even if you couldn't exactly describe it as graceful yet by any stretch of the imagination, there was certainly an improvement of sorts. All that optimism evaporated very quickly, however, when Lesley tried to get him to do a few basic steps. His mind understood what she was asking of him, but his body had apparently no inclination to co-operate and whatever he tried to make it do, it just went ahead and did its own thing anyway. Now he was sitting there dispirited and sore, and Lesley was still telling him he was going to be fine. He didn't know how she did it and said so.

"Do what? Be patient? It's something else you learn when you've been doing this as long as I have. Don't forget, I couldn't dance either at one time."

"I find that hard to believe."

"It's true. I think anyone who says they can't dance has either never found the right dance or the right teacher. Everyone can do it to one degree or another. You go to any wedding reception and everyone dances, especially once they've had a few. The thing is, they're all having a good time, and nobody cares what they look like. But the one thing they're all doing is moving their bodies in time to a great song. You can't tell me that isn't dancing."

"Not like this, though."

"No, not like this, but no one has ever taught them how. Now of course some are better at it than others, but you could say that about anything. I bet there are things you can do that you'd have to teach me, even if it's only your job."

"That's not very exciting, I'm afraid."

"It doesn't have to be. It's something you can do right now that I can't. Now, reverse our positions. It's the same thing."

Andy took a moment or two to think about this. It nearly made sense, but only nearly.

"You have world champions in dancing, though," he said. "And I've never seen a programme on the telly called Strictly Come Insurance."

"Don't get me wrong, Andy, there are exceptional dancers who can compete at the highest levels with a hell of a lot of hard work and dedication, but they will also have had a natural ability in the first place. I think it's the same with any artistic endeavour, whether it's dancing, playing an instrument, painting, whatever. I'm convinced that anyone can be taught to do it, but some people have an inborn talent and they're the ones who reach the top. Luckily for you, we're only trying to reach the top of this competition, not the top of the world rankings. I'm sure we can do it."

"If you say so."

"I say so. But not by sitting around talking about it. Are you ready to go again?"

Chapter Twenty-Nine

"She's fucking relentless, lad. I think she's a machine."

"I know what you mean there, Liam. I'm spending six days a week knackered and one day *getting* knackered. I think she's trying to kill me."

"You know what Julia said yesterday? She said that as we get nearer, we'll probably have to start increasing the number of training sessions."

"What, to more than one a week?"

"Two for sure, maybe three."

"I hope she's not talking to Lesley. That would finish me off. It's bad enough that she expects me to practice at home. Practice? I can hardly move!"

"Do you do it, though? How does that work? I'm okay, like, because I'm on my own, but how do you do it with a houseful?"

"I've had to start going into the garage. Can you believe that? Ali had a go at me. Said she couldn't stand the noise I was making in the bedroom."

"Andy, mate, I really don't want to know about the noise you make in the bedroom."

"Get lost. There's none of that going on. I haven't got the energy. Ali's made up. She wants me to take up dancing full-time."

"It's not just the pain, though. It's doing my head in trying to learn all the language. It's not even English. It's bad enough trying to learn all the steps, but how are you supposed to do it when she uses words you've never heard before? She keeps going on about my frame. I didn't know I had a frame 'til now. A frame's what you put pictures in."

"Or what coppers do to you."

"Or that. Whatever it is, apparently, mine's all wrong. I *slouch*, she says. I stick my arse out when I'm supposed to be tucking it in. She told me she was going to stick a broomstick down my trousers to keep my back straight. I told her she wasn't getting anywhere near my trousers, thanks very much. I signed up to learn how to dance, not go along and have the piss taken once a week. She sends me pictures and videos of people doing it properly. I wish I'd never given her my number."

"I know. Lesley's the same. She sends me clips of these insane dancers doing stuff I could never dream of and thinks it'll encourage me."

"Yeah, what's that all about? I wouldn't send you a clip of Mo Salah scoring and tell you that you could do it too if you try hard enough."

"And the bloody stupid pictures. Memes is it, the kids call them? Those stupid pictures of sunsets and stuff with things like *believe in yourself* and shit like that. What are they meant to do? I'm not going to look at one of them and go, 'You know what? You're right! I believe in myself now!' It's more likely to make me puke."

"She means well, I suppose. At least she's not sending you pictures that say, 'You're a bag of shite'."

"That would be a bit more honest. Not that I need it. I've got kids to do that for me. Stevie doesn't say a word about it, but Amy... The other day, she came into the garage to see what I was doing. She stood and watched for a bit, then just sort of snorted and went out again. She told me last night I was making a laughing-stock of her. I pointed out that it wasn't going to be her getting on a stage and making a knob of themselves in a couple of months. You know what she said?"

"What?"

"'It might as well be.' After all I've done for her, that's the gratitude I get."

"Freya and Del keep asking me to send them videos of me training."

"You don't, do you?"

"Do I hell. I don't need to. Julia's only gone and friended them both on Facebook and *she* sends them videos. Del sends me little messages of encouragement and helpful bits of advice from stuff she's seen on *Strictly*. Freya just takes the piss. Bloody kids. I wish I'd never told them."

"I wish I'd never had mine."

"No, you don't."

"Do you want to adopt them?"

"No thanks."

"Well then. You know what I reckon?"

"What do you reckon, Andy?"

"I reckon this is all Mike's revenge. All those years we never got in touch with him and I bet he's up there now wetting himself watching us."

"At least we're keeping him entertained, hey?"

"Yeah, he always did have a sick sense of humour. Remember that time I found out about Nic?"

"Oh God, yes. I can never hear The Communards without remembering that."

Chapter Thirty
1987

Liam wasn't sure whether Mike put the song on the jukebox to cheer him up, as he claimed, or whether it was his idea of a joke, but 'Don't Leave Me This Way' was about the last thing he wanted to hear at the end of what could have been the worst day of his life.

It had started well enough. He woke up early, not feeling tired for once and got some reading in to prepare for that morning's lecture. He stayed alert throughout the lecture, enjoyed it and made copious notes. It was only when he headed down to meet Mike and Andy for lunch that things began to go wrong.

His friends had already claimed a table at Fat Freddy's, the Union's café. Liam ordered himself lasagna and coffee and went over to join them, waving hello to Claire and the two Donnas at a table behind them. He chatted with Andy and Mike about their day so far and they made tentative plans for the weekend until the food arrived. He was happily tucking in when he overheard the conversation that was going on at the next table. Claire and the Donnas seemed to be discussing someone they knew, and their voices were loud enough to carry. Mike and Andy were enjoying their food and not speaking much, so Liam was able to listen in.

"I don't know what's up with her," one of the Donnas said. "She's not herself."

"Well, it isn't boyfriend trouble," Claire replied. "She hasn't got one."

"She has, you know," the other Donna said.

"What? No, she hasn't! Has she? Who?" Claire sounded very excited at the prospect of some juicy gossip.

"No one we know. He's not here; he's back home. She let it slip once. This was last year, so don't say anything. I don't think they've split up. It sounded pretty serious to me."

"Donna! Why haven't you ever said? What did she say?"

"It was when we were talking about what we were going to do over the summer. She said she was going to Crete with James and his family. It sounded like they were quite well-off. I tried to press her on it, but she just shut up and then changed the subject. She's not mentioned it since."

What Claire said next nearly made Liam choke on his coffee.

"Bloody hell. She's a dark horse, our Nic, isn't she?"

Liam didn't hear the rest of the conversation. He could barely hear anything and felt faint. It was like he was standing at the top of a tall cliff and looking down and could fall at any second.

"You okay, Liam?" Mike asked.

"Yes, fine," Liam managed to say, then he stood up on jelly legs. "Sorry. I've got a banging headache. I'll see you later."

Without waiting for a response, he walked downstairs, out of the building and sat down on a low wall, trying to breathe in as much air as he could and slow down his pounding heart. He lit a cigarette and smoked it, staring at the ground. A Twix wrapper was caught in some grass at the edge of the wall and a procession of ants was marching across it. He watched them go and tried not to think about what he had just heard but failed.

It explained everything. No wonder Nic wanted to keep everything dark. She wouldn't want word getting back to her rich boyfriend that she was seeing some scally from Liverpool. Liam was just her dirty little secret, someone to occupy her time while she was in Bangor and away from her real boyfriend.

Of course, there was a possibility that Donna had got it wrong; she did that sometimes, but it didn't sound like it. He thought briefly about going to the bar and getting rat-arsed but thought better of it for two reasons. One was that he was supposed to be seeing Nic later and wanted a clear head. The other was that he had no desire to be around other people who might ask stupid questions.

He walked back up the hill to his room, feeling lost and alone. To think that tonight was the night he had planned to tell Nic how he really felt about her, that he thought he loved her and had hoped that she might say the same back. He paused halfway up the hill and leaned on the wall, anger rising in him. He aimed a punch at the wall but couldn't quite bring himself to hit it as hard as he wanted and pulled back at the last second, grazing his knuckles instead of breaking his hand as he had intended. If he'd broken his hand, Nic might have given him some sympathy, but he couldn't even do that right. No wonder she didn't really want him.

Why did he have to have heard that today? He was meeting Nic that evening to go and see the film *Little Shop of Horrors* at the Theatr Gwynedd, partly because they both wanted to see the film (Nic more than Liam) and partly because most students went to the cinema to watch the latest releases. The theatre tended to show more arty, interesting films and so attracted much smaller audiences. Liam had hoped that he and Nic would be able to watch the film like proper couples do, but now he could only imagine being trapped in the theatre with someone who didn't want to be there.

He spent the afternoon trying to read, but he was all too aware that he was just staring at words on a page that could have been written in Swahili for all they meant to him. In reality, he was trying to imagine what this James character might look like, what he had that Liam didn't, and what he would say to him to cut him down if ever he met him. Some posh get from down south would be no match for Liam's Scouse wit and he would tear him to shreds.

When the time approached to go out, he got himself showered, shaved and dressed in his best shirt (that would show her) and walked slowly down to the theatre. They had arranged to meet in the foyer so that if, by chance, anyone saw them, they could say that they had met by accident, but Liam timed it so that he entered the foyer just before the film was due to start. Nic was standing near the box office, looking at her watch and glancing around. Good. Let her wait.

157

"There you are!" she said when she saw him come in. "I've got your ticket. We'd better get in; it's about to start."

"I'll pay you later," Liam said.

"Don't worry about that. Come on."

The auditorium was already in darkness as they went in and from the silhouettes Liam could see, barely half-full. They found seats on a row that was completely empty and sat down.

"I thought you weren't coming," Nic said.

"I'm here, aren't I?"

Whatever Nic might have been going to reply was cut short by the film starting. As the opening sequence began, Nic leaned in towards Liam, but he folded his arms and focused his attention on the screen. He had been looking forward to seeing this film but his mood soured it for him. He found the songs annoying and the special effects stupid. The romance between Seymour and Audrey annoyed him and he wanted to give Seymour a bloody good shake for being such a wimp. Even Steve Martin, whose cameo as the dentist had the small audience laughing and cheering, couldn't raise a smile. He hated dentists and the thought of it set his fillings on edge. When the final credits rolled, he stood up and walked out of the auditorium with Nic hurrying behind to keep up with him.

"That was brilliant!" Nic said when they were out in the foyer. "Better than the stage show if anything. At least this one had a happy ending."

"It's not as good as Rocky Horror," Liam said.

"Well, that goes without saying. All the same, I loved it. I want to get the soundtrack. I loved Rick Moranis. I didn't know he could sing like that."

"I thought you said they all die in the stage show. That would have been a better ending."

"Oh, no. That's really sad. I'm glad Audrey got her happy ending."

"Yeah, well, it's nice someone does."

"Wow, we're cynical tonight. What now? Do you want to come back to mine? Gill and Ravi are away for the weekend."

"No, I think Mike and Andy are in the Belle Vue. Unless you want to come with me."

"I'd love to," Nic said, "but...I don't know. I don't know if I'm quite ready for that yet. Maybe next time. You understand, don't you?"

"Oh, I understand," Liam said through gritted teeth, pushed open the theatre door and walked out onto the street.

"Why did you say it like that?" Nic asked as she joined him on the pavement outside. "You're in a terrible mood tonight. Are you okay?"

"I'm fine," Liam snapped. "Just great."

"Have I done something? What is it?"

"Look, forget it. I'm going to the pub."

"No, wait a minute. I don't want to leave you when you're like this. Something's upset you. I know you want to tell everyone about us, but..."

"Don't worry. I'm not going to tell anyone. We wouldn't want James to find out, would we?"

The colour drained from Nic's face, and she looked like he had slapped her.

"James?" she stammered. "What do you know about James?"

"Enough."

"No, Liam. What exactly do you know?"

"I know that if you want to keep your boyfriend back home a secret, it's probably best not to tell anyone about him. Or are you only good at keeping secrets when it's me?"

"Look, I don't know what you think you've heard, but you've got it wrong."

Liam turned away and lit a cigarette. He knew that he should be careful about what he said next but was past caring.

"I get a lot wrong, don't I?" he said quietly. "I thought you liked me, but I got that wrong, didn't I?"

"No, you didn't. I *do* like you."

"Not as much as James, though. You're better off with him."

159

He knew as soon as he said it that he had gone too far, but the words hung in the distance between them, and it was too late to take them back. He expected Nic to be hurt. What he didn't expect was her fury.

"How fucking dare you!" she shouted. "How dare you accuse me! You know nothing about it. Nothing! For your information, I finished with James last summer. He took me away to bloody Crete with his snotty family and then left me with them while he shagged some waitress. He completely fucking humiliated me, so don't you even mention his name."

Liam was stunned and didn't know what to say. He couldn't have got this more wrong if he tried.

"I'm sorry," he said, stepping towards her. "I didn't know."

"No, I gathered that," she said, holding up a hand to stop him from getting any closer. "But you didn't bloody ask, either. You just assumed that I was some tart playing two men at the same time. Thanks a lot, Liam. If that's what you really think of me, then there's nothing more to say."

"So why didn't you want anyone to know about us?"

"Because James broke my heart and everyone knew about it and I didn't want that happening again. His whole family knew what he was doing and thought it was a big joke. I had to stay there for the rest of the holiday because I couldn't get home on my own. Have you got any idea what that feels like? I thought I'd never trust anyone again. Then I met you, and, believe it or not, thought I might just be able to love someone again, but there was no way I was going to risk anyone knowing until I was sure."

"You can be sure," Liam said. "We can still..."

"No, Liam. We can't. Not now you've shown me what you really think of me. Fuck off to the pub with your mates. I'm done."

"But..."

"Just go away, Liam. I'm not doing this anymore."

With that, she turned away and walked off, leaving Liam standing outside the theatre. He watched her go and wanted the ground to swallow him up. He had behaved like a stupid child and made the biggest mistake of his life and there was almost certainly no way of putting it right.

He should have gone home then but wanted a drink and trudged up the hill to the pub instead. That was a mistake too. Mike and Andy were already in high spirits when he got there and the last thing he felt like having was any kind of a good time.

"Here he is!" Andy said. "I'll get you a pint."

"Didn't think you'd come," Mike said. "We thought you might be a bit busy with your girlfriend."

"My what? I haven't got..." Liam protested, but Mike slapped him on the back and laughed.

"You were seen, you sly bugger. I've just seen Richie off my course who said you were getting very cosy in the theatre with the lovely Nic."

"How long's that been going on?" Andy asked, handing him a pint. "Or was that your first date?"

"No," Liam said and took a long pull on his pint. "That was the last one. We broke up."

"What? How come? What happened?"

"I fucked everything up," Liam said. He wanted to cry but was damned if he was going to do it here. "I don't want to talk about it."

"Oh, mate," Mike said. "Sorry. Tell you what, I'll stick some tunes on to cheer you up."

He went over to the jukebox and made some selections while Liam concentrated on his pint and said nothing.

"Here you go," Mike called. "You like The Communards, don't you?"

'Don't Leave Me This Way'. It bloody had to be, didn't it?

Chapter Thirty-One

Liam had just finished work for the day. He had spent the afternoon fitting a video camera doorbell for a lovely old lady in Bethesda, who insisted on plying him with so many cups of tea and Tunnocks' Teacakes that Julia would explode if she ever found out. He had absolutely no intention of telling her because she was starting to reveal a fiercely determined streak, especially as far as Liam's physical fitness was concerned. She had even started to sniff him when he arrived at practice to check whether he had been smoking on his way to the rehearsal room.

He pulled into the industrial estate, but when he arrived at his unit, he was quite surprised to find a blue Toyota already parked outside it. It was very rare he received visitors at the unit; in fact, the only person who had called there in the last year had been his accountant, Rhodri, who came to pick up his paperwork to do the end of year accounts and he didn't stay. What was even more surprising was that the occupant of the car was a young blonde woman who appeared to be filming herself on her phone.

Liam parked the van outside the next unit, went over to the Toyota and tapped on the driver's window. The young woman was so startled that she nearly dropped her phone but regained her composure and slid the window down.

"Can I help you at all?" Liam asked.

"No, it's okay," the woman replied. "I'm just waiting for the owner of this unit."

"That would be me," Liam said. "Would you mind moving your car, please? I need to park outside the unit to unload my gear."

"Are you Liam Rawlinson?"

"It depends. Who's asking?"

The young woman got out of the car and held out her hand.

"I'm Michelle Leyland," she said.

"Sorry. That doesn't ring a bell."

"I'm a content creator. You know, Mish's People?"

She looked at Liam as if he were supposed to know what that meant. All he heard were words but didn't recognise the order she had put them in.

"No, sorry. I don't even know what a content creator is. What can I do for you, Ms – Leyland, was it?"

"It's more what I can do for you, Liam. Is there somewhere we could have a chat?"

"Well, like I said, I need to unload my van and then get home and change. There's somewhere I need to be tonight."

"Dance practice?"

"Okay, this is getting a bit weird now. You seem to know a lot about me, but I don't know anything about you. Do you want to start at the beginning?"

"Can we go inside? I think it's starting to rain."

Liam sighed and opened the door to the unit. He showed her to the small office area and cleared a spool of cable off a chair so she could sit down.

"Right then," he said. "I got that your name's Michelle Leyland, but after that, I sort of lost track."

"I'm a content creator," she said, again making it sound like the most obvious thing in the world. Seeing Liam's blank look, she explained further, speaking slowly and clearly as if she were explaining to a toddler how to use a fork. "I make videos about things that interest me and post them on TikTok. You *have* heard of TikTok, haven't you?"

"Yes, I have. Why?"

"Why what?"

"Why do you do it? What's it for?"

"I've got nearly two million followers."

"Congratulations."

"Thanks. I make videos of people and things that I find interesting, and people seem to like them." She tapped her phone and brought up her page on TikTok and showed it to him. If that was anything to go by, she certainly made a lot of

163

videos. The page was full and as she scrolled down, there were more and more of them.

"That's very impressive, but I don't know what it's got to do with me."

"I saw a clip that someone called Freya did about this dance thing you're doing and tracked you down. Clever idea to show your business card at the end of the clip."

Liam resisted the urge to tell her that Freya was his daughter or that he hadn't watched any the clips all the way through. He had heard more than enough about what goes on online not to trust her just yet.

"You're lucky I came back here today. I don't always. You could have been waiting a long time."

"It would have been worth it. I really want to talk to you about it and do a piece on you if you agree."

"No."

Liam stood up and went over to open the door.

"If you don't mind, I'm very busy," he said. "I've seen some of the stuff you people post and I don't want any part of it."

"You don't understand," Michelle protested, staying where she was.

"Oh, I think I do. You might be under the impression that the idea of a fat, old bloke dancing is funny, but it really isn't. Could you just leave, please?"

"I don't think it's funny. Honestly, I think what you guys are doing is awesome." Michelle paused, then tapped her phone again and showed the screen to Liam. On it was a photograph of an elderly man lying in a hospital bed. He was attached to an array of monitors and drips but was giving a thumbs-up to the camera. His mouth was concealed behind an oxygen mask, but Liam could tell from the visible part of his face that he was smiling.

"My granddad," Michelle said. "He had lung cancer. He fought to the end, but we lost him two months ago. He was in Larks House and they were amazing. They made it so easy for them. Sorry." She rooted in her bag for a tissue and wiped away the tears that were spilling from her eyes. She blew her nose and did that thing young people do when they think that waving their fingers to waft air at their eyes is somehow going to make them stop crying. "Can we start again?" she asked.

Liam came back and sat down again.

"I'm sorry for your loss. He looked a great old fella."

"He was. The best. Me and my brother used to go round there after school most days because my mum worked shifts. My nan and granddad were like second parents to us. Then he got ill, but by the time they found it, it had gone too far. He was wasting away in hospital, like he was shrinking in front of our eyes, but Larks House made him comfortable and as happy as he could be. My nan used to come away from the hospital crying and didn't really want to go to see him there, but she spent hours with him every day at Larks House and it helped so much. So I want to help you to help them."

"I'm sorry, Michelle. I jumped to conclusions when I should have heard you out. What do you want from me?"

"You really don't know how this works, do you? Wow. It's easy. I have two million followers, like I said. So anything I post gets seen by all of them. If even a few donate or share, it will boost your profile and I mean a lot."

"That's very kind of you, but..."

"But nothing. I'm happy to do it for my granddad and all the others like him."

"Well if you put it like that, what do you want me to do?"

"Brilliant!" Michelle beamed and jumped to her feet. "I've got some props in the car, so we'll get some photos and then have a chat about what you're doing and why."

She was out of the door before Liam had a chance to ask, "What props?" As if the contortions Julia was putting his body through weren't enough, this complete stranger was going to make a complete show of him. As he did when his dance partner insisted on manoeuvring his neck or his legs into positions they were never supposed to reach, he held his tongue and reminded himself that this was all in a good cause.

Whatever humiliation he was put through, it was nothing compared to what Mike had endured. He heard Michelle's car boot slam, and she came bustling back into the unit with several large carrier bags.

"Right," she said. "What look shall we go for?"

"I'm in my work clothes," Liam said, gesturing at his baggy, stained sweatshirt and scruffy jeans.

"Doesn't matter," Michelle replied, foraging in one of the bags.

"At least let me take my hi-viz off."

"No! That's the point. That's the story, don't you see? The idea of an ordinary working man swapping the hi-viz for the high glamour of the ballroom? It's perfect! Now, what about this?"

She held out a top hat. Liam looked at it as if she had offered him a rat sandwich.

"Really?"

"No, it isn't quite right. Hang on." She put the top hat down on the desk and fished in the other bag. What she pulled out was even worse.

"Now this is perfect!" she exclaimed, showing him an object that appeared to be a plastic bowler hat covered in gold glitter and sequins.

"Are you taking the piss?" Liam asked.

"Come on, Liam. You need to enter into the spirit of it. Let's get some photos first, then I'll do a bit of an interview. How does that sound?"

"It sounds bloody awful, but you know what you're doing, I suppose."

"Yes, I do," she said and handed him the hat.

"What do you want me to do with this? Oh, no. You don't expect me to put it on, do you?"

"Not yet. First of all, hold it out in front of you... No, both hands... On the brim, Liam... No, one hand each side! Come on. Haven't you ever seen *Cabaret*? Or *Chicago*?"

"Have a guess."

"Hold the hat out in front of your chest with straight arms... That's it. Now smile!"

"You want me to smile as well?"

"Of course. A great big, cheesy showbiz smile... No, that looks like you're in pain."

"I am."

"Look like you're enjoying yourself. Think of all the money you're going to raise. That's it!"

Michelle raised her phone and Liam heard click after click as she took photographs from a variety of angles.

"That's great, Liam. Now, how about we go for the full Bob Fosse?"

"You're doing it again. I have literally no idea what you just said."

"Bob Fosse is only one of the most famous choreographers ever. How can you be dancing without knowing things like that?"

She consulted her phone and, once she had found what she was looking for, held it up for Liam to see. It was a picture of three lithe young people standing in a row and leaning back in what looked to Liam like a most unnatural pose. They were all wearing bowler hats and looked like they were trying to brush something off the brim.

"What in God's name is that?" Liam asked. "No. You can't expect me to do that. I'll look stupid!"

"It's called The Rake. And you won't look stupid. You'll look like you know what you're doing. So come on. Stand sideways on. Lean back a bit...no, at the waist!"

"I haven't got a waist!"

"Shut up and lean back. That's it. Now point your left leg straight out and turn your foot to face me."

"I'll fall over!"

"No, you won't. Don't be a baby. Like this."

She bent down and grabbed his leg and pulled it straight, then took hold of his foot and turned it nearly at right angles to his leg.

"Have you ever thought it might be time to buy some new trainers?" she asked.

"You wanted the working man look."

"True. Okay, bend your right leg at the knee a bit...good. Now hold that."

Liam did his best to hold the pose while Michelle consulted her phone again, but he felt seriously off-balance. If she didn't hurry up, the only photos she would get would be of him in a heap on the floor.

"Right. Hands now. Put your left hand on your thigh and then you're going to hold the brim of the hat like this, okay?"

She showed him the picture on her phone again.

"That's impossible," he said.

"No, it isn't. They're doing it."

"Yes, trained professional dancers are doing it. Don't know if you knew, but I'm not one."

"Just try it, Liam. You're doing great."

Liam consulted the picture again and tried to copy the dancers, pinching the brim of the hat between his thumb and forefinger as if he were picking up a delicate china cup in a posh tearoom, something else that was totally out of his field of experience.

"That's fantastic!" Michelle said and clapped excitedly. "Hold that!"

"I don't have to smile, do I?"

"Not this time."

"Thank God for that."

Once again, Michelle snapped away until she photographed Liam from almost every angle possible.

"Awesome!" she said. "You can relax now."

"Are you sure? You don't want me to jump through hoops of fire or anything?"

"No," she said and laughed. "Now we're just going to sit and talk and you're going to tell me all about your friend and why you're doing this.

Chapter Thirty-Two

"Is that the star of TikTok?"

"Don't start, Delyth. I look like a right idiot."

"No, you don't, Dad. You look incredible. Have you lost weight, too?"

"I bloody hope so. I'm getting enough exercise."

"You sound a bit out of breath. Sorry, are you in the middle of training?"

"No, it's okay. I'm on a break. Miss Whiplash lets me have five minutes every couple of hours or so. She just said she's not that bad, but she is, you know. She's a sadist. Could you send me a file in a cake or something? I think I need to escape."

"I hope she isn't listening to that."

"Oh, she is. Now she's threatening me with a banana, so I'd better not stay on long."

"Have you seen how many views that TikTok has had?"

"No, I haven't. Has it had many?"

"You don't know how to look, do you?"

"No."

"Thought not. Okay, open TikTok. Have you done that?"

"Yes. Bloody hell. There's some strange stuff on here."

"Ignore it. Now find the clip. Got it?"

"You're not going to make me watch it, are you?"

"No, but look on the right-hand side. See the heart? Now look at the number under it."

"It says...14.6k. Is that...? That can't be right."

"It is. Looks like you're a hit. Mish has a really big following, so loads of people will have seen it. Have you had many donations?"

"I don't know. I doubt it."

"Have you checked your emails?"

"Only the work one, for quotes and that. Why?"

"Oh my God, you're hopeless. They tell you when you someone donates. I can't believe you didn't know that. I thought Frey told you what to do."

"She might have done. I'm not sure I was listening."

"Well, check now."

"Okay, but I don't know if... Fucking hell! There's one, two, three...are those all donations?"

"Look at your Just Giving page, Dad."

"Hang on."

"You still there, Dad?"

"I am. I just can't...There's over five hundred quid there, Del. Thirty-one people have donated. I don't know who a lot of them are. This is insane!"

"Isn't it? You're doing brilliantly, Dad. We're proud of you, me and Rainie. And Freya is."

"Thanks, sweetheart. That means a lot."

"You know who else is going to be proud of you? One day, your grandchild is going to look back and see what you did and be so impressed."

"I'm just doing my best, Del. Wait a minute. What did you just say?"

"I said your grandchild is going to be impressed."

"Does that mean...?"

"Yes."

"Which one of you?"

"Me."

"Oh, Del. That's wonderful! And how are you? Are you okay? Is everything...?"

"Everything's fine, Dad. The clinic is keeping a very close eye on me, and so is Rainie. It's all good."

"I'm really pleased for you both, Del. Give Rainie my love, will you? I'll tell you one thing. That baby is going to have the best two mothers it could wish for. You are both going to be amazing."

"Thanks, Dad. I had a very good example."

"Yes, that's true. Your mum was great with you, both of you. I'll grant her that."

"So were you, Dad. You still are. Not many girls have got the Dancing Electrician for a dad."

"I'm not sure many would want it."

"Of course they would. You're boss, lad. Mum thinks so too, you know. She follows everything you do."

"Probably waiting to have a good laugh when I fall flat on my face."

"No, Dad. I know she's proud of you but she'll never say. You know what she's like. You should talk to her."

"I do talk to her."

"No, I mean *really* talk to her. Have you ever wondered why she never found anyone else after you left?"

"I've never asked about things like that, Del, you know that. It's none of my business. Look, I've got to go. Julia's got the cattle prod out."

"Okay. Talk to Mum, Dad. Please."

Chapter Thirty-Three

Liam didn't speak to Nic for the rest of the term. He had tried to apologise to her the following day, waiting outside the drama building until she came out of a tutorial, but she was in the company of some of her friends (including the insufferable Geoff), laughing and joking as if she didn't have a care in the world. Rather than risk her blanking him, he hid around the corner until they had gone. If she had been on her own, he would have tried to speak to her, but not when she had her mates with her. After that, he stopped trying. He thought about writing to her, even going so far as to opening a notebook at a blank page and putting his pen to the paper, but when he considered what to say, he realised that there were no words to justify or explain the way he had behaved and gave that up too. He saw her at a distance in the bar sometimes, but she was usually with the drama crowd. Even Claire and the Donnas remarked that they didn't see so much of her these days. Liam's friends had the decency not to mention her at all.

There were other distractions to take Liam's mind off his perhaps not broken but certainly wounded heart. The end of year exams were approaching a bit too rapidly for his liking and they included the dreaded Shakespeare paper that would count towards his finals. He also had to decide on a topic for his dissertation and have his choice agreed by the English department. He was thinking of doing something on the poetry of Seamus Heaney, partly because he liked it and partly because there were relatively few books on the subject, which meant he would have less research. Writing the dissertation was going to take up enough of the summer without having to do a lot of reading too. The one good thing, as far as anyone who was going to read his dissertation was concerned, was that when he was home at Christmas. His mother lent him a typewriter ("I'm only lending it so make sure you look after it."), so that the English department wouldn't have to employ any of the former staff from Bletchley Park to decode his handwriting. He had been trying it out and was getting quite proficient at it, provided that you called pecking at the keys with two fingers proficient and there was a plentiful supply of Tipp-Ex to hand.

He hoped that his parents would be equally understanding about his other major plan for the summer. He had been talking with Andy and Mike, and they had all agreed that at such a crucial time in their academic life, it made perfect sense to stay in Bangor over the summer rather than go home. Liam and Andy had to prepare for their final year, and Mike, who had taken his finals, was now waiting for his results. He had signed on to do a Postgraduate Certificate of Education, which meant he would be around for at least another year. They could study with few distractions, encourage each other and have the university library close at hand. They couldn't stay in halls, so would have to rent a house, but had already earmarked a likely candidate, a large house towards Bangor Hospital, owned by a local landlord who was prepared to let it out for the summer. The only two potential sticking points were that Liam had to get his parents to agree (and hopefully assist with the rent) and that there needed to be four of them because the landlord, a Geordie named Howie Coleman, insisted that all four rooms in the house be taken before he agreed to the lease. Howie Coleman was reputed to be somewhat dodgy and well-connected in places you wouldn't necessarily want connections, so it was best not to argue.

The first problem was solved rather more easily than Liam had expected. When he made his weekly phone call to his parents (or rather to his mum because his dad's contribution was still "I'll get her"), Liz surprised him by getting in first.

"Me and your dad have decided to take a longer holiday this year," she said. "We've always wanted to go to France. We're going to be away for three weeks, though how your dad's going to get on with the language, I don't know. Shout probably. I just hope we can get some decent English food because you know how he is with garlic. Anyway, you don't mind being on your own, do you?"

Liam spotted what, if he played it right, could be a perfect opportunity.

"Well, if that's what you want," he said, doing his best to sound shocked and perhaps a little sad. "I'll manage, I suppose."

"You're not to be having any parties, though. I know what you young ones are like. I want to find the house in exactly the same condition when we get back."

"I hope you can trust me. I mean, I know I'd be okay, but...maybe it would be better if I stayed here for the summer."

"No! We can't ask you to do that. They won't let you stay in halls anyway."

"I might be able to find a room somewhere. I could probably put up with it for a few weeks, if it would make you feel happier."

"But I know what student bedsits are like. I've heard that some are really grotty. You know, dirty and damp and falling to bits. I don't know, Liam. It's good of you to offer, but..."

"It's fine," Liam said, resisting the urge to punch the air. "I'm sure I can find somewhere that's not too bad. Or too expensive."

"We'll help you with that, of course. No, Liam. I insist. If you're sure..."

And just like that, it was done. All they had to do was find a fourth and the solution to that arrived far quicker than Liam had expected.

He had just come out of a lecture and was on his way down the hill for a spot of post-lecture lunch when he spotted the familiar figure of Becky up ahead, going in the same direction. She was walking with her head down, lost in a world of her own. She hadn't been quite the same since she and Paul had split up a month or so earlier, particularly because of the circumstances. She had found out, purely by accident, that the verdant, snow-capped mountains of Snowdonia weren't the only attraction that the Mountaineering Club held for him; there was a first-year student called Sharon who had been very keen for Paul to show her the ropes in more ways than one. Becky was devastated, hurt and angry in equal measures and Liam, Mike and Andy, like Three Musketeers, had given her plenty of support. Liam especially felt she was a kindred spirit after his breakup with Nic. They had offered a number of solutions, many of which involved Paul's mountaineering tackle and his personal tackle and had made Becky laugh for a while at least.

Liam jogged down the hill to catch her up, calling her name as he did so as not to startle her. She turned and gave him a weak smile.

"Hi," she said, and Liam could tell by her tone of voice that something was wrong.

"Are you okay?" he asked. "What's up? Is it Shitbag again? What's he done?"

"No, it's not Paul," Becky replied. "It's Jo. She's just told me she's signed up for that Camp America thing, so she's going to be away all summer."

"That's a shame. Why don't you go, too? You've always said you want to see the States."

"I know, but I want to *see* the States, not be stuck on some camp entertaining kids. If I wanted to do that, I'd get a job at Pontins. I don't really want to be stuck in that house on my own and Jo won't let the room out, so I guess I'll have to go home. I'm just on my way to the Union to ring my dad now. He'll hate the idea. I'm sure he was glad to get rid of me."

"Tell you what," Liam said, "I'm going to Fat Freddy's. You make your call and then come and have lunch. We'll get our heads together and see if we can come up with an answer."

"No, there's no need. I'll sort something out."

"Hey, what are friends for?"

"Okay," she said as they reached the door to the Union. "I'll see you up there in about then minutes."

It turned out to be less than ten minutes. Liam had only just sat down with a cup of coffee when Becky arrived.

"No answer," she said. "They must be out."

"That's a bugger. Come on, let's order. I've had an idea."

175

They ordered their food and while waiting for it to come, Liam put his hastily concocted plan into action.

"It's probably just as well your folks weren't in," he said, "because you mightn't have to go home."

"I'd be bored out of my head on my own," Becky said. "And I don't think I'd feel that safe. So unless someone can come and sleep on the settee, I think I'll have to go back."

"No, you won't. Here's the idea. Me and Andy and Mike have been talking about renting a place here over the summer and one of the places we were looking at has four rooms. I could have a word if you like. You could come and stay with us. I think Mike might have someone else in mind, but I can talk him into it."

"What, me in a house with three lads?"

"It's not like you don't know us, is it?"

"I know, but won't it be a bit weird?"

"It doesn't have to be. At least you know we're okay. It's not like strangers or anything."

"No, I suppose you're safe enough. I mean, it's you, isn't it? And I've wondered about Mike."

"Wondered? What about?"

"I don't know. There's *something*. The way he dresses and everything and he never has a girlfriend. I've wondered if he might be gay."

Liam, who had never even thought about it, was just about to protest but stopped himself. Anything that might strengthen his case...

"I'm not sure," he said. "He's never said, but you never know."

"Okay," Becky said, "you have a word and see what they say. My folks are going to go mental if they knew I was going to be the only girl in the house, though."

"So don't tell them. Just say you'll be sharing with some mates and let them think whatever they want."

"That's very devious," Becky said, winking at him. "I like it."

"Good," Liam replied. "I'll speak to the lads later and get our names down for the house. This is going to be a brilliant summer."

He was partially right. It was a very memorable summer, but not necessarily for the reasons he hoped.

Chapter Thirty-Four

Andy had just finished a Zoom call and was about to get stuck into some paperwork when his mobile rang. He reached out to answer it when a bolt of pain shot up his arm. This bloody dancing was using muscles he never knew he had, and they all ached. Each time he had a practice session, he woke up the next morning as stiff as a board and just as it was beginning to ease, it was time for the next session, and it all started again. The one consolation was that the dance had really begun to come together, and whereas at first the moves he was being expected to do felt completely unnatural, now he had a much better understanding of what was expected of him. However, understanding it and being able to do it with any degree of competence were two different things.

He managed to get to his phone before the voicemail kicked in and saw from the screen that it was Alison. She didn't normally ring from work, so it was probably something important.

"What's up?" he asked. "You okay?"

"Yes, I'm fine, but I've just had a call from the school. They wanted me to go up there straight away, but I'm about to go into a meeting. Can you go?"

"Yes, of course. I'm free for the next couple of hours. Did they say why? Don't tell me Amy's done something stupid."

"No, it's not Amy. It's Stevie. He's been fighting, apparently."

"Stevie? *Our* Stevie? That doesn't sound like him. He's never been in trouble."

"Well, he is now. So you'll go?"

"Yes. I'll leave now. Don't worry, Ali. I'll get it sorted out. I'm sure there's been some kind of misunderstanding."

As he drove to the school, Andy remained convinced that this was all a mistake. In all his time at the school, Stevie had never been in trouble of any kind. He worked hard, did what he was asked to and although he wasn't exactly a high-flier, his results were always on the good side of acceptable. Every parents' evening, the comments were much the same, that Stevie was giving no cause for concern. At one such evening, his maths teacher, Mr Park had even joked, "There's nothing to talk about. Fancy a game of cards?" Amy was the one who was always being told off for talking in class or, on one occasion, answering a teacher back, for which Andy and Alison had both had a word. She hadn't, as far as they were aware, ever done it since. They were good kids, both of them, unlike some of the little brats at the school, who were clearly running out of control and must cause their parents sleepless nights, if they cared at all. Amy and Stevie were both polite (usually) and respectful and when he looked around at others, Andy was proud of them and of himself and Alison for the job they had done.

The last thing he expected to find when he reported to the headteacher's office was Stevie sitting outside with his tie askew and a face like thunder. He was just about to ask his son what was going on when the headteacher's secretary emerged from the office and asked them both to come in. Andy had always found Mrs Blackler, the headteacher, to be a pleasant, fair person, and by and large, her pupils spoke well of her. Today, however, she was sitting behind her desk with the sort of face that Andy was used to seeing on his own high school headmaster's face on the few occasions he was summoned to the office. It was a face completely devoid of humour or friendliness and Andy's heart sank.

"Thank you for coming in, Mr McGovern," Mrs Blackler said. "I'm only sorry it was necessary."

"Not at all," Andy said, looking at Stevie, who was staring down at the carpet. "What's happened?"

"The first thing I must say is that we do not tolerate aggressive behaviour here, do we, Steven?"

"No, Miss," Stevie said, though it was barely audible.

"Mrs Blackler."

"Sorry, Mrs Blackler."

"Better. We pride ourselves on discipline at this school and we are very concerned when one student is aggressive or threatening to another, especially when it is out of character. Do you want to tell your father what happened today, Steven, or shall I?"

Stevie didn't reply but remained fixated on the carpet.

"Well, I wish someone would," Andy said.

"Very well," Mrs Blacker said. "I will. At break-time this morning, Mrs Templeman heard a disturbance and when she went to investigate, she found Steven, who had another boy pinned up against the wall. She heard him say, 'You say that again, I'll knock you out.' Mrs Templeman had to pull him away from the other boy."

Andy looked at his son, at the headteacher, and then at Stevie again.

"Say what again?" he asked.

"I'm sorry, Mr McGovern. I'm not sure..."

"This other teacher says Stevie said, 'Say that again.' I was just curious as to what that meant."

Mrs Blackler consulted her notes. "Neither Steven nor the other boy was prepared to say," she said eventually. "The point is that Steven was clearly threatening the other boy, and as I said, we will not tolerate it. Because it is out of character for Steven, however, I have decided to be lenient and I will only send him home for the rest of today to cool off, as long as he assures me that there will be no repeat. I suggest that he might take the time to write a note of apology to the other student."

"I'll see that he does so," Andy said. "There is something I want to say, though. You said you don't know what the other boy did to provoke this, and at the same time, you admitted that this is out of character. I'm not a teacher, but it seems reasonable to me to assume that whatever it was must have been quite something to make Stevie react like that. Don't you think that if you have no idea what it was, then you haven't got the full picture here?"

"If neither of them will tell me, then all I have to go on is what Mrs Templeman saw, which was Steven behaving aggressively," Mrs Blackler suggested. "The point is that we do not accept aggression as an appropriate response to any provocation. If one student says something unacceptable to another, we expect it to be reported in the appropriate way so we can deal with it. We don't permit students to deal with it themselves under any circumstances."

"And the other boy? What is happening to him?"

"He is also going home for the rest of the day. It's all in hand."

"Fair enough. I'm glad that you are trying to run a safe school here, Mrs Blackler, so thank you. Stevie, let's get you home. You've got a bit of explaining to do. Have you apologised to Mrs Blackler for disrupting her day?"

"Sorry, Mrs Blackler," he said, and it sounded, to Andy's ears at least, sincere.

"I'll see you tomorrow, Steven. And I don't expect to see you in this office again."

Both Andy and Stevie were silent during the drive back home. Andy was dying to find out what had been said but deliberately gave his son the silent treatment to make a point. Once they were in the house, he ushered Stevie into the living room and sat him down.

"Right," he said. "Are you going to explain exactly why I have been dragged away from my paperwork this afternoon?"

"It doesn't matter," Stevie replied quietly.

"Wrong answer. It *does* matter, son This isn't like you at all. So go on, spill. Who was the other lad, for a start?"

"Ryan."

"Ryan? Which one's he? Is he the one with...?"

"With the ears, yes."

"That's not a reason in itself. What did he say to you?"

"It doesn't matter, Dad. I won't do it again."

"No, I know you won't. But all the same, we've not brought you up to fight. I've only ever been in one fight in my life, and I'll always regret it. So we're still going to sit here until you tell me why you did it this time."

Stevie looked away and didn't answer.

"Stevie, tell me. What's the problem?"

"You are!" Stevie exclaimed and looked like he could cry at any second, which wasn't like him at all. "It was about you!"

"Me? Why?"

"It's this bloody dancing! You had to go and put it online, didn't you? Everyone's laughing at it! And Ryan said...he said you were gay."

Andy let that sink in for a second, then stood up.

"The little bastard!" he said. "I'll kill him myself."

"Dad!"

Andy laughed and sat back down again.

"I won't, don't worry. Okay, Stevie, there are a couple of things I need to say about this. One, you threatening to give this Ryan lad a dig for saying that is completely out of proportion. If he thinks 'gay' is an insult these days, then he's not very enlightened and so isn't worth your attention. We know some very fine gay guys and I'd take it as a compliment to be compared to them. That's the first thing. The second thing is – I'm sorry, Stevie. I'm sorry if what I'm doing has caused you embarrassment. Believe me, I'm finding it embarrassing enough for both of us, but I never stopped to think about how it would impact on you and Amy. So I apologise. If it's going to cause you problems, then I'll give it up right now."

"No. I don't want you to do that. It's important. You wouldn't be doing that if it wasn't."

"Thank you. I don't want to give it up either."

"I wish everyone else could see how important it is."

"Then tell them. But tell them with your mouth, not your fists."

"What if they still keep laughing?"

"*Then* you can knock them out. But for God's sake, don't be stupid enough to do it in school!"

Stevie laughed and Andy was very glad to hear it.

"Tell you what, though," he said. "If you think it's bad now, did I tell you we've all got to get spray tans before the final in December?"

Stevie poked his fingers in his mouth and made gagging noises.

"Oh, thanks," Andy said. "That's charming, that is."

"So who was it?" Stevie asked. "Who did you fight?"

Andy hesitated, but if Stevie had been honest with him, then the least he could do was treat him the same way.

"Liam," he said. "It was a long time ago."

Chapter Thirty-Five

"Hi, Liam?"

"Hi, Becky. How are you?"

"I'm fine, thank you. I just had a rare free period and thought I'd give you a ring. Am I disturbing you?"

"No, it's okay. I'm just burying myself under piles of papers, trying to find the one receipt my accountant needs. Can I find it?"

"I'm guessing no."

"You'd be guessing right. One bloody receipt from Screwfix, that's all, but you know what accountants are like. He thinks it's the end of the world."

"Do you want me to call back?"

"No, I'm glad of an excuse to stop for a minute before I rip my office apart. I have no idea where the bloody thing's got to."

"Now, think carefully. Where did you have it last?"

"Don't you start. The accountant's bad enough. You'll be telling me next I need a proper filing system."

"Haven't you got one?"

"Listen, if I spent as much time as he wants me to do all that stuff, I'd never have time to do anything else. There would be nothing to invoice, no business, just a bunch of neatly filed receipts from B&Q. Anyway, that's my problem. How are you doing?"

"Yeah, pretty well, mostly. I have my ups and downs. There's songs I still can't listen to. I cried when 'The Safety Dance' by Men Without Hats came on the radio. I heard Mike singing, 'We can dance, we can dance, everybody look at your pants.'"

"I always thought it was 'Everybody look at Joanne'!"

"Joanne? Who's Joanne?"

"I don't know. I didn't write the song. Wasn't that one you lived with called Joanne?"

"Jo? Yes, I suppose she was."

"Do you ever hear from her?"

"No. She got a bit miffed when I never moved back in with her for the third year. She got some nightmare of a lodger and never forgave me. So, speaking of 'You can dance if you want to', how's it all going with you and Andy? I've seen your videos. Bloody hell, Liam. I never saw that coming!"

"That's my daughter. She does all the editing and the captions and stuff. It's all her fault."

"You're getting quite good from the look of it."

"Freya's editing would make anyone look good. You should see all the stuff she cuts out. Just taking out all the bits where Julia swears cuts it down by half. Tell you what, when I first met her, she seemed so nice, but she hasn't half got a mouth on her. She's an amazing teacher and a lovely person, but she scares the shit out of me."

"She must be a good dancer."

"She is. She's brilliant. She showed me some footage of her when she was a junior champion. It was dead grainy, but you could see how good she was. Her dad used to go everywhere with her, to all the competitions and that, and he filmed everything. That takes a bit of dedication. I couldn't see my dad doing that."

"No, neither could I."

"Oh, of course! You met him at graduation. I'd forgotten that. He didn't approve of you, that's for sure."

"That's because he thought we'd been living in sin. Wouldn't believe me when I said there was no sin involved."

"Yes, well, if he knew I was learning how to dance, he wouldn't be following me round with a film camera. He'd have me sectioned. Not that he'd have anything to worry about. It's not like I'm ever going to hit the big time."

"How's Andy doing with it?"

"He seems to be doing really well. He sent me a video yesterday and he and Lesley looked great. It was actually funny. I mean, funny in the way it's supposed to be, not funny like I look."

"You don't look funny."

"I do. I catch sight of myself in the mirrors and it looks stupid, this attractive, slim woman trying to steer a big lump round the dance floor."

"Oh, behave. You're not that bad."

"I am. I always was, even back then."

"You weren't. You pulled Nic, didn't you? And she was gorgeous. Sorry, *is*."

"Yes, well, look how that turned out. I fucked that up properly, didn't I?"

"Not permanently. Not if you got married! How did that happen, anyway?"

"It's a funny story, really. After she did her PGCE, she got a job in Manchester and off she went. I didn't think I'd ever see her again because I stayed in Wales. It was either that or go home and there weren't many jobs in Wales *or* Liverpool then. I tried the Civil Service for a couple of years, but I didn't like it and they didn't like me. I was working in a shop at the time. It was all I could get – that's what an English degree does for you. Anyway, Nic was on holiday in Anglesey and came over to Bangor to, I don't know, revisit her old haunts or something. I don't think I was an old haunt she expected to see. Anyway, we went for a coffee and had a good chat."

"And that was that? Passion over the lattes?"

"Hardly. We did stay in touch, though, and when a job came up in Colwyn Bay, she came and stayed with me for a couple of days for the interview. She got the job and didn't leave."

"It sounds idyllic."

"It was for a long time. Well, idyllic with the usual arguments over money and kids and that sort of stuff. We got married a year or so later, and then the girls came along. We did okay."

"So how come you split up? Sorry, I'm really nosey. Don't tell me if you don't want to."

"No, it's okay. It was my fault, as ever. I got really insecure and jealous. She was doing so well in her job and I was

186

fixing plugs, you know? And her looks just got better with age and mine...didn't. Do you remember meeting her at a conference a few years ago?"

"God, yes, I do! I'd forgotten about that. We had one hell of a session that night."

"It was that conference that did it. She came back full of some bloke who was there, one of the speakers. She went on and on about what an inspiration he was, how well he spoke and how bloody nice he was. We ended up having one hell of a row about it and I accused her of having an affair with him. She denied it, but I couldn't let it go. I was drinking a bit more than I should have back then, too, which didn't help. We had another blazing row about it, and she threw a few plates at me, which I've got to say I deserved, and then suggested I went somewhere else for a bit. It wasn't my finest hour. I'm only glad the girls had grown up and moved out by then."

"Sounds like a mess."

"My mess. I got it completely wrong."

"If it's any consolation, she didn't sleep with anyone at that conference. By the time we'd finished, she could hardly stand, let alone do anything else."

"I'm not sure if that makes it better or worse. I knew that, really. I've thought ever since that if I'd only kept my mouth shut, we'd probably still be together. I know you can't say that for sure – I might have done something else stupid, but in all likelihood, I think we'd have probably been okay."

"Well, they say an affair is a symptom of problems in a marriage, not a cause in itself."

"Whoever 'they' are, might have a point. Nic didn't even have an affair. It was all in my head."

"Did you tell her that?"

"I tried, but the problem was me, not her. It's always been me. So I stayed away rather than do it to her anymore."

"So rather than sort yourself out, you walked away."

"I'm not proud of it."

"Quite right too. You need to have a word with yourself, Liam. What the hell were you thinking? You threw away everything you'd built just because you couldn't be arsed changing. How old are you?"

"Now, wait a minute—"

"No, *you* wait a minute. Have a think about this. Mike and I would have loved a long and happy life together and do you know what? I think we would have made it too. There was never any question of anyone else, not from the minute we fell in love with each other. But we never got the choice, did we? The fucking cancer sorted that out for us. I'd give anything to get him back. I'd fight anyone and anything. And you? You walked away from Nic without even trying to fight for her. Over *nothing*."

"Yes, I know. I've regretted it every day since."

"But you haven't done anything about it."

"No."

"Do you think maybe you should?"

"No, it's too late."

"There you go again. Giving up before you even start. It's not too late, Liam. I've spent the last few months with so many 'ifs' going through my head. *If* we'd had children, I wouldn't be on my own now. *If* Mike had gone to the doctor sooner, he might still be alive. If if if. While there's life, it's never too late. What if something happened to you tomorrow? Or to Nic? Tell me to mind my own, but it sounds to me like there's unfinished business between you two. I think you need to talk to her."

"Do you think she'd listen?"

"I don't know, Liam. I don't really know any of you anymore. But if you don't want to spend the rest of your life wondering about might-have-beens, you need to sort your head out and talk to her."

"Yes. You're right. Thanks, Becky."

"Don't thank me yet. You've got work to do and I don't mean on your heel leads or whatever. It's not like you haven't got form for this. Don't keep making the same mistakes."

Chapter Thirty-Six
1987

The day they all moved into the house they would be sharing for the summer would have gone a lot more smoothly had it not been for a complication in the very large, furry shape of a cat called Raymond.

They had decided to club together and hire a van because although the house wasn't far from where they all lived, they all had bags and boxes to move, so doing it all in one trip made more sense. Mike could drive a van (although when they picked it up, it appeared at first that this was very much in theory, and he had never actually driven one, but he soon got the hang of it). He, Liam and Andy loaded their possessions onto it and then went to collect Becky from her house. Becky lived in a narrow street and Mike had to park the van half on the pavement. It was a Sunday, and the hope was that it wouldn't get in anyone's way for the short time it would take to get Becky and her things onto the van and set off. It was only when Becky answered the door that they discovered a problem.

"I don't know what to do about Raymond," she said. The cat was sitting in the hall, washing himself intently, unaware that he was the subject of discussion.

"I'd forgotten about him," Liam said.

"I can't just leave him, not with Jo being away too."

"Do you not think you might have mentioned it before?" Mike asked. "It's not like we haven't talked about this much."

"I thought he'd wandered off to live somewhere else," Becky said. "He disappeared for a couple of months, and we thought he'd gone. But he came back the other day and it looks like he plans to stay for a bit."

"He's got a surprise coming to him, then," Mike said. "We can't take him."

"I can't leave him here," Becky protested. "What do you want me to do? Just dump him on the pavement?"

"This is Raymond we're talking about," Liam said. "Won't he go and live at one of his other houses?"

"What if he doesn't? What if he waits for me to come back and I don't? He'll be sad. Who's going to feed him."

"Look at the bloody size of him," Andy pointed out. "*Everyone* feeds him."

"Can't we take him?" Becky pleaded. "Please?"

"How?" Mike asked. "Have you got a carrier? Or a crane?"

"I'll hold him," Becky said. "He trusts me."

"I'm not driving a van with a cat roaming around in it. This heap of shit is hard enough to drive as it is."

"He'll be good. I promise."

Liam, Andy and Mike looked at each other, none of them wanting to be the one to make the decision. In the end, it was Mike who caved in.

"Okay. But the first sign of trouble, I'm stopping the van and he can go and live where he likes."

"Thanks, Mike," Becky said and gave him a quick hug. "I'll just get his things."

Raymond's 'things' consisted of a cat bed, food bowl, litter tray, a big bag of litter and two carrier bags of cat food. Raymond had nearly as much to bring as Becky had. Fitting it all into the van, however, wasn't the problem. Getting Raymond into the van was. He might have been perfectly happy to live with Becky, but clearly, no one had told him that meant going on his holidays. He allowed her to pick him up, but when she tried to carry him outside to the van, he squirmed and jumped out of her arms and back into the house.

"Ow!" Becky cried. "The little shit scratched me!"

"Well, you wanted to bring the little shit," Mike observed. "If he doesn't want to come, he doesn't want to come. I can't stay parked here much longer."

"One more try," Becky said. "If he doesn't come this time, I'll have to leave him."

It took ten minutes to coax Raymond out from under the table where he had taken refuge. Becky had to entice him out with cat treats while Liam waited with a towel to wrap him in if she was successful. When Becky finally managed to get him out from under the table, and Liam had wrapped him in the towel, from which only his head was visible, looking like a large, angry, furry mutant baby, Becky was able to carry him onto the van.

They set off and spent the short journey to the new house with Becky making soothing noises about what a good boy Raymond was and Mike muttering dark threats about what he planned to do should the cat be any more trouble. Once they reached the house and opened the door, Raymond, now free of his towel, shot upstairs and disappeared, only emerging later on to enquire if perhaps there was any dinner going.

They spent the rest of the day settling into the house. It had three bedrooms upstairs and a further one down a few steps on a lower level to the ground floor, which looked out onto what, under other circumstances, might be called the garden. In fact, it was a large yard which looked like a construction site. When they viewed the house, the landlord had explained that the bricks and wood that filled the yard were left over from the renovation work he had done and it would all be going. He didn't actually say when, though, and it clearly wasn't yet. Even in the bright summer sunshine, it looked a state. When they looked at the place, Liam offered to take that room and no one tried to talk him out of it. Mike, Andy and Becky had claimed the bedrooms upstairs. Liam quite liked the idea of being out of the way, imagining it was somewhere he could retreat to and shut himself away to work. The rest of the ground floor was taken up by a large living room, which looked like it might have been two rooms knocked through, and a kitchen big enough to accommodate a pine dining table and chairs.

Once they had unpacked and Mike had returned the van, they gathered together in the living room. Andy had thought far enough ahead to get in a couple of bottles of wine and there was a very handy pizza place just up the road. As he sat with a glass of wine in one hand and a cigarette in the other, laughing and joking with his friends, Liam didn't think he had ever been happier. This was where he belonged and these were the people he belonged with. Becky looked relaxed and content, all the upset over Paul apparently forgotten. Liam had to admit that she looked good in her summer dress and wondered if, perhaps, she might be ready to move on. They had weeks ahead of them to get to know each other better and who knew what might develop? If it did, he might be able to put the mistakes he had made with Nic behind him once and for all. It was going to be a brilliant summer.

Chapter Thirty-Seven

"No, you're making the same mistake again. Heel lead, Liam. No, *heel* lead...All right. Stop there and take a break."

Liam sat down and mopped his face with a towel. His hair was soaked, and his T-shirt felt like he'd been walking in the rain. Julia gave her forehead a quick dab and came over to him.

"Don't look so down," she said. "You're mostly there. You've got all the moves, but the judges will be looking for technique too."

"They can look all they like, but at this rate, I don't think they're going to find any."

"Of course they will. Don't say that. We just need to eliminate the little errors. If you can drive the dance, we'll really glide across the floor and that's exactly what the foxtrot should look like. You'll get there."

Liam laughed humourlessly, drank some water and buried his face in his towel. It felt like all the water he drank leaked straight out through his skin. The trouble was that he knew the steps well enough; he practiced them at home and occasionally in the unit when he had a moment. He had, at Julia's insistence, watched video after video of beautiful, elegant couples dancing the foxtrot. They made it look so easy and effortless, but he couldn't see himself achieving that. These were professionals with years of experience. He was a bumbling amateur who had been playing at dancing for a matter of weeks. Every time he tried to picture himself doing it or caught sight of himself in the studio mirrors, he saw the fat, clumsy idiot who was useless at sports and could never get clothes to look right.

In a way, it was his mother's fault. He found out late in her life that after she had Liam, she had two miscarriages and then she and Stan gave up on their hope to have more children. She told him this while he was visiting her in hospital after the heart attack from which she never fully recovered. After the initial awkwardness of visiting times, and, perhaps mindful of her own mortality, Liz had opened up to Liam about his childhood, how she had felt guilty that she hadn't been able to provide a brother or sister for him and because he was such a solitary child, she had compensated by over-indulging him in all his favourite foods. She urged him to look after his own heart and not end up like she had, and he promised he would. He nearly managed it for a while, too. While things were good with Nic and the girls were growing up, Liam and Nic cooked food that was good but healthier than the stodge he had always eaten at home. The girls kept him on the go and his weight remained constant. It was slightly more than the ideal for his height but still okay, and his waist measurement, while never getting as low as the twenties, stayed firmly in the thirties. That seemed like a long time ago now. Since he had split up with Nic, he had stopped bothering with the healthy cooking and existed on microwave meals and takeaways. It was little wonder he didn't possess a pair of decent trousers that felt particularly comfortable. And in about four weeks, he was supposed to dance in public, looking like this. Still, every series of *Strictly* had the one celebrity who was a crap dancer but was kept in for entertainment value. Maybe that was a role he could fulfil.

He wanted to be better, partly for Julia's sake but also because the girls had bought tickets for the final, so had Nic and he didn't want to make them ashamed to watch him. Even Michelle Leyland had said she would be there. There was also the reason he was putting himself through all this was for Mike, and despite having a go at him that time on the phone, Becky had also promised she would be there. If he was honest, he wanted to be better than Andy, but from the clips he had seen of his friend's rehearsals, that would take some doing. He had plenty of reasons for wanting to do well and knew how the dance was supposed to be in his head, but communicating that to his reluctant body was where the problem lay, and he didn't know how to get around that.

"Are you okay?" Julia asked. "You seem to be having a bit of difficulty focusing today."

"Today?"

"Yes, today. You've been better than this. Is there anything you want to talk about?"

"Do you really think I can do this?"

"Where's that come from? Yes, of course I do. Do I think you're going to look like a professional dancer? Probably not, but then you haven't got the time to do that. I've got to say, I've worked with plenty of people who didn't pick the steps up as quickly as you. You've got a very good memory and that's a big plus."

"I know. It's in my head, but I can't convince my body to do it. I don't know why."

"You're overthinking it. I'll tell you something. When I was at school, I could never do the high jump. I should have been able to – I could do a really fast run-up and I knew how it was meant to work, but I'd do the run, take a look at the height of the bar and something in my head would go, 'Don't be stupid. You can't do that' and I couldn't. It didn't make any logical sense that a human being could jump that high, yet lots of other kids could do it."

"I was like that with climbing ropes. Remember those ropes that used to hang down from the roof of the gym and they'd make you climb up them? The other kids would shin up them like monkeys, but I never did it. I'd do the first bit, get my feet on the rope and that was it."

"That's the point. The human body is capable of doing all sorts of things, but a lot of them don't make sense if you analyse them too much. You sometimes have to trust and let your body do it, no matter how ridiculous you think you look."

"There's that too. I don't look like a dancer. As soon as I start worrying about how I look, I can't do it."

"Then don't think about it."

"That's easy for you to say. Look at you."

"That's enough of that. I'm going to tell you something now that I haven't told many people. Have you got any idea what it's like to be in a job where physical fitness, to say nothing of how you look, counts so much and then to get cancer? Can you imagine how it feels when dancing has always been the biggest part of your life and you're lying in bed because the chemo has made you so weak you can barely walk? Or when your job relies on looking good and you can't imagine ever doing that again with one boob and no hair? The first time I went back into a dance studio after that, I felt like a complete fraud. I hadn't just left my boob in the operating theatre; it was like I'd left everything. But I put some music on and tried a few basic steps and my body remembered. I cried a lot during my treatment, but that day might be the day I cried the most. It was still a while before I was able to let anyone watch me dance, but when I did, it was like getting *me* back. So, yes, Liam, I get what it feels like to look at yourself and think you can't do it."

"I'm sorry. That puts it into perspective."

"It should. I'm not trying to make you feel bad, but that shows how your mind can influence your body. I still catch sight of myself in the mirror and remember how I looked at my worst. I have to blot it out, or I won't be able to dance a step. That's the thing about cancer, Liam. The doctors may tell you your body is free of it, but your mind never is. People say you look great and it's like you've got over a cold. They don't want to talk about it anymore, but you never forget. It's always there. Dancing takes my mind off it. It's somewhere I can go and be happy and be me."

"I had no idea. I must admit, I look at you dance, and I forget you ever had cancer. It shows how much I know."

"You're by no means alone. Tell you what I do know, though. We've got this studio for about another hour, so let's make it count, shall we?"

They did. For the next hour, Liam did his best to forget everything else and concentrate on getting the dance right. He got the heel leads when he was supposed to and swung and swayed when that was what was required. He felt the music flow through him and danced. He ignored the mirrors and the way they mocked him and instead pictured himself gliding across the dancefloor like the dancers in the videos he had watched. He didn't exactly feel graceful, but he certainly felt lighter. By the time Julia told him to stop, he was beginning to feel like something had changed and a burden he had never known he was carrying was starting to lift.

As they left the studio, Julia switched the lights off and turned to him with a cheeky grin.

"Hey, Liam," she said. "Have you lost some weight?"

Chapter Thirty-Eight

"Hello? Is that Mr Rawlinson?"

"Yes, it is. How can I help?"

"My name is Elis Gruffydd, Mr Rawlinson. I own the cheese factory in Porthmadog, Caws Madog. I don't know if you've heard of it."

"I'm not sure. It rings a bell..."

"So, no, then. It doesn't surprise me. We're only small, but we're growing. That's why I wanted to speak to you as a matter of fact. We're based on an old farm, which has been okay so far, but we've seen an upswing in orders lately and we need to expand a bit to cope."

"Right, I see. So how can I help?"

"Well, we've got an outbuilding that we've earmarked for the expansion, but it's not been used since God knows when. It's got lights, but they don't work and nothing else. It's going to need completely rewiring, new lights, sockets, the lot. Is that the sort of thing you do?"

"I certainly do. It sounds like a big job, though, so it's not going to be cheap."

"I didn't think it would be, Mr Rawlinson. I've got the budget for it, though. I just need a formal quote."

"I'd be happy to do that. I could call over – let's see – Friday if that's convenient?"

"Friday would be ideal, thank you."

"No problem. Could you text me the address, please?"

"I'll do that now."

"Great. Can I ask, how did you find me?"

"I was going to look online, get a few names like, but then I saw you in the paper, you know, this dance thing you're doing."

"In the what, sorry? In the paper?"

"The Times, I think it was."

"Sorry, the line's a bit...Did you say The Times?"

"Yes, the North Wales Times. You know, the free paper. I don't usually read it because it's all ads, but I was using it for packing and saw the interview you did."

"But I haven't done...Never mind. So you saw this article..."

"Yes, and I thought I'd give you a call. Anyone who's prepared to make a fool of themselves for cancer charities is all right by me."

"Thanks, I think."

"No problem. It's something that means a lot to me. It's sort of why I do what I do. I've not always been in the cheese business, you know. It's only been the last five years, really. I used to be a footballer, believe it or not. I wasn't bad, either, even I say so myself."

"Sorry, how does a footballer end up making cheese?"

"Well, that's quite an interesting story. I'll try and keep it short, though, because I'm sure you're busy with work and rehearsing and everything. So, I'd been doing okay, played for a couple of decent clubs – nothing Premiere League but Division 2 and 3, that sort of thing. I even got looked at for Wales once, but nothing came of it. Anyway, I was playing in a cup tie against Charlton it was. It was one-all and looked like it was heading towards a replay, when we got a corner. The ball came right at me, and I did a diving header. I won us the match but also finished my career at the same time."

"How come? What happened?"

"It was quite famous at the time. The thing is, I scored the winning goal in a cup tie and didn't know anything about it. Apparently, I went down like a ton of bricks and had to get stretchered off. By the time they got me to hospital, I was having seizures. They got it under control and did all kinds of tests and that's when they found it—a brain tumour. Quite a big one, from the sound of it. Heading the ball had done something to it, but it could have happened any time, when I was driving or anything, so it was lucky, I guess. They got the little bastard, though, or most of it. I still needed chemo to mop up what was left. And that was it. Football career done. It was my own fault, really."

"How so? You weren't to know."

"I was in a way. I'd been getting headaches, see. Bad ones sometimes, but I just put them down to stress and hangovers. I'd just split up with my girlfriend because she was shagging some lad who played for Wrexham and they were above us in the league. I was hitting the clubs quite hard and thought it was that. I should have got it checked out earlier. That's why I like what you're doing, mate. Everyone needs telling what they need to look out for and to get to the doctor if there's anything going on they don't like."

"Thanks, Elis. I appreciate that."

"Funny thing is it was the best thing that happened to me in some ways. I met my wife while I was getting treatment, which I wouldn't have done otherwise. I actually married a nurse; can you believe that? And I wouldn't be making cheese, either. I'd just be an ex-footballer who wasn't well known enough to get a job on the telly."

"How did you get into the cheese business? Seems a bit of an odd choice."

"It isn't really. There's always been a bit of a football/cheese connection. Nobby Stiles was famous for being partial to a bit of stilton and then there's Lineker and his crisps. It's always been there. It started as a bit of a hobby while I was convalescing, but I didn't ever expect to make a business out of it. It just sort of happened. And now I'm expanding and that's why I need you."

"It would be my pleasure, Elis."

"That's great news, Liam. Thank you. Oh, and would you mind if Caws Madog sent some sponsorship money your way? I'd love to help with what you're doing."

"That's very generous. There's no need, but..."

"No arguments. I'd love to. And I might just get onto the Times about it myself. See if we can't both get a bit of publicity out of it. That is, if you don't mind."

"No, I don't mind at all. Anything that gets the word out and the money in is fine by me. And I never thought I'd hear myself saying that."

"Good. I think it's also important to tell people that there is hope, you know? It doesn't have to be the end, especially not if it's caught in time. Mad as it sounds, it was actually the start for me. I don't know if you can be glad about cancer, but you know what I mean."

"Yes, I think so. Let's see what we can do then."

"Excellent. I'll send over my address right now and see you Friday."

Chapter Thirty-Nine
1987

It was a beautiful summer day. Sunshine bathed the back yard, which they had discovered to their joy, was the perfect sun-trap during the afternoon. They had cleared some of the rubble to one side to create an area where they could sit and had found some deckchairs and a small table in a charity shop so they wouldn't have to sit on masonry or timber. Mike and Andy, dressed in T-shirts and shorts, were drinking beer and passing the time with some Jenga-like activity they had devised using the bricks that were scattered around and judging by the good-natured arguments that kept breaking out, neither of them was very clear as to the rules.

Fortunately, the neighbours on one side had gone away for a fortnight and the guy who lived on the other side never bothered them. He was a strange man in his sixties called Larry or Gary or something, who was never seen without an over-sized set of headphones clamped to his head. Everywhere he went, he left behind the scent of patchouli lingering in the air and Mike had joked that he had tracked him around town one day, just following the trail. They all speculated about whether he wore his headphones round the house, which would explain why he was never bothered by the antics of the students next door. It all gave Mike and Andy free rein to make as much noise as they liked. Becky had gone into town to meet a friend and do some shopping and wasn't due back just yet. It would be a perfect August Tuesday were it not for the fact that Liam was sweltering in his room.

It wasn't as though Andy and Mike hadn't tried to tempt him to come outside; they had, but Liam had to decline because the dissertation wouldn't write itself. Since this sunny spell had begun and they had all discovered how warm it was in the yard, he had lost too many days sitting about pretending to read but getting nowhere. Now he had a lot of work to do and far less time to do it than he would have liked. He had no choice but to get on with it and try to ignore the fun everyone else was having around him. He felt like he did back when he was taking his A levels and his parents insisted he did at least two hours work every evening. They practically locked him in his bedroom, from where he could see the other kids who lived in the road outside playing football as if they didn't have a care in the world. Liam had no great desire to play three-and-in or headers and volleys, and probably wouldn't have done so even if he could, but he resented not having the choice. He didn't much want to spend the summer building towers out of builders' detritus now, either, but he didn't want to be left out. Pretty soon, the others would start going to the pub without him and would eventually forget he existed at all.

He wasn't completely alone; he had Raymond for company, which was something of a mixed blessing. While it was nice to have someone to talk to (or rather complain to), and it was even better that they didn't answer back, apart from letting out the occasional rather pathetic miaow around mealtimes, Raymond's form of unconditional love wasn't really conducive to getting much work done. He was intrigued by the typewriter and sat on the desk staring at it while Liam typed. Liam wasn't sure whether it was the sound or the movement of the keys that was the object of the cat's rapt fascination. It would have been very amusing, were it not for the fact that Raymond was such a large cat and when he plonked himself down by the typewriter, it was sometimes tricky either to reach around him to type, or even see the paper, something Liam needed to do.Even two thousand words into his dissertation, his typing skills hadn't improved greatly and he needed to see what he was doing or he would type nonsense. He made plenty of mistakes anyway and was already on his second bottle of Tipp-Ex. His tutor had also advised him to use carbon paper and make a copy of the dissertation to keep for his own records, which he had done, but he wasn't sure there was a great deal of point. The sheets he had saved so far were such battlefields of alteration that the carbon copies were rendered so wholly illegible that Raymond might have typed them. In fact, there were times when he thought that even the clean copy might make more sense if he had asked the cat's opinion on the poetry of Seamus Heaney and written those thoughts down instead of his own.

The idea behind the dissertation had been a good one, or so he thought at the time. He had set out his stall from the start; this was going to be his reaction to the poems and what he understood of the poet's life and beliefs. The thinking was that if he said from the beginning that this was his aim, back up everything he said with quotes, and write as in-depth an explanation as he could manage, then nobody could tell him he was wrong. There was, as far as he could see, such a dearth of critical writing on Heaney's poetry that he could more or less say what he wanted without anyone contradicting him. It seemed like a pretty foolproof plan. It was only when he came to write the damn thing that he discovered the fatal flaw in his idea. He found many of the poems to be completely impenetrable, and without any reference works to consult, he had absolutely no idea what they meant. All he could do was write as much as he could about the poems he at least partly understood and hope that this was enough. He had the horrible feeling that it wouldn't be and wondered on more than one occasion if he could contact his tutor and ask if he could change the subject of his dissertation to something else. There were two very compelling reasons why he decided against that and to press on regardless. One was the time factor; he had already lost enough time and couldn't afford to lose any more. The other was that he had absolutely no idea what he would do instead. He had no choice but to stick to his chosen path and hope that at some point Raymond revealed himself to be a secret expert on contemporary poetry and would actually help, rather than sitting on the desk like an oversized furry paperweight.

Staying inside and away from his housemates was easier for Liam when Becky wasn't around. Mike and Andy were his best friends and he couldn't imagine life without them, but sometimes they weren't very mature. Wherever they were, there was noise; whether it was music or laughter, it was always at full volume. Liam liked a good laugh himself and he couldn't fault his housemates' taste in music, but they had no appreciation of how much work Liam had to do. He made a point of letting them know why he was retreating to his room but stopped short of asking them to keep the noise down because he didn't want to be a killjoy. He could only hope that they would get the hint, but it wasn't working yet.

The house was calmer when Becky was around, though Liam couldn't easily say why. It wasn't that she was in any way disapproving or anything. She liked a laugh as much as any of them and Liam hadn't fully appreciated what a great sense of humour she had until now. But for some reason, Mike and Andy were not quite as boisterous when Becky was in this house. This presented Liam with something of a dilemma because a quieter house meant that, in theory, he could concentrate on his dissertation, but when Becks was around, he preferred not to be closeted in his cell. It wasn't just her sense of humour that he had come to appreciate that summer; it was everything else about her as well.

He hadn't expected it to happen. True, he had always liked Becky and the fact that she was attractive couldn't be ignored, but he had always seen her strictly as a mate, one of their group. Over the past few weeks, he had talked to her more and in greater depth than he had over the two years he had known her. They talked about their home lives, beliefs and hopes for the future. Becky, he learned, had been one of those kids who worked hard and behaved themselves in school but weren't among the high achievers and, as such, remained anonymous. She was overlooked by the teachers, whose attention, out of necessity, was pulled towards those at the top and bottom of the class. They weren't pushed to achieve anything better and, therefore, didn't and ended up staying exactly where they were. Becky had been smart enough to recognise this while still having time to do something about it and worked as hard as she could to scrape the grades she needed to get into university. At least here, she received the individual attention she needed to build up her confidence and start to flourish. One of the reasons she wanted to go into teaching was to help the many pupils who were as overlooked as she had been, to support and encourage them to reach their potential. She was under no illusions about the challenge she would be facing, but the fact that she was still prepared to try only made Liam admire her more. Admire was a bit of an understatement if he were truthful. The fact of the matter was that he thought he might be falling in love with Becky and didn't know what to do about it. Daydreaming about her was yet another thing that kept coming between him and his attempts to concentrate on the poems of the great Seamus. He even allowed the stupid damn cat to come into his room and park his fat, furry arse on the desk. Becky was so fond of Raymond and Liam thought that if the cat liked him, it might mean Becky would too. So far, the only sign of affection he was getting from either of them was cat hairs in his Tipp-Ex.

Liam was about to start considering the next of Heaney's poems when there was a sudden howl of guitars and a thrash of drums. Andy had apparently gone upstairs and flung open his bedroom window so the whole neighbourhood could be treated to a bit of Jesus and Mary Chain. Liam heard Andy's feet thundering down the stairs and his friend burst through the back door and into the yard. The sight of Andy with his arms flailing around like a windmill in a cyclone was enough to persuade him to close the lid on the typewriter, shoo Raymond off the desk and go outside to catch a bit of sunshine and join in the fun. It was, after all, possible to work a bit too hard.

Chapter Forty

"Steady on, Andy! You nearly had my eye out!"

"Oh God. Sorry! Are you okay?"

Lesley rubbed the side of her head where Andy's finger had caught her and smiled.

"Yes, you missed, fortunately," she said. "Now, come on. That's not like you. I thought we'd got those arms under control."

"So did I."

Andy sat down on the floor where he was, breathing heavily. They had been training hard for two hours now and he was feeling it. His muscles were burning, and it felt like someone had applied industrial-grade sandpaper to his heels and the tops of his toes. Lesley was pushing him harder than ever, but there wasn't any choice; time was getting very short.

"You look shattered," she pointed out, not that it needed pointing out. Now he was sitting down, Andy wasn't sure if he would be able to get back up again without using a block and tackle. "I'd be tempted to say let's leave it there, but there was so much good in that, and I don't want to finish this session here, not when we've only got one more."

"So much good? It felt like a mess to me."

"Just as well I'm the expert then, isn't it? The swivels were good. Most of the side-by-side work was good and pretty much in synch. You were nervous in the lifts, but you still did them and I felt safe. That was all great work."

"There's a but coming, isn't there?"

Lesley joined him in sitting on the floor, though she did it far more gracefully than he had. Where he had flopped, she lowered herself gracefully, sitting and crossing her legs in one fluid movement.

"There's always a but with me," she said. "That's what I'm here for. The steps are nearly there. The technique is nearly there, *but* where's the performance gone? I was watching your face in the mirror and it gave virtually nothing. It's such a big part of this dance, Andy. Without the facial expressions, without the essential kookiness, I guess you'd call it, you can hardly call it a Charleston. You've been so much better, even though I know you feel really self-conscious. What happened?"

"I don't know. I think I was concentrating on everything else. It takes me all my time to keep my arms where they should be, and even then, I nearly belted you. I don't know if I can get it all right at the same time."

"Well, that's nonsense," Lesley said. She got up with the same ease with which she had sat down and went to retrieve her phone. She poked around on the screen for a bit and then, once she had found what she was looking for, sat back down with Andy again.

"Watch this. This was only last week. I know you hate watching yourself, but you need to see this."

She shoved the phone under his nose and pressed play on a video file. It was a clip of Andy practicing part of the dance on his own. He wanted to cringe as he watched it, but he had to admit it looked pretty good, so much so that he barely recognised himself.

"I didn't know you were filming," he said. "You said you had to send an email."

"I lied. But do you see what I mean? The face and everything was so much better."

"That's probably because I didn't know you were watching."

"I hate to tell you this, pal, but two weeks tomorrow, there's going to be more than just me watching you. Do you know how many tickets they've sold?"

"No. And I don't think I want to know."

"I won't tell you it's two hundred then."

Andy thought he had misheard at first, but then the awful truth about what Lesley had said started to sink in. It felt as though the ground was moving under him and he had to put his hands firmly on the floor to hold on.

"I can't do it," he said. "I can't dance in front of two hundred people."

"Yes, you can, Andy," Lesley said, placing a reassuring hand on his arm. "It's easy."

"When you do it all the time, sure. But I've never done it before. Two hundred? Shit. That's too many."

"You need to calm down. Let me tell you something my first dance teacher told me. This was when I was seven and about to go on stage for the first time and I was every bit as terrified as you are. I said I couldn't dance in front of all those people and what she said has stuck with me all my life. She said, 'What difference does it make?' She told me that it didn't matter if I was dancing in front of a thousand people, or one person, or none because the music is the same, the steps are the same steps and the dance is the same dance. She was right, too."

"So just ignore them? Is that what you're saying?"

"Ignore them or use their energy to lift you, whichever works for you. Some say picturing the audience nude helps, but I can't say I've ever tried that one. Some of the judges we get, you really wouldn't want to do that."

The mention of the word 'judges' sent Andy to a whole new level of horror. He had been so concerned about performing to an audience, especially one containing his wife and his children (luckily, it was a bit far for anyone from work to commit to going), that he'd shoved the judges to the back of his mind. He wished they had stayed there.

"Oh God," he said, "the judges are going to take me to bits. Alison and the kids are going to have to watch me getting verbally murdered in front of them."

"You don't need to worry about the judges. We do when we're competing properly, but that's their job. If you're sensible and listen to what they're saying, they only want to offer constructive criticism. It's not like it is on the telly when they want to be the stars themselves half the time. This will be different. They understand why you're all doing this, and they'll be nice."

"Do you know them?"

"I do. Chris Croft loves the sound of his voice a bit, but he's very fair. Peg Blanchard is one of the most experienced judges round here and is just lovely. She can come over as a bit stern when she can see things need improving, but all the young dancers absolutely adore her. Then there's Dame Philippa. She's a bit of a funny one."

"Dame? We've got a Dame?"

"Not really. She gets called that behind her back because she can be a bit of a drama queen. Philippa DeVine isn't her real name, either. There was a rumour floating round that her real surname is Snodgrass, but that's never been proved. Anyway, they will all be on your side, so you don't need to worry. So, are you ready to go again? Once more with feeling?"

"I don't know. All that talk of judges..."

"Then concentrate on something else. Think of why you're doing this. Think of your friend. What's the first thing you think of when you remember Mike?"

"His hair, I suppose. He always had great hair. Mind you, this was the eighties and there was a lot of great hair around. It breaks my heart to think he would have lost it."

"What else?"

"He laughed a lot. I think back on those days, and we always seemed to be laughing. I mean, we probably didn't laugh all the time, but that's how it feels."

"Then concentrate on that. Do your routine. Exaggerate every gesture and facial expression and be funny. Imagine how Mike would have laughed along."

"He'd have been the first to take the piss out of me!"

"But in the way only friends can. Now, come on. Once more for Mike."

She cued the music up on her phone and they took their positions. As the music started, Andy tried to clear his head of everything but an image of a young man with perfectly gelled blonde hair in a leather jacket and an Icicle Works T-shirt, sitting watching him with that smile on his face. Andy hit every position and step harder and with more enthusiasm than he ever had before. He imagined Mike laughing at the bits of comedy schtick they had put into the routine and made them bigger to make him laugh more. He was hardly aware of what he was doing, but when the song finished, he had given everything he had, and he and Lesley collapsed on the dance floor and lay flat on their backs, giggling like children.

"Now that's how you do it!" Lesley said once she had regained a degree of composure. "What do you reckon Mike would have thought of that?"

"He'd have thought I was an idiot," Andy replied, still laughing, "but he'd have bloody loved it."

Chapter Forty-One

"You okay to talk, Andy?"

"Yeah, I've just finished practice. What's up?"

"How did it go?"

"Yes, good, I think. Good as it's going to get anyway. That was the last one, well, apart from the dress run on Saturday. Feels really weird, you know?"

"Yes, I get that. We had ours yesterday. It was a bit sad, actually. I gave Julia some flowers and she cried. I nearly joined her. I can't believe we're here. It all seemed like such a long way off when we began. I don't know what I'm going to do now!"

"You going to keep dancing?"

"Behave. This was enough, thanks. I'm glad I did it in a way, but enough's enough. You?"

"I doubt it. Lesley said she'd give me more lessons, but I could tell from her voice that she hoped I'd say no. Anyway, I think once we've got Saturday night over, I'll be glad to see the back of it."

"How do you feel about that? Saturday, I mean."

"Honestly? I'm shitting it. It's one thing doing it in the studio when it's only Lesley there and we can stop when things go wrong, but on Saturday, there'll be no stopping whatever happens. It's giving me nightmares."

"Have you had that one where you've forgotten to put trousers on?"

"No! I'm usually just standing there waiting to go on and I know, like you know in dreams, that I can't remember anything. It's bloody horrible."

"I dreamed the other night that they suddenly gave us different partners and I had this bloke who looked like a long-distance lorry driver. He seemed nice enough, though."

"A psychiatrist would have a field day with you. It sounds like it's not the dancing you're worried about."

"Get lost. Christ, who'd have thought all those years ago that one day we'd be talking about anxiety dreams caused by ballroom dancing? We used to think we were so cool."

"You were never cool, Liam. Neither was I. Mike was always the cool one. We just tried to fit in."

"That's true. Still, we got the last laugh, though, didn't we? Where's Mike now?"

"That's sick, lad. Anyway, Mike did all right for himself, didn't he? He got Becky, after all, and I think that's forever, whether he's around to see it or not."

"Have you spoken to Becks? Is she coming on Saturday?"

"She said so. She's going to book in somewhere overnight. I said she could stay with us, but she said no. Probably just as well. Alison said she was fine with it, but I got the idea that there was something she wasn't saying. She could stay with you though, couldn't she? You've got a spare room."

"Well, no, she couldn't. The spare room's – er – being used this weekend."

"Who by? Hang on, it's not...? Is it? Is your ex staying over?"

"Yes, Andy, Nic is staying over, but there's nothing going on."

"Oh, really?"

"Really. It's just to save her the cost of a hotel. The girls are coming over on Saturday morning because Freya wants to follow me round with a camera for the socials. I've told her no one wants to see me trying to squeeze into a tailcoat, but she seems to think it's a good idea. That's something else I'll be glad to get rid of. I'm sick of seeing pictures of myself on bloody TikTok or whatever. It's not me at all."

"You're a star now, mate. You'll have to keep it up, or you'll disappoint your fans."

"Sod that. I'm going straight back into obscurity after all this. Never again."

"So what's Nic going to think when she sees you dancing with another woman? It was your wedding song, wasn't it?"

"I don't think she's arsed to be honest. A wedding song doesn't mean much when the marriage has gone down the pan. She probably doesn't even remember."

"I bet she does, mate. I reckon you'd be surprised. You should talk to her while she's here."

"I don't think so. You can't go back. There are lots of things I'd have done differently, but it's too late now. I've been looking back a lot since we heard about Mike, but the only thing it's shown me it that I'm okay as I am. It's best to leave the past in the past."

Chapter Forty-Two
1987

Liam had tried to ask Becky out twice now, and neither occasion had gone according to plan. He was starting to wonder whether or not he should give up. Whatever forces guided his destiny (if there were any) were clearly trying to tell him something. Maybe it was time he started listening. But he clung onto the hope that next time things might go better and she would say yes. It was a very slim hope, but a hope all the same.

He had run the conversations through in his head time and time again while he was supposed to be working or trying to get to sleep. In theory, Becky should have been impressed by his wit and unable to resist his charm. But the problem with imagining how a conversation is going to go in advance is that conversations generally involve more than one person, and no matter how many variables you have planned for, you can't always predict what the other person is going to say. The chances are, they will come out with something completely random that you hadn't predicted at all. That was usually where it all started to unravel.

The first occasion came one Friday afternoon. Liam had planned to spend the day working to allow some free time at the weekend, but while he was in the kitchen making himself a Cup-a-Soup for his lunch, an unmissable opportunity presented itself. Since he had made up his mind to ask Becky out, he had found it impossible to get her on her own; Andy or Mike, or more often both, were always around and there was no way Liam was going to do it with an audience. So far, today was much the same as every other. Andy was sitting at the dining table eating toast and Becky was rooting around in the cupboard under the sink while Liam boiled the kettle and watched a blackbird digging about in the brick dust, looking in vain for something tasty for lunch.

"Are we out of binbags?" Becky asked. "I'm sure we had some."

"Yes, I think we are," Andy said. "I looked yesterday."

"And when you didn't find any, you didn't think to say or anything?"

"Sorry, I forgot."

"I bet we're out of loo roll as well," Becky sighed. "I suppose I'd better pop down to the shop and get some." She paused, presumably waiting for another volunteer to step forward, but when they didn't, she stomped into the hall to get her coat. "I'll go then," she said.

"Hang on," Liam said. "I'll come with you. I could do with some air." The nearest newsagent and general store was a good ten minutes' walk away and there was a small greasy spoon café next door. His hastily concocted plan was to accompany Becky to the shop and, while there, offer to treat her to a coffee and maybe some cake. He could steer the conversation around to telling her how he felt. It all seemed pretty foolproof.

"Oh, okay," Becky said, "I'm going now though."

"I'll just grab my jacket," Liam replied, delighted that things were going exactly according to plan.

As they walked down the road, Becky chatted happily about somebody Liam didn't know, but he thought he managed to sound sufficiently interested. When they reached the shop, Liam put the second phase of the plan into action.

"Oh, look," he said, "the café's open. I could murder a coffee. Fancy getting one, my treat? I'll throw in a piece of that chocolate cake too." And that was when it went wrong. While they were walking, he had been rehearsing what he would say, but Becky ruined everything simply by saying, "No, it's okay, thanks. I'd better be getting back. Don't let me stop you, though." Liam didn't get to ask Becky out. He had to buy a cup of coffee he didn't want and could barely afford, then sit there sullenly drinking it. Worst of all, he didn't even get to walk back to the house with her. There was no part of his plan that had gone right at all. The second time he tried, it didn't go any better.

A couple of days later, he was sitting in the living room, leafing through the local free newspaper, with Raymond sprawled across the back of the armchair like a giant, furry antimacassar. He didn't know why he bothered with the paper; there was never anything in it, but it was something to read in an idle moment. Becky was reclining on the sofa reading an Armistead Maupin book and occasionally half-sniffling, half-laughing, an effect those books usually had on her. As Liam reached the What's On section, an idea struck him, and he acted on it immediately.

"Hey, Becks," he said. "*The Lost Boys* is on at the cinema this week."

"Oooh Kiefer," Becky replied with a somewhat lascivious grin.

"Thought you'd say that. Fancy going?"

"Definitely."

"Brilliant. What about Friday night?"

"Sounds good to me," Becky said, but before Liam could celebrate, Mike wandered into the room and Becky ruined it. "You coming, Mike? To see *The Lost Boys*?"

"Isn't it a bit scary for you?" Mike laughed.

"Get lost," Becky replied. "I sat through *The Fly*, and *Hellraiser*. You're the one that was shrieking like a little girl."

"I'll tell Andy," Mike said. "We haven't been to the flicks for weeks."

They all went, and Liam pretended to be pleased about it. He pretended to enjoy the film, even though when they sat down, he was at one end of the group and Becky was at the other with Mike and Andy between them. He pretended not to be bothered about the fact that Becky and Andy spent the whole film huddled up together giggling or that in the pub afterwards went on and on about how gorgeous Keifer Fucking Sutherland was. Liam kept quiet, but his frustration and jealousy had begun to eat away at him. Time was getting short, too. He knew that he had the best chance of asking Becky out while they were

217

all living in this house, but the summer was ebbing away and so were his hopes. The sight of Andy and Becks getting so cosy in the cinema bothered him most because the thought that Becks might be interested in anyone else in the house had never occurred to him, but once it had, he saw the signs everywhere. They were always laughing together over some private joke, and it didn't take much of a leap for Liam to imagine that it was him they were laughing at. Did Becky know how he felt? Was that the big joke? Were they laughing about the fact that they were secretly seeing each other? Liam watched and waited for his chance to do something about it.

It came one night towards the end of the summer when Mike suggested that they all walk over to Menai Bridge on Anglesey and go for a drink there for a change. Becky elected not to go, so Liam, Mike and Andy set off. It wasn't that long a walk, and it was a pleasant, warm evening. They had a laugh and a game or two of pool, but as the alcohol took hold, Liam noticed that Mike and Andy were leaving him out of the conversation more and more, and the more he saw it, the quieter he became. By the time they made their way home, Liam was barely speaking to them at all. As they crossed the Menai Bridge, Liam began to walk more slowly, letting his friends pull away in front of him, waiting for them to spot his absence and care enough to come back for him. They didn't, and this just upset him more. He'd never really fitted in with them and it was pretty obvious that they didn't give a shit about him. Well, sod them. He had too much work to do next year to make sure he passed his degree, so they could just do without him, and after that, they'd all piss off back where they came from and never have to bother with each other again. He was surprised, then, to round a corner and find Mike and Andy waiting for him.

"You all right, Liam?" Mike asked. "We'd thought you'd fallen in or something."

"I'm fine," Liam snapped and tried to walk past them, but Andy caught his arm.

"What the hell's the matter with you?" he asked. "You've had a face on you all night."

"Yeah, like you're arsed," Liam said and pulled his arm free. "Maybe I should have jumped in. It would have given you something else to laugh about."

"I don't know what you're on about."

"Don't give me that. You're always laughing at me. You and your bird."

"My...what? Who are you talking about?"

"Becky. You know damn well who I mean. I thought you were my fucking friend."

"Mate, I don't know what you're talking about!"

"Yes, you do. You know I like Becky, but that hasn't stopped you, has it?"

"Becky? What the fuck...?" Andy said and took a step towards him, but Liam pushed him away. Andy stood there stunned for a second and then pushed him back. Before either of them knew where they were, they were grappling with Liam falling backwards into a bush and dragging Andy down after him. There was a frantic rustling and they both emerged, faces covered in scratches and leaves and twigs in their hair.

Later, they would be hard-pressed to say who started laughing first, but as the onlooker who had been treated to the show, it was probably Mike. However it started, they all sat beside the road and laughed until they cried. Gasping for breath, Liam just about managed to say, "Don't ever breathe a bloody word of this. Either of you." This made them all crack up again. Once they had calmed down, Mike got to his feet and held a hand out to each of his friends, which they both took and hauled themselves to their feet.

"Seriously," Liam said, brushing his clothes down and picking foliage out of his hair. "We never ever mention this again."

"Yeah, like I'm ever going to tell anyone about this," Andy said. "Just so's you know, Liam. There's nothing going on between me and Becks. We're just mates, that's all."

"Doesn't matter," Liam replied. "It's none of my business. We just don't tell anyone about this, yeah?"

"Too bloody right," Mike agreed. "I'm taking this one to my grave."

Part Three
Finale

Chapter Forty-Three

It had been a very long time since Liam had felt this nervous. His stomach was in a knot, his heart was beating at a rate which surely couldn't be healthy, and his palms were damp against the steering wheel. He kept telling himself that this was ridiculous, but somehow his body wasn't taking any notice. This was only the dress rehearsal, for God's sake. How was he going to feel later when they did it for real? The last time he had been as anxious as this was the day Freya was born. Before that, he remembered the panic that had set in the morning of his first finals exam. He woke up convinced that nothing he had revised was going to come up and that even if it did, he wouldn't be able to remember it. Mike had walked him to the cavernous Pritchard-Jones Hall in the main university building, where the exams were taking place in case Liam bottled it and didn't turn up. He didn't help Liam's nerves by regaling him with some of the apocryphal stories of previous students who had allegedly freaked out in exams, like the one who suddenly stood up, said, "I shouldn't be here, I'm an orange!" and ran out. Despite the banter, Mike was a reassuring presence and Liam would not forget the hand his friend had laid on his shoulder just as he was about to go in.

"Whatever happens," Mike had said, "in three hours, it'll be over."

Liam had carried this message with him for the rest of his life and whatever situation he found himself in, he could always look ahead to the time when the situation would inevitably be over. He wished Mike was with him today to offer some similar words of wisdom, but then, in a way, he was, in spirit, if nothing else. Liam tried to focus on the fact that he had to dance for about a minute and a half twice more, then it would all be over, and he'd never have to do it again. He tried to convince himself that it didn't matter, that it was just for charity and nobody's life depended on it (or at least not like that) and that everybody there wanted them all to do well. Nobody would be laughing or mocking. Somehow, though, it still took a huge amount of courage to peel his hands off the steering wheel and get out of the van.

"Nobody's going to judge you," Nic said that morning before he left.

"Well, the judges are," Liam argued. "That's kind of what they're there for. Clue's in the name."

"None of the audience, I meant. Think about it. None of them are doing it, are they? You and Andy and the others, you're the better people. You should all be really proud of yourselves. I know I'm proud of you."

She'd given him an unexpected hug then, and she had felt so familiar in his arms that he didn't want to let go. He'd suggested that she come along to the dress run, but her pride in him apparently didn't stretch to watching him dance twice in one day. Besides, she said, she wanted to watch the final performance with everyone else, with no knowledge of what to expect. Freya had wanted to come early, too, to record the dress run for the posterity of social media, but Liam had asked her not to. If it all went wrong, he didn't wany any record of it in the public domain.

He got out of the van and scanned the hospice car park for Andy's car. It didn't seem to be here yet, so with no friend or ex-wife to accompany him, he went in alone.

The Larks House Hospice was a converted Georgian manor house. It had served as an emergency hospital for soldiers returning from the Second World War and had continued as a medical establishment ever since. The owners had sold it to the charity around twenty years earlier, but the building retained much of the original brickwork and ornate, vaulted ceilings that provided a reminder about its original purpose. Liam signed in at reception and was directed down a long corridor to what had once been the manor's ballroom. If he had been nervous before he went in, nothing prepared him for the sight that greeted him when he swung open the ballroom door and went inside.

The room was nothing short of magnificent. It looked like very little had changed since the days when beautiful rich people would gather here to dance the night away. Elaborate gold-painted mouldings adorned the walls, and the ceiling and walls were hung with some of the biggest mirrors Liam had ever seen. Forget seven years; if one of them broke, you'd be looking at seven hundred years of bad luck. He didn't envy whoever had the job of cleaning them. The wooden parquet floor had been polished to an immaculate sheen and he hardly dared tread on it in his battered old trainers. It was hard to believe that a room like this could exist in a building whose purpose now was to nurse people through the last years of their lives. It seemed somehow incongruous and wrong.

The centre of the room had been left clear, presumably as a stage, because it was surrounded on three sides by chairs that had been laid out in tiers. At one end was a desk with three chairs, which was clearly the judges' area, and there were two other chairs alongside, which Liam guessed were for whoever was hosting the evening. A giant disco ball hung from the ceiling, casting splinters of light over the whole room as it moved gently in a breeze that was coming from somewhere. Members of the hospice staff hurried backwards and forwards, making last-minute adjustments, and Liam could see a couple of the other competitors standing at one side, looking every bit as over-awed as he was.

"They've done a pretty good job, haven't they?" a voice said. Liam turned to see Carol, the event organiser, standing behind him.

"That's one word for it," Liam said. "It's incredible."

"Before you ask, no, we don't keep it looking like this. It's locked up most of the year and just cleaned for special occasions and then it takes the best part of a week. It's worth it, though."

"It certainly is. I just hope I can do it justice."

"You're here, Liam. That's all we can ask. You're all doing the most wonderful thing and we really appreciate the way you've all embraced it. The main thing is that you try and enjoy your day. You've earned it."

"Thank you. I'll do my best."

"Good. Right, if you go out of the side door over there and turn left, you'll see the signs that'll take you to the rooms we've commandeered for dressing rooms. It's boys in one and girls in the other, and the girls have got the bigger one, I'm afraid, but at least you'll all be able to keep each other company. Go and drop your stuff off and make yourself comfortable. There's tea and coffee-making facilities in the dressing rooms, but don't drink too much once you've got your costume on. There's still a couple of hours to the dress rehearsal and it can be a bit of a bugger when you're all dressed up, I believe."

"I'll remember that," Liam said. "I think I'm hyped up enough without caffeine."

"I'm telling everyone this, but there's no need to be nervous. Just do your best and have fun and remember everything you've been taught and it'll be fine."

"Yes, that remembering bit is one of the things that makes me nervous."

"You're an electrician, aren't you?" Carol asked. She sneaked a look at her clipboard that Liam didn't think he was supposed to see.

"Yes, I am," he said.

"Well then, just think of everything you remember every day when you're doing your job. I bet most of it's second nature to you now, isn't it? Your memory's an incredible thing. You retain all sorts of stuff without realising it."

"Yes, and I google the rest," Liam said. "I can't really do that in mid-routine, can I?"

"You won't need to. You'll be fine. Oh, look, here's your friend."

Liam turned and saw Andy enter the ballroom with Alison, Stevie and Amy in tow. They all stopped dead as soon as they saw the room, and Liam imagined he heard the sound of four jaws simultaneously hitting the floor.

226

"All right, lad?" he said, going over to them. "Bit disappointing, isn't it? You'd have thought they'd have made a bit of an effort."

Chapter Forty-Four

"Bloody hell, lad, look at the state of you!"

Liam was self-conscious enough about how he looked in the charcoal-grey tailcoat, starched collar and bow tie without Andy killing himself laughing. The suit felt like a straitjacket, and he looked like he'd stepped off a wedding cake. It wasn't his usual look at all.

"Yeah, thanks, Andy. Like, I don't know. I look like the frigging Penguin. This is supposed to look *elegant,* for God's sake. I think someone misheard. Elephant is more like it."

"No, I'm only winding you up, mate. You look sound."

"Anyway, you can't talk. What have you come dressed as?"

"What's wrong with this?" Andy looked at himself in the full-length mirror and gestured to his red suit. "This is the latest thing. Everyone's going to be wearing these soon."

"It's the latest thing if you live in 1976," Liam said. "Are those trousers flared?"

"They are not. They're...roomy. Some of the moves we're doing, I need a bit of space. I can't be constricted, or I'll burst out of it."

"I can't breathe, or I'll burst out of mine."

Andy sat down in front of the mirror and started to brush his hair.

"Mind you," he said, "I'm glad Lesley decided against the wig."

"Wig?"

"Have you ever seen 'The Rockafeller Skank' video? It's got these two lads with big afros. I told Les it would make me look like Harry Enfield's Scousers and people would start shouting, 'Calm down, calm down.' I also pointed out that it could be considered insensitive and that's what decided it really. The real reason I didn't want to wear it is because in this suit, I looked like a bloody matchstick."

"You think yourselves lucky," came a voice from the corner of the room. One of the other contestants, who Liam thought was called Pete, was sitting on a chair next to a clothes rack, eating corned beef sandwiches from a Tupperware box. He was perhaps a little older than Liam and Andy and was dressed in a teal, sequined mesh shirt, open to his waist and very tight trousers. "All I can say is I'm glad I've fathered my children because I don't think I'll be doing it again after wearing these pants," Pete said.

"You look great," Liam said. "Very...stylish."

"We both know that's crap, but thanks. Mind you, when you've had prostate cancer, you can pretty much do anything. I've had that many fingers poking around up there that I've forgotten what dignity's like. But at least I'm still here to tell the tale."

"Are you all sorted now?"

"Pretty much. I was lucky, really. They found it when I went for my MOT, as I call it, you know, those men's health checks they do when you reach a certain age. You had one?"

"No," Liam said. "I think I got a letter about it, but I haven't been yet. I've been putting it off, I suppose."

"Well, don't," Pete said. "It's not the most fun you can have, but it probably saved my life. I hadn't had much in the way of symptoms, I don't think, but there it was. It was seven years ago before I started working here. I still have check-ups, but they're all clear. They're just a bit of a day out now. Gives me the day off work."

"What is it you do?" Andy asked.

"I work here," Pete said. "I'm a porter. I'll tell you what, though. It gives you a whole different perspective on things. I complained about some of the things I had to do, but the poor buggers here don't get a say. They have to have everything done for them while they wait for the end. You don't hear them complain though, none of them. I thought this would be a really depressing place to work, but it isn't. The staff here are incredible, so kind and caring. They do everything they can to make it as easy as possible, not just for the patients, but for their families too, because it's not just the patients who are waiting. I wouldn't work anywhere else now. That's why I'm doing this, though when I signed up for it, I didn't think I'd be wearing something like this. They asked me if I'd get my chest waxed, but I told them to get lost. I'd rather have another prostate exam."

"So, how's the dancing been going?" Liam asked.

"Let's put it this way: it doesn't matter how bad you lads think you are; you've got absolutely nothing to worry about from me. Bless her, Andrea has done her best, but some people are never meant to dance and I'm one of them. Still, if it raises a bit of cash..."

"Can't wait to see you shimmy," Andy laughed.

"I promise you'll never forget it," Pete said. "Oh, here he is. Hope you've left some bog roll for the rest of us."

As he spoke, the other male amateur dancer, a young man called Jason, came into the dressing room. He had long hair tied up in a man-bun and was dressed in a very traditional black tailcoat. It contrasted nicely with the slightly green pallor of his face.

"I think I ate something," he said. "I can't stop throwing up."

"Try not to do it on the dancefloor, eh?" Pete said. "Don't want anyone slipping over."

"I don't think there'll be anything left by then," Jason said. "Oh God."

With that, he turned around and ran back out of the dressing room. Pete laughed and helped himself to another sandwich. "Kids," he said. "No bloody stamina."

"Does he work here too?" Liam asked.

"Yes, he's not long started. He's a good kid, really. I would say that, though. He's my son."

"You're competing against your boy?" Andy asked. "Wow. What's that like?"

"Well, it's driven his mother round the bend, but I've got to take my hat off to him for doing it. Plenty wouldn't."

"I know what you mean. It was all I could do to get my lad to come here at all. Luckily, we don't live round here. If there was any chance of Stevie's mates seeing him, we'd never have got him out of the house. He'll just be glad when tomorrow comes and I stop embarrassing him."

"We'll all be glad when tomorrow comes," Pete said. "If I ever hear that bloody *Hot Hot Hot* again, I'll do something desperate."

They were interrupted by a knock on the dressing room door. It opened slightly and Julia's voice called out, "Are you all decent?"

"Come in and find out, love," Pete replied.

Julia opened the door fully and came in. Liam hardly recognised her. In a long, dove-grey dress made of some floaty material Nic would have been able to identify, which was covered in crystals and with her hair up in an elaborate style that probably also had a name, she looked stunning.

"Julia," Liam said. "Bloody hell, look at you! You look amazing."

"Why thank you," Julia replied. "You scrub up quite well yourself. I came to warn you that they're going to be calling us all into the ballroom in five or ten minutes. Just so you're prepared."

"Already? Oh God."

"Don't panic," Julia said. "It's only the dress run. It's nothing to worry about. I'll see you there."

With a rustle of her dress, she disappeared back through the door.

"Here we fucking go," Liam said, catching the nervous look on Andy's face.

"What's the worst that could happen?" Andy replied.

"We could all be about to make massive tits of ourselves," Pete said, putting the lid back on his sandwich box and tucking it away in his backpack. "Still, at least we'll all be doing it together, eh? I'd better go and drag Super Mario out of the bathroom."

Chapter Forty-Five

Liam would have preferred it if they had each done their dress rehearsals in private, but Carol of the Clipboard explained that it was useful to get used to having an audience, even if it only comprised the other competitors, hospice staff and the volunteers who were helping out with the running of the event. Along with Andy's family, there were a few other people who looked like they could be friends and family of the competitors. Nic and the girls weren't due until the evening. Nic said she couldn't cope with being around Liam while he was so nervous because he'd have her up the wall too, and Liam agreed fully with her decision. If the dress run went as badly as he feared it might, he didn't want her to witness it either.

The judges were obviously much too important to allow themselves to be seen in their finery just yet, so three of the volunteers sat in their seats to get the dancers used to someone being there. They found their new roles highly amusing and entertained each other by doing very bad impersonations of the judges from the television show. Liam wished with all his heart that the organisers had put shop dummies or something there instead because at least they would have shut up and been considerably less irritating.

The nearer it got to his time to rehearse, the more Liam's patience was being tested by just about everything. Some of the other dancers stood at the side of the ballroom, practising steps or doing stretching exercises, but it was obvious to Liam that they didn't really need to; they were already good enough. They were clearly trying to psyche out the opposition by proving how high they could kick or how fast they could spin. Julia saw him watching and came over to him, holding up the hem of her dress so it didn't drag along the floor.

"Is there anything you want to run through?" she asked. "Might as well make the most of the time while we're waiting."

"Look at them," Liam replied. "They're just showing off. It's like when you did exams at school and it was always the dead bright kids who went round afterwards going, 'What did you put for question six?' when they know damn well they've got it right and you probably haven't."

"They're just trying to keep limber, Liam. Go easy on them. They're just as nervous as you. Everyone handles it in different ways."

"I'm not nervous," Liam said. "I'm terrified. Is it too late to pull out and go home?"

"Don't you dare! I'm not doing this on my own."

"Don't you get nervous?"

"Of course I do. Every time. You've just got to focus on what you're doing and ignore everyone else. Only you can dance your dance, and only they can dance theirs."

They were interrupted by a sudden burst of music blaring out of the speakers that were mounted on the walls around the room. Liam hoped that none of the patients were trying to sleep because that was loud enough to wake everyone up.

"Sorry!" Carol called from somewhere at the back of the room. "Just testing the levels."

The music subsided and Liam saw Andy and Lesley emerge from the door at the side of the ballroom. They spotted Liam and Julia and came over.

"Where have you been?" Liam asked. "Thought you'd chickened out and got off."

"We were just having a bit of a run-through in the corridor," Andy explained. "Have they not started yet?"

"Any minute," Julia said, glancing at her watch. "I must remember to take that off for the performance."

"I wish they'd hurry up," Liam said. "I want to get this over with."

He instantly wished he had kept his mouth shut, because Carol appeared again, waving her clipboard and clapping her hands.

"Is everyone here?" she asked, looking around, silently counting heads. "Right. Good. We're just about ready to start. If you could just listen up for a minute, I'm going to give you the running order, which will be the same for tonight. We've pulled names out of a hat to try and make it fair, so unless there's a real problem, we'd like to stick to it. Okay, here we go. Pete and Andrea will be going first – sorry guys, but someone had to – then Kelly and Matt, Jason and Hayley, Jade and Keith, Liam and Julia, Estelle and Johnny, Andy and Lesley and then finally Emma and Bill. Sorry, you two have to wait 'til the end, but again, someone's got to. Have you all got that?"

A murmur of assent ran around the room. Liam glanced over at Pete, who was whispering something to his dance partner. He didn't look at all happy, but she shrugged apologetically as if to say *What can you do?*

"So if everyone could clear the dancefloor, please – thank you – we'll run through the programme as accurately as we can so I can see the timings. Any problems, we can have a chat at the end."

Carol walked over to the chairs next to the judges' area and tapped the microphone that had been set up there.

"Good evening, everyone, and welcome to the Larks House Strictly Amateurs Dance Competition!"

The makeshift audience applauded as wildly as a handful of people can applaud. Clipboard Carol seemed to enjoy it.

"Please welcome to the dancefloor our first couple, Larks House's very own Pete Kearney and his dance partner Andrea Patrick!"

Liam watched as Pete took his partner's hand and led her onto the floor. There was a pause, and then the music started and off they went. Liam was dismayed to see that for his age (not that he was very much younger), Pete was a very agile and enthusiastic dancer and matched his partner step for step.

234

His hips moved in ways that Liam could only dream of. To Liam's untrained eye, the performance looked flawless and when the routine ended with Andrea executing the splits to perfection, he thought that the contest might as well end there, even before it had begun. Pete was obviously going to smash it and there were still another six dancers (not including Liam himself) to go.

"Bloody hell," he whispered to Julia, "he's amazing."

"He's no more amazing than you," Julia replied. "He's only got the same experience as you have."

"No, I could never have done that."

"You could if you'd been trained, but you've been trained in the foxtrot instead, which is much harder, honestly. Now shush. Focus on yourself."

It was a bit easier for Liam to do that during the next two performances. A young girl called Kelly did a tango with her partner, a very serious-looking young man named Matthew, but she looked very nervous and made such a mess of the steps in the middle of the dance that they had to stop and start again from the beginning. She was followed by Jason, who managed to stay out of the bathroom long enough to give his version of a paso doble. Liam wasn't quite sure what the dance was supposed to look like, but he was pretty sure it wasn't like that. Jason did quite a lot of standing around with his arms raised, trying to look macho and failing completely, while Hayley, his partner, did the majority of the dancing. The fact that she was very good only highlighted his deficiencies and made him look worse. The performance these two dancers gave should have made Liam feel better, but if anything, they made him more anxious, particularly when the watching volunteers and staff laughed at Jason's attempt. Any minute now, he and Julia would be called to the floor and then everyone would have a chance to laugh at him, too. Jason finally finished and made his escape back into the audience, where his father was waiting for him, completely unable to hide his laughter. Jason appeared to be taking it well. He was very red in the face but was joining in with the laughter.

Carol called the next couple, Jade and Keith onto the dancefloor. Liam was aware that Julia had taken hold of his arm and was squeezing it, trying to provide reassurance. Jade and Keith took their positions, the music started and...

The lights went out. For a moment or two, nobody was sure what was going on, but then Carol called out.

"So sorry, everyone. And I'm really sorry to ask this, but is there an electrician in the house?"

Chapter Forty-Six

Andy watched in the half-light as Liam had a brief, hushed conversation with Carol and hurried out through the main ballroom door.

"I'm sorry once again, everyone," Carol called out. "Luckily, whatever has happened has apparently only affected this room, so the rest of the hospice is okay and all the patients are safe. We're equally lucky to have an expert in our midst and Liam says he expects to be able to get things up and running again very soon. In the meantime, just relax for a bit, but please don't wander too far away from the ballroom. We don't want to have to track everyone down when the lights come back on."

She laughed nervously and followed Liam out of the room, leaving the doors open so at least some light filtered in from the corridor outside.

"I've got an idea," Andy said to Lesley. "Why don't we do our dress rehearsal now while no one's looking?"

"That's a terrible idea," Lesley replied, though she laughed when she said it. "We've got no music for a start, and I've heard you sing. Just wait. I'm sure your friend will get it sorted out."

"While we're waiting, come and meet the family," Andy said and led her over to the audience area where Alison was watching what was going on, but Stevie and Amy had their heads buried in their phones, their faces illuminated by the screens. "Alison, kids, this is Lesley."

Alison stood up and leaned over the seats to give Lesley a hug.

"Lovely to meet you," she said. "It's nice to put a face to the name I've been hearing so much in the last few weeks."

"I'm sorry," Lesley replied. "It does take over a bit. You'll have your husband back after today."

"No, it's fine. You can keep him a bit longer if you want. It's given me a few hours peace every week and I've just about caught up with *Drag Race*. Kids, put your phones away and say hello to your dad's other woman."

Amy and Stevie looked up from their phones and acknowledged Lesley's presence without going to the extremes of put them away altogether. As soon as they could get away with it, they went back to catching up on whatever urgent business they had been engaged in before they were rudely interrupted.

"So, how do you think it's going?" Alison asked. "Some of them look really good. I was a bit surprised, actually. I mean, a couple of them were a bit dodgy, but there were one or two...you'd never know they were amateurs."

"Hey, that's my competition you're talking about," Andy said. "You're supposed to say they're all crap and I'm brilliant."

"I haven't seen you yet," Alison said. "But I'm sure you are. Is he, Lesley? Have we uncovered a new superstar?"

"If he dances like he has in practice, then we've uncovered a dancer, certainly. Did you know your husband has natural rhythm?"

"I've got to confess that after all these years of marriage, that's news to me. Well, well, well. Who knew?"

"I wouldn't take too much notice of the dress rehearsal, though," Lesley said. "I've been involved in enough to know that they are no real indication of how the performance is going to go. They're really there to iron out any issues with costume and to get the dancers used to the floor."

"So is it true that a bad dress rehearsal means a good first night? That's what they say, isn't it?"

"The only people who say that are ones who've had a terrible dress rehearsal and they only say it to make themselves feel better. It can go either way and usually does."

"I wish Liam would hurry up," Andy said, "or there'll be no time for a dress rehearsal at all. It's half four already."

"The dance is only ninety seconds, Andy," Lesley pointed out. "I'm sure we'll squeeze it in somehow. You're not getting out of it like that."

They made rather uncomfortable small talk for another half an hour or so before Carol came bustling back into the ballroom, slapping her clipboard for attention.

"Won't be long now, everyone!" she shouted. "Liam knows what the problem is and he's fixing it right now. If the remaining dancers could get themselves ready, you'll have your turn on the dancefloor very soon."

"Oh God," Andy said. "Here we go."

Almost as soon as he said it, the lights came back on, and a spontaneous round of applause burst out. It increased in volume when Liam came into the room, still in his tailcoat but with his workbag slung incongruously over one shoulder. He gave a rather embarrassed wave and went over to join Julia, who hugged him and brushed dust off his jacket.

Carol called Jade and Keith back onto the floor and the dress rehearsal resumed. Apparently unperturbed by the delay, Jade, whom Andy had found out was one of the hospice nurses, was whirled around the floor by her partner Keith, an older dancer, whose greying ponytail looked completely at odds with his suit. He would have been more at home at Glastonbury than in the ballroom. He was incredibly light on his feet, though, and together, they performed what, to Andy's eyes at any rate, was a very impressive quickstep. Then it was Liam's turn and Andy could only look on in horror as just about everything that could go wrong did so.

It was impossible to say what would have happened were it not for the delay and for Liam having to get back to his day job for a while. It was obvious to Andy, though, that his mind was anywhere but on the dancefloor. They had to start the dance twice because he wasn't ready the first time and started a couple of beats late, meaning the timing was off from the start. When they did begin again, Liam looked like he had lost all confidence and every step he did was tentative and cautious. At one point, he went to go the wrong way into a spin, and although Julia caught him and put him right, he stumbled and almost dragged them both over. If Julia had not been such a good dancer, they would have looked like two drunks at the end

239

of a wedding, clinging to each other for grim death while the lights came up around them. At the end, Liam looked utterly shellshocked and, rather than waiting for the somewhat muted applause to finish, fled from the ballroom through the side door.

"Jesus," Andy whispered to Lesley, "what the hell happened there?"

"Very bad dress rehearsal," Lesley replied. "That's sort of what they're for."

"I need to see him. I know Liam. He'll be beating himself up right now."

"You haven't got time. There's only Johnny and his partner and then we're on. You need to concentrate on your own dance, Andy. Liam will still be there in ten minutes."

He knew she was right and that he owed it to her to do the best he could. He didn't take much notice of the couple who were currently rehearsing, though the audience's reaction at the end indicated that they had been pretty good, and he tried to put Liam out of his mind too. He concentrated instead on his breathing and trying to remember the steps he was about to perform. Suddenly, Carol was calling his name, and he took Lesley's hand and walked out onto the floor.

The routine went well, far better than Liam's had. He remembered most of the steps, only going wrong once, but a shouted reminder from Lesley set him right again. He focused on the moves and the facial expressions, on the music and on Lesley. They got through to the end and he looked over at Alison and the kids. Alison and Amy were on their feet, clapping loudly and even Stevie had managed to tear himself away from his phone and was grinning. As they left the floor, Lesley squeezed his arm and said, "Now *that* was a dress run. That was amazing, Andy, well done."

"It was more you than me," he said. "But thank you."

Alison rushed out of her seat and flung her arms around him.

"That was actually pretty hot," she said in his ear. "I think I fancy you as a dancer."

240

"That was just the dress," he replied. "Wait 'til you see the real thing."

"I look forward to your performance later, then," she said and kissed him. He ignored the looks the kids were giving them and kissed her back. Alison pulled away from him and said, "Do you think you'd better go and find Liam?"

"I suppose I should. I'll be back, though."

"You better."

He made his apologies to Lesley and slipped out through the side door and into the corridor. He was about to go to the dressing room when he saw Julia hurrying down the hall towards him.

"Julia! Where's Liam?"

"I don't know," Julia replied, tears glistening in her eyes. "He's gone!"

Chapter Forty-Seven

Liam sat in his van and thumped his hands on the steering wheel. He turned his phone off, trying to ignore that he already had two missed calls from Julia and one from Andy. He lit a cigarette and smoked it, glaring through the windscreen at the hospice. Evening was drawing in, and the outside lights had been switched on, bathing the building in a golden glow. It looked beautiful and almost magical, and he hated it. The car park was filling up, and people, all dressed in their best clothes and laughing and joking, were making their way inside. Well, there was one joke they weren't going to be laughing at tonight.

He should have known better. Of course, it was a stupid idea, and he should never have got involved. He should have left it to Andy, who at least had some idea what he was doing. What the hell was he thinking of? Whatever persuaded him that a big, fat, clumsy bastard like him could possibly learn to dance? At least he'd got the lights back on, but that was all he was good for. It was only a fuse anyway and anybody could have fixed that. Dancing was something that he should have left to better people, slimmer and fitter people who wouldn't make idiots of themselves. He was going to let Julia down and let his daughters down and Nic would never look at him the same way again if she had any sense. It was all he could do to stop himself from starting the van and driving off. He had the keys in his hand, and it would be the easiest thing in the world, but if he did that, would he be letting everyone down even further, or would they be glad that he had gone?

He watched as a white, soft-top Mini pulled into a parking space and Nic got out. Fortunately, she didn't look at his van but hurried into the hospice. Freya and Del would be here soon, and probably Rainie too. What kind of example was he going to be to his grandchild? Was it better to be an idiot or a quitter? Either way, it wasn't going to be much of an example at all, except maybe in how not to turn out. Becky would also be arriving at any time and what would she think? He'd sort of hoped at one time that he might have a life with her, but it had never happened. She chose the right man, even if he wasn't here anymore. Liam didn't know if he believed in an afterlife and Mike was up there looking down, but if he was, he'd almost certainly be pissing himself laughing at all of this. He checked his watch. An hour until it was all due to start. There was still time to get away.

Suddenly, Nic rushed out of the hospice and looked frantically towards the car park, her phone to her ear. First Julia, then Andy came out and joined her. Liam tried to sit as low as he could in his seat so they wouldn't see him, but Nic pointed towards the van and, after a brief conversation with Andy, began to walk towards it. He shouldn't have made himself so easy to find. That was another mistake.

Nic reached the van and rapped on the window of the passenger door. The look on her face was one with which Liam was all too familiar, a combination of anger and disappointment. Without waiting for an invitation, she opened the door and climbed in. For a few long seconds, neither of them spoke. Liam had too much to say but didn't know where to begin. In the end, it was Nic who broke the silence.

"Well?" she said. "Do you want to tell me exactly what the fuck is going on?"

"It was shit," Liam said. "*I'm* shit."

"I heard."

"I'll bet. They couldn't wait to tell you, could they?"

"Julia told me. She's lovely, by the way. I could almost get jealous if she wasn't so professional. She's really upset because she thinks she pushed you too far and didn't give you enough support, which is really unfair. I'm sure she gave you loads of support. She didn't realise just how needy you are."

"Needy? Me?"

"Yes, you. The rehearsal didn't go according to plan, so Liam's doing what Liam does and running away when things get tough."

"No, I'm not. I haven't left, have I?"

243

"Probably because you can't decide what's easiest, staying or going. Do the hard thing for once."

"You didn't see it, Nic. I got everything wrong. I'm going to let everyone down. I'm going to make a fool of Julia and you and the girls. I can't do it."

"You can and you're bloody well going to. You're not going to run away this time. You need to remember why you're doing this."

"I know why I'm doing it."

"Do you? Don't you think Mike would have liked to have had the choice? He couldn't run away, could he? And what about Becky? I bet there were times she wanted to give up and run away too. But they couldn't, so you're not going to either. You're going to be a grown-up and get on with it. It doesn't matter if you win or come last; you're going to do it, or I'm done with you."

Liam felt as though she had punched him in the face. He wanted a cigarette but didn't dare with Nic in the van.

"I thought you were done with me anyway," he said. "Isn't that what divorce means?"

"Do you know what, Liam? I wish sometimes I could be done with you once and for all. Sometimes, I wish we'd just left it in Bangor and never met again, but then I look at the girls and wouldn't have missed them for anything. And I wouldn't have missed the good years we had, either."

"But I ruined that."

"You walked away from it, and I thought I'd never forgive you for that. You could have stayed and fought for me, but you didn't. Do you know what's funny? That song you're dancing to, 'Someone to Watch Over Me' when we danced to it at our wedding, I really thought you meant it. I thought you were going to watch over me, but you walked away and left me to watch over myself."

Nic wasn't looking at him and he could hardly bring himself to look at her. Out of the corner of his eye, he saw her swipe her sleeve across her face and thought she might have been wiping a tear away.

"I meant it at the time. I still do. But I let you down and didn't trust you when you did nothing. I didn't think I deserved you," he said.

"I know. Maybe if you'd stuck around, I might have had a chance to show you that you did. You're a good man, Liam. Yes, you're a bit of a jealous, insecure dickhead at times, but you're kind and funny and you were a great dad. But all the times you thought you were a joke, or not good enough, or whatever, it was you that made it happen. No one else. You make yourself into the person you think you are, but that person isn't you at all."

Liam thought about it and knew what she said was, without question, true, every word of it. There was no way he could argue with it, so made a joke out of it instead, as he always did.

"Have you ever thought about writing greetings cards?" he asked.

"Fuck off," she said but smiled despite herself. "So come on, Anton du Berk, are you going to be a big boy and dance or what?"

Liam looked out of the window and saw that another car had pulled up a few spaces away. Freya got out, followed by Rainie, who held the rear door open and helped Delyth out, taking her tenderly by the arm. Liam nodded at Nic and got out of the van.

"Dad!" Del called. "What are you doing out here?"

"Your dad's the hero of the hour, apparently," Nic said. "They blew a fuse or something and he fixed it. He's just been putting his tools in the van. Come on, let's get you inside. You look like you could do with a sit-down, Del. Let's just hope tonight isn't too exciting for you."

With his daughters and daughter-in-law on one side of him, and Nic on the other, Liam walked back to the main door of the hospice, where Andy and Julia were waiting for him.

"Are you okay?" Julia asked.

Liam let the girls go past him to check in and once they were more or less out of earshot, he said, "Yes, I'm fine, Julia.

Bit of stage fright, but Nic talked me round. I'm so sorry for the scare."

"Don't be daft," Julia said. "We all have wobbles. Are you okay to dance?"

"Raring to go," Liam said as bravely as he could manage. "I'll be with you in a minute. I just need to ask Carol a small favour."

Chapter Forty-Eight

Everything else was forgotten for a while and it all came down to the dancing.

The ballroom was full of people who had made an effort to get into the spirit of the event by putting on their best evening wear and Carol had changed out of her usual sweatshirt into a midnight-blue silk ballgown. The judges were assembled at the desk, with their notepads and score paddles at the ready and, in the corridor outside the ballroom, the dancers were lined up, some chatting excitedly, some standing silently, contemplating the dance they were about to do. Two volunteers wearing headsets guarded the door to the ballroom, ready to usher the couples through when it was their turn. One of them received a message and turned to the dancers.

"That's it," she said. "We're about to start. Good luck, everyone."

Andy and Liam glanced at each other, and Andy gave an encouraging thumbs-up. Liam drew a finger across his throat but did his best to smile. From inside the ballroom, music and applause rang out and the show began.

One by one, when it was their turn to dance, the dancers went through to the ballroom. A space had been set aside at the back of the room so that each couple could sit and watch the rest of the show. This meant that the remaining couples had no real idea how each dance had gone. The heavy doors muffled the sound of the judges' voices, but they could hear the clapping and cheering as each couple finished their dance and received their marks. It sounded very similar for everyone, which was hardly surprising because everyone had their own partisan section of the audience and because it was a charity event, the audience as a whole applauded each pair with equal enthusiasm.

The time flew by and suddenly Liam and Julia found themselves at the front of the line and next to perform. Liam looked at the volunteers who had their hands on the doors, waiting for their cue to open them and froze.

"I can't remember anything," he said.

"You can," Julia replied, giving him a warm hug. "It's all in your head. Just feel the music and let it come out. I'm proud of you, whatever happens. Come on. Let's do it."

And they did. Liam took Julia's hand, and the doors were flung wide. He kept his head up as he led his partner onto the dancefloor and tried to ignore the fact that somewhere in the audience, Freya, Del, Rainie, and Nic, especially Nic, were all watching. The music started and he did as Julia had said and let it flow through him, trusting his body to remember the moves.

Afterwards, he wouldn't remember much about it. There was one little stumble, certainly and he was pretty sure he nearly went the wrong way into the spin again, but Julia was there to stop him, and he corrected himself quickly. He concentrated on the song, his frame, and feet and danced like he had never danced before and for those few seconds, it felt wonderful. Then as suddenly as it had started, the song hit its final chord and it was over. Liam and Julia went over to the judges' desk and stood with their arms around each other. Liam felt weirdly dislocated; was that applause for *them*? He could hardly concentrate on what the judges were saying, but it didn't sound as bad as he was expecting. They praised his 'musicality', whatever that meant, and seemed to think his timing was okay. With each comment, good or not so good, Julia clung onto him and when the judges had finished delivering their verdict, she whispered, "See? I said you could do it." Their scores, two sixes and a seven, weren't the disaster he had been convinced they would be, and he didn't care. Julia was right. He had done it, but there was still one more important, even scarier thing he had to do and that would have to wait. They walked back through the audience to the rest of the couples, and as he did so, he could see his girls clapping and beaming at him. Del looked like she was in tears and Nic...did she actually blow him a kiss? He could see that Becky was sitting just behind his family and it looked like she was in tears. None of it felt real, the applause, the pats on the back and hugs from the other dancers, none of it. Whatever this feeling was, he wished he could bottle it and keep it forever.

All too soon, it was time for Andy's dance. It was the first time Liam had seen it all the way through, and he could scarcely believe that he was watching his old friend out there on the floor, dancing with what mostly looked like impeccable timing and control. His facial expressions were as funny as any Liam had seen and the one lift he did, where he somehow managed to whirl Lesley around his back and onto her feet again without missing a beat, was incredible and he could hear gasps from the audience. There was one bit when Andy and Lesley were dancing side by side when they were perhaps slightly out of time with each other, but otherwise, from what little Liam knew about such things, they appeared to execute the dance brilliantly. The judges were equally impressed and when it came to giving their scores, two of them raised paddles with eights on them, though Phillippa, the head judge, who seemed a bit picky and miserable, only gave them a seven. All the same, when Andy came over to join Liam and the others, he was obviously delighted with his performance. He hugged Liam, something he rarely did and said, "We did it! I hope Mike was watching that."

The final results didn't really matter after that. Liam was made up for Pete and Estelle, whose scores from the judges were equal, which meant they had to share the trophy. All that mattered was that they had done what they set out to do. They had challenged themselves to do something that was about as far out of their comfort zone as it could get and they had done it. They had done it to honour Mike and everyone else whose lives had been affected in any way by that horrible, insidious disease and proved that it's never too late to do something amazing. Good as it felt, though, Liam was still unable to relax properly because the moment was fast approaching when he had the chance to try and put the past behind him once and for all. Carol took to the microphone once more and that moment was here.

"Ladies and gentlemen," Carol said, "some of you might know this, but earlier today, we had a bit of an electrical problem, which meant we were worried that this brilliant evening might not have gone ahead. We were rescued by our very own hero; someone you have just seen dance. He didn't want paying for his work, but he did ask a favour and we were delighted to grant it. Liam, could you come over and tell us what it is, please?"

Liam ignored the look Andy gave him and made his way back through the audience to the microphone.

"Hi, everyone," he said, "sorry. I don't make a habit of this, and it won't take long. So...yeah, it's been an incredible night and I hope we've raised lots of money. Andy and I did this for our friend Mike and I hope his wife Becky wasn't too embarrassed by us." In her place in the audience, Liam could see Becky shaking her head *No*. "But there's another reason I did it. That song I danced to was a special one because I danced to it with my wife at our wedding – not like that of course! It was one of the best moments of my life, but because I was stupid and didn't realise what I had, I let her go. So, if you don't mind, I'd like to try and make up for it, just a little bit and do the dance one more time."

He put the microphone back in the stand and walked over to where Nic was sitting in the audience, hiding her face in Freya's shoulder. He held out his hand to her.

"Nic," he said, "may I have this dance?"

Nic looked up, and for a moment, he wasn't sure whether she was about to punch him.

"No!" she hissed. "I can't!"

"Please? Just this once?"

"I don't know how, Liam. This is ridiculous!"

"Follow me," he said. "I'll lead."

She took his hand, and he helped her out of her seat and over to the dancefloor as the audience erupted around them.

"You bastard," Nic said quietly as they reached their position, "I'm going to murder you for this."

But she didn't. She allowed him to take her in his arms and as 'Someone to Watch Over Me' started once again, they soon forgot that there was anyone else in the room.

And they danced.

Chapter Forty-Nine

Before they all went their separate ways that night, Liam, Andy, Becky and Nic made a small diversion and went back into Bangor together. They had agreed to meet up at Liam's house for a celebratory drink. Liam had given Freya the keys so that she could let everyone in, and Andy had given Alison directions so she could follow on with Stevie and Amy.

They stood together outside what they had always known as Top College and looked out onto the lights of the town below. All around them, students passed by on their way to a night out, all looking very young.

"Did we look like that?" Andy asked.

"We looked worse than that," Becky said, taking his arm. "It was the eighties, after all."

"We thought we were great," Liam said.

"I think we were," Nic replied. "All of us. But especially Mike."

As one, they all looked up to the sky and said a silent farewell to their old friend. Then, Becky still holding onto Andy's arm, and Liam with Nic's hand held tightly in his own, they left the university behind and went back to their families.

Epilogue
1988

They'd done it. Somehow, Liam, Andy and Becky had finished their final year and were standing looking down onto the town, dressed in their caps and gowns, graduates at last. The year had flown over; it seemed like it had hardly begun before they sat their finals. Mike was doing his teacher training and kept them entertained with horror stories of his work placement when they met up at the Union. They still gathered there at least once a week, but far less frequently this year than in the previous two. With their finals looming up ahead of them, everything suddenly seemed more serious. The exams went reasonably well in the end, despite Liam having one paper that he thought he had cocked up badly and possibly failed. When their results came through, Liam and Andy achieved upper second-class honours, while Becky surprised everyone, not least herself, by getting a first.

The graduation day had passed by in a blur and one by one they had processed onto the stage in the Pritchard-Jones Hall to shake the hand of the vice chancellor and process off again. They had their official photographs taken in their hired gowns, in front of a fake wood-panelled board, proudly holding a scroll tied up with ribbon, which wasn't a degree certificate at all, and had managed to slip away from their parents to meet up here. Groups of graduates were celebrating all around them. Claire and the Donnas were celebrating together, and even Spanner, who somehow managed to make a cap and gown look scruffy, was passing a surreptitious spliff around with his mates.

Liam looked over to a group on his left and saw that Nic was chatting with some of her drama department friends. She caught his eye and gave him a smile and wave. They had started speaking to each other again during the last year, and although things weren't quite the same, at least the outright hostility had ended, so Liam greatly appreciated that smile. He also didn't expect to see Mike coming up the stone steps towards them. Having graduated the previous year, he looked slightly out of place in his leather jacket and Psychedelic Furs T-shirt, but it wouldn't have been the same without him.

"You made it, kids," he said.

"We all did," Andy said. "Who'd have thought it?"

"It doesn't seem real," Becky said. "I still can't believe this is it."

"Off into the real world," Liam said. "Jobs. Families even. Is that it? Are we grown-ups now?"

"It had to happen," Andy said. "It was always going to. It's all gone so fast."

"Well, you lot had better stay in touch," Becky said.

"Of course we will," Mike said. "We haven't come this far to lose touch now. We're always going to be friends."

"Always is a long time," Liam said.

"Of course it is," Mike said and put a hand on his friend's shoulder. "But we've got a long time. We're going to live forever."

The End

The story on the preceding pages was purely a work of fiction.

The stories that follow are all true.

Jason's Story

The Best Kind

"There's no easy way to say this, get your pants off."

I've done the very British thing, whereby I've told the doctor what I think the problem is and what he, the medical professional, should do about it. This is obviously an injury caused by riding my bike to work and back every day. All I need is a rest. Couple of weeks off work. Maybe a better saddle? Better underwear even? I'm stalling. Milliseconds become hours as the request hangs in the air...

He had to say the C word, didn't he? ... no, not that one, *cancer*. Then again, Wade Wilson had cancer, riddled with it. The result? Deadpool has regenerative powers, pretty much a superhero... I'm still stalling. And that was a comic.

I've come this far. For those who know me, the bike bit is true; I was actually quite fit at one point. I'd noticed the swelling and asked my then partner if she could feel the swelling. She told me something along the lines of she'd heard that one before. Unanimously, we agreed it was time to get checked. Appointment made, easy. Stroll to the docs, easy. Laugh with the receptionist, easy. Get your pants down... actually quite difficult.

Men can handle being injured pretty much anywhere and parade their injuries like they stormed the beach at Normandy, except this one place.

Time to swallow my pride and down go the pants. It's the point of no return and maybe if it hadn't been for people around me telling me to go, well, maybe I wouldn't have. I'm supposed to be the strong one, the one that others look to when they need to. The one that my kids look up to. The brother that isn't terminally ill. The son who will help hold everything together when the time comes.

My doctor's voice turns into the teacher's voice from the Charlie Brown cartoons, just a warbling that isn't making any sense and it won't until I get my pants back up. I should have legged it, rested up and it'd be fine in a few weeks.

With everything back where it should be, I say my thanks, avoid eye contact, and wait for my scan appointment.

Our amazing National Health Service don't hang about. In a whirlwind, I'm tossed about for scans, appointments, results and finally dropped into the surgeon's chair. Excuse the pun, but they were on the ball. I'm trying to keep a positive attitude but something inside you switches when you know that lurking in your body is something that could kill you. This is where it's important, as far as any advice I can give, don't start looking on the downside.

That, and don't look on the internet. Fifteen years ago, the internet was a very different place, not like today's version where you can find positive stories and motivation. That's very much a new concept for the internet that exists in the upside down. Everyone who has a horror story has a medium for telling it.

"This is the best kind of cancer to get because it can be isolated. Plus, you've caught it at an early stage, so the chances of us completely removing it are improved."

Nobody wants to hear that they have cancer and if you do, you want to hear that the odds are in your favour.

"When we remove the testicle, we can put in a fake one. Would that be something you'd be interested in?"

I'll be honest, I just want it out of me and replacing it with something else is the furthest thing from my mind. But I can't help but question. What is it? Who makes them? Is that all they make? Maybe Bluetooth. Could you put something in there with Bluetooth? Everything's better with Bluetooth. What did Hitler pick? As it turns out there aren't that many options. There's no catalogue to choose from. In fact, the option is to either have it or not. I agreed because they told me it may be more comfortable for my partner. For the curious among you, it's basically a mouse ball. I don't mean the creature; that would be ridiculous. I mean the old-style computer mouse.

I know my approach to this might not be to everyone's taste but it's *my* approach. I'm a firm believer that positive mental attitudes can aid physical recovery, so this story reflects my mental outlook. As it is, I sit here and in the past three years, have been made a grandad twice over. The eldest keeps messing with the keyboard, which I think covers me for typos. My five kids are all enjoying life and I'm enjoying watching them live it.

Sadly, a family friend passed away from exactly the same thing that I had: testicular cancer. He didn't go to the doctor's, he didn't act, and before long, it had spread to his shoulder and then consumed him, eating at him from the inside. The scariest thing about this disease is that you don't know, and every day a little thought pops into my head that maybe just a little bit of it is in there, eating away. So when it raises its head, when you feel something that isn't right, take that step. Men especially, there really is no excuse here. You are talking about an area of the body that you regularly fiddle with anyway.

That's it. It's nothing exciting, but I am here to tell my little story, and if it helps someone, then all the better. Because I overcame that fear and caught it early, they were able to isolate it, which also meant not needing chemotherapy. And to conclude, I leave you with the words that I will never forget on my last examination before being given the all-clear. Professor Clarke, holding my testicles in his hand:

"You are my superstar."

And I looked him in the eye and smiled.

Jason Pinnington

Estelle's Story

After checking myself, I was diagnosed with breast cancer four years ago and have since had surgery, and I am still receiving some form of treatment for legacy conditions that it has left me with.

Now, I could sit here and tell you all about how terrible it is—which it is! From the day you walk into the clinic and are delivered the news, having to tell your family, followed by all the treatment itself, is a pretty grim affair. But I always try to see the positives in all situations, and even cancer offered some lovely moments that I would never have experienced if it hadn't been for the dreadful disease. The main things for me are the new friends I have made. I always tell people that having cancer puts you in a shitty club, but this is the most loving club you could ever belong to. It's the club where people truly 'get' you! It's the club you need to be a member of to understand why people say certain things or feel a certain way. I know some of you reading this may think you know what I mean because you looked after a loved one who has/had it, and they tell you EVERYTHING, but the fact of the matter is that you cannot truly understand until you are part of the 'club.' Pray it is a club you never need to join.

But apart from cancer warriors all feeling the luuuurve and supporting one another, I thought I would give you the top ten things we all experience, whether you have breast cancer or any other type.

1. When you are first diagnosed, you are overwhelmed with hunger for some reason. I'm sure there is a scientific explanation for this, so I'll let you google it and educate yourself, but all cancer patients just accept it. My husband was diagnosed twice before my own, and both times, we went straight to a greasy spoon caff and had a fry-up. With my diagnosis, we sat in the hospital car park where we should have been wailing and crying after having just been delivered the news.

259

But instead, we sat in silence for a few minutes until one of us piped up, "You hungry?" Within half an hour, we were seated in another café with a huge breakfast in front of us. We sat there discussing surgery and chemo while buttering our toast and asking the waitress for more coffee. The thing is, you know it's odd behaviour, but you can't help it. I've heard of people going for an 'all you can eat' Chinese buffet, going straight to the chippy for pie and chips, and someone else told me they managed to eat three Big Macs in the space of twenty minutes. So if you are thinking of opening a caff anywhere, open it by a hospital and just make sure you have plenty of sausages and tissues, of course.

2. Talking of food, everyone who has been diagnosed will have that person who will all of a sudden become your nutritionist. They pontificate about what you should eat while they shove their seventh Jaffa Cake in their gob and spit custard cream crumbs all over you as they tell you that their aunty cured their cancer by eating snail antenna sprinkled with the remnants of a packet of Monster Munch. Yes, we all know we have to eat healthier, and cancer will undoubtedly make you reassess your eating habits. I did. I went on the Keto diet for many months as I heard it was beneficial. I also don't use sweeteners anymore or drink diet drinks. I recently spoke to a nutritionist who said all diet drinks should be removed from the shelves. Not just because they have highly suspected carcinogens in them but because what it does to your sugar levels is quite incredible. Her advice was to drink the non-diet if you ever have one and just keep these at a minimum. I now only drink full sugar carbonated drinks but seeing as I may only have one glass a week, if that, I'm not going to worry. Many breast cancer patients can't have orange juice anymore due to its effect on our tablets. A friend of mine was told she should only eat a rainbow diet. This was something she had to explain to me. Apparently, this is a diet where you eat food that are all different colours. I thought all people did this anyway, but then I figured the person giving the advice clearly

lives on a beige diet—similar to some wedding buffets I've seen (sausage rolls, sausages, sandwiches, vol-au-vents, chicken drumsticks—you get the gist).

3. In addition to the 'nutritionist' above, you will also come across the 'know-it-all.' These tend to be people who have never had cancer but know someone who has, making them experts. They will tell you that your cancer can't be that bad because you look good, or your cancer might kill you because the milkman's nan had it, and she was dead within a week. Some people who just hear the word cancer think the victim will no doubt die. You discover that no one at work is asking for your lottery money anymore, or do you want to pay a deposit for the Christmas do. The worst thing about all that is that you know people have been talking about you in whispers. WE HATE THAT! It is these 'know-it-alls' that spread the gossip about you. Their ill-informed views are deemed gospel, and your birthday fund has now been renamed 'Funeral Flowers.' Someone once told me that their department had a discreet meeting about them all having the same day off for the funeral. The girl was diagnosed, had treatment and was back in the meeting room within five months. She had even managed to replenish the aforementioned Jaffa Cake supply.

4. While there is a lot of this in people who have never had cancer, you would be surprised at how many victims have a cancer hierarchy mentality. "I have stage three. Oh, you only have stage two..." "Is skin cancer a proper cancer, though?" "I had a mastectomy. You were lucky only having a lumpectomy." "You only have chemo for 'bad' cancer." "I had the worst cancer you could possibly have." "Oh, you only had surgery. I was zapped with Gamma rays, put in a radioactive chamber for a fortnight, had my head replaced with a Lindt chocolate bunny and now have to sleep upside down listening to Barry Manilow to stop it coming back!" Okay, the last one might be a bit untrue, but the rest, unfortunately, are not. These have all been said to me or friends of mine.

5. Are all cancer clinics the same? From what I hear, I think yes. The chairs might be set out differently, and some bed curtains are better hooked up than others, but what they all have in common is the TV. All the waiting patients stare at it while their partners sit next to them, googling every term they can think of about your cancer (all the knowledge leaves your brain as soon as your consultant shakes your hand, by the way). My appointments were always in the morning, so our staple viewing was Homes Under the Hammer. This was a good distraction, as I am sure many readers are aware of the piss-taking soundtrack, which made me and my husband laugh. Some friends said they discovered 'How to Dress for Summer' with their morning magazine shows. I also have a friend who said she now makes the best sticky pork ribs with spicy sweet potato fries, thanks to the cookery slot she managed to catch before being told she had to have a double mastectomy. My husband and I also discovered that non-payment of numerous parking fines can result in a couple of men turning up and taking away your Sony TV or Nissan Note, depending on how many tickets you ignored. Who knew daytime telly could be so educational?

6. Talking of parking, why are hospital car parks so bloody expensive?! If you must go daily for treatment, this can soon mount up. But apart from the costs, there is also the fact that they are always full. These patients feel pretty rotten anyway and worse when they come out after their appointment. To then have to walk for miles back to the car can sometimes feel like a killer. I know some hospitals don't always charge, but some do, and at five pounds a day and fifteen rounds of radiotherapy, it's hard to know what to feel sadder about. And before you start with getting a bus, taxi, lift, tuk-tuk, private jet, blah blah, just know that sometimes this isn't an option. Moan over!

7. I am sure that all cancer medical staff are given a 'Cancer Vocabulary Guide' as part of their training. Classics include- *That doesn't look right. That doesn't*

feel right. That doesn't sound right. That looks sinister.
That looks suspicious. Let's see what the biopsy says.
This won't hurt. Sorry, did that hurt?' This will hurt—
deep breath. I'll find a vein. I know best. Stop
wriggling. Stop crying. Don't move.
And they apologise—a lot!

8. Talking of staff, like all professions, there are the good, the bad and the ugly. I have had the privilege of dealing with all three. I'll start with the ugly. I'm not talking of someone we traditionally think of as ugly according to their appearance; I'm talking of the members of staff who think it's amusing to dismiss all of your opinions in your treatment. They usually like to put the fear of God into you, and they smile all the way through it. I had one that gave me a leaflet on every treatment known to man. I think he would have given me one on how to cure impotence if my husband hadn't stepped in and, with a few choice words, wiped the smug smile off the doctor's face. Then we have the bad. I had a few, but what they all had in common was their 'big hands.' No offence, but if you look like you have hands that could throw up a garden wall before the lunchtime news, you have no place in wielding a syringe or any medical equipment requiring a delicate touch. I have heard stories of patients looking like they have been through ten rounds with Rocky Balboa because the nurse was determined to find a vein with the wrong needle. A nurse, who I will call Minnie, had nothing mini about her, including the meat hooks hanging off the end of her arms. Put it this way, she hurt me that much. I insisted on having surgery so I didn't have to have the monthly treatment from her. I don't mind saying that when I watched the coronation of King Charles and saw his hands, I broke out into a cold sweat.

9. One thing most of us have in common is all the new sports gear we now have. You might have bought it because you wanted to get fit (I took up running), but you will undoubtedly participate in some sort of charity walk/run/abseil/crocodile fight. I have more trainers

now than Foot Locker and discovered a condition called Plantar Fasciitis through my cancer diagnosis.

10. What most of us have in common is humour, though. Tumour humour, we call it. Not everyone can find the laughs, but that depends on you. I have seen people still laughing at their cancer and then have been to their funeral a month later. Some people laugh to the end, and I personally applaud these people. While it helps them come to terms with their shitty situation, it can also help those around them to cope. People find it easier to smile than to frown—that's a fact! So as long as it's appropriate, and the patient gives you the nod, then find the laughs, offer those smiles and take the piss. As I have said before now, if anything deserves to have the piss taken out of it, then cancer has to be at the top.

Bless you, all who have read this, and before you turn to the next page, give your body a little check. It'll take you two minutes. You spend hours on your phone and think nothing of it, so it's not a big ask. Checking yourself doesn't stop you getting cancer, but it can make all the difference between life and death. Tell your loved ones, too and teach your young ones how to do it. Stay healthy, you beautiful lot!

Estelle Maher

Estelle is the author of four novels, including *The Killing of Tracey Titmass* (a fictional account of her own breast cancer journey) and the latest, *Dear Jane, Love Daisy*. She is also the co-creator and co-host of the *Get It Off Your Chest, The Funny Side of Breast Cancer* podcast, available on all good platforms.

Pete's Story

My story won't be as witty or as professional as Estelle's, but when she asked me to consider writing about my own cancer experience(s), there was a common theme in that I thought I could share. That is, quite simply, to be vigilant and aware. This, of course, echoes Estelle's check yourself campaign, but maybe mine is from a male perspective, where we tend to ignore pretty much everything even when we know we shouldn't.

So, when I was much younger, I was aware that my dad was always going into hospital to have polyps removed. As a kid, this didn't mean much to me other than I knew it had something to do with backsides, and that was, quite frankly, enough information for me as a 14-year-old. My dad passed away at 77 and was officially diagnosed with bowel and lung cancer. He was a lifelong smoker with a poor diet and no exercise, but hey-ho, gyms and cucumber shakes weren't popular with Irish immigrants in the 60s and 70s.

Fast forward to 2012, when I was forty-six, I noticed something happening when I went to the loo. There was a change. (I will be graphic here as I think the messaging requires it.) My poo was more runny than usual, and of course, I ignored this for a time, assuming it was too much curry or a 'bad pint'. I, for one, have never been a fan of scrutinising my deposits, but after some time, I noticed some red stuff which I didn't think should be there. Again, I left it for a little while and eventually called in my forensic partner, Estelle, to carry out an examination. Her professional opinion was, "That doesn't look right. Get checked out."

Well, here is where the delay and male awkwardness comes in. It's one thing to summon your wife to come and look at your poo, but it's quite another to sit in a doctor's surgery with the knowledge that, at some point, he's likely to ask you to bend over whilst snapping a latex glove on. So, I did what every other middle-aged male would do in the circumstances; I prevaricated, and even being berated by my well-intentioned wife to do something was better than picking up the phone to make an appointment.

That was until I was sitting in my car behind a bus on Water Street in Liverpool and I started to read the NHS campaign poster on the back. It said if you had any of the following symptoms, which had persisted for three weeks or more, make an appointment.

• Rectal bleeding
• A persistent change to normal bowel habits
• Abdominal pain or tenderness
• Right lower abdominal mass or palpable rectal mass (intraluminal and not pelvic)
• Weight loss
• Unexplained iron deficiency anaemia

I wouldn't have minded number five and didn't know what number six was, but I knew I had numbers one and two.

At this stage, I did not consider cancer a possibility, but things started to click, and I got very worried very quickly and made the appointment. This story is not about my cancer journey; it's about being vigilant and looking for signs. I will leave the main cancer journey detail out but suffice to say, I was treated for bowel cancer and slightly chuffed about being called 'young'. This is because most bowel cancer symptoms show in the over-fifties, hence the current screening campaign but cancer doesn't follow the rules as we know, so you are never too young to be aware and on the lookout.

As a postscript to the main event but still very much on the be vigilant theme, my post-bowel screening activity largely ceased after five years. However, my superpower is growing bowel polyps faster than anyone, so they regularly check and harvest them via a colonoscopy.

But five years on, am I declared cancer-free? No, unfortunately not and because I am a persistent individual, I was having an old man's MOT and during my blood tests for the usual diabetes/cholesterol, etc. I persisted in asking for a cancer marking test. After much reluctance, they relented. I thought no more of it other than they would tell me off for being overweight and me lying about how much I drink. That was until a call on Good Friday when they advised my blood showed an abnormality on the cancer marking test. After the MRI, they did indeed find a nasty relative of bowel cancer sitting on my liver, very quietly growing away. If I had not persisted with the receptionist and doctor, that tumour would have got me in the end as it grew slowly and silently.

There is a lot of luck, good and bad, with everyone's cancer story, and as the cliché goes, everyone's story is different. However, you can help stack the odds in your favour by doing a lot of things, but some of the easiest don't involve jogging and giving up red meat, but rather remaining vigilant and making a nuisance of yourself when your gut is telling you to do so.

Pete Maher

Andrea's Story

'Don't make me angry. You wouldn't like me when I'm angry.'

For anyone who has been diagnosed with cancer, once you have been through the total daze of diagnosis followed by the 'why me?' stage, the next stop is often anger.

Now I'm writing this because when the tsunami of pink you see every year is coupled with the words 'have to fight it' ringing in your ears, suggesting that every cancer patient is a heroic warrior, it is enough to wind anyone up. Being anything but stoic and strong doesn't fit how you are meant to behave but those companies painting pink ribbons on their products are not going through it – you are.

So, for me, the angry stage was more than raging at the kids who nonchalantly tell you at 8.00am: 'Mum, I forgot I've got Home Economics at 9am. Have you got any mince for spaghetti Bolognese or do you need to go to Tesco's?' That isn't such a great example as that's enough to turn anyone into a serial killer.

The anger that comes from a cancer diagnosis is the type that suddenly grips you—you're unreasonable, grumpy, snappy, but mainly explosive.

The fact is any little thing can turn you into a screeching banshee making the household run off in different directions. Once the post-anger exhaustion hits you, then berate yourself that you're not the brave Boudicca champion fighting the cancer war. At times, I turned into the Incredible Hulk and my children gave me a wide berth. Suddenly, their grandmother found the kids calling on her a lot more frequently.

So, anger to me needs to be acknowledged and talked about. Why do I feel I am qualified to comment? Apart from the obvious that I've had cancer, it was also because I was a probation officer for eight years and one of my roles was to run cognitive behaviour group work programmes for drunk drivers and chaotic youth who didn't think of consequences (my favourite). I also ran the anger management groups or anger replacement therapy to give it its posh name.

These groups were made up of men twice my size covered in tattoos before they were trendy or builders who wore shorts even when there were ten inches of snow outside. They were tough and high-risk, and the group work was the last stop before prison. Getting to know them better I learnt a lot about anger and where the emotion comes from.

There is nothing wrong with anger; it often tells you something is wrong. It's not the emotion but the way that you deal with it. Anger has a specific pattern that you can recognise and if you can recognise it, then you can deal with it. You can then learn to understand why you are angry and put in coping techniques.

Intellectually, it all sounds very easy, doesn't it? As a probation officer, I worked with the offenders to help them recognise patterns. It was only when cancer reared its head that I realised how hard those men worked to control the thing that was wrecking their lives.

When I was diagnosed and going through treatment, sometimes I couldn't even articulate why I was angry. It didn't seem to have a beginning or a trigger. The symptoms of being angry, however, remained constant: headaches, difficulty breathing and a tightening in the chest. If you feel these things, you might not even recognise that you're angry. You might notice more in your inability to cope with little setbacks.

Don't berate yourself for being angry; you have to deal with the shock, fear, and confusion of cancer, along with the frustration of not being able to do all the things you normally do. When having chemotherapy, you can't drive, you lose your independence, and for women who are so often the glue that holds the house together, you must rely on the rest of the household to do it for you.

Things that made me uncontrollably angry included:

- the toothpaste lid being left off
- losing my glasses
- the dog not being walked
- not being able to get through to the doctors
- Tesco's

269

I once walked all the way to Tesco, as I couldn't drive to buy a chicken because, probably fuelled by guilt, I decided to cook the family a Sunday roast. This is no mean feat, as most food made me nauseous. I opened the chicken and it stank rotten and I had to put it straight in the outside bin. I then stomped back to Tesco's and demanded to see the manager. He asked me if I had bought the offending chicken with me. I'm ashamed to say he got both barrels. I asked him, as someone who was having chemo and vulnerable to infection, did he think it was a good idea to bring a rancid chicken with me?

It was only when I stopped raging I realised he meant the batch number so he could take the other potentially dangerous chickens off the shelf. Despite being given a bag of baby carrots as compensation, it was only hours later that I calmed down. Lucky for me, because I sported a chemo turban and massive shades, he won't be able to recognise the rude, unreasonable woman that confronted him that day.

Later, I was told that anger is very normal for cancer patients. Certain medications can also cause it, such as steroids. I was massively relieved to find out that the steroids they regularly shove into you can cause anger which is affectionally titled 'Roid Rage'. I loved this and wanted to create a T-shirt range which would become an instant hit with cancer patients and bodybuilders. My T-shirt empire is yet to see the light of day.

You will be glad to know that the anger stage gives way to acceptance, or it did with me. If, however, you find it going to the depressive stage, which I flirted with as well, it's important to know you're not alone. I write this to let people know who get a diagnosis that you will go through a myriad of emotions and that's okay.

You do not have to be a 'warrior'; you feel how you feel and remember:

'Cancer isn't an opponent in some war game you can stomp out by mindset and determination.' Nancy Stordahl

Being brave and heroic isn't something that comes naturally and if you must go through a bit of anger along the way, that's okay.

Andrea Moulding

Andrea is the author of *Throwing Salt at the Devil* and *Stay on the Bus* and is the co-host of the *Get it Off Your Chest: The Funny Side of Breast Cancer* podcast.

Hayley's Story

My story as a single mum. How my world was shaken. Being diagnosed with uterine cancer, and then just six weeks later, being diagnosed with Hairy Cell Leukaemia - a rare and incurable cancer of the blood and bone marrow.

It's that moment you thought would never happen to you. I vividly recall THAT moment when I received the news of my diagnosis of uterine cancer. Saturday, 17th June 2023; walking into my gynaecologist's room alone to find him sitting there with the support nurse was a gut-wrenching moment that will forever be etched in my memory. My gynaecologist, who had been my consultant for over ten years, was usually such a happy, upbeat person. However, upon seeing his demeanour, I sensed that the news would not be favourable. It was at that moment he revealed the devastating news that rocked my world - I had uterine cancer and that a full hysterectomy was the only viable cure, a hysterectomy that would result in induced menopause.

Denial struck me. I was in shock. I was in panic. I was incredulous, unable to fathom the reality of the situation. "This can't be happening to me. I am a single mother to my ten-year-old son, Lorenzo. I have to be OK. I have to be," I told my gynaecologist.

What we thought was a harmless polyp removal two weeks prior was indeed uterus cancer. The gravity of the situation hit me like a thunderbolt, and I struggled to come to terms with the diagnosis, the prospect of a hysterectomy, and the ensuing menopause much before my time. I was quickly scheduled for a hysterectomy a mere two weeks later, and the weeks leading to the procedure were scary with intense emotional turmoil. Sleepless nights, fear, sadness, anger, pain, and worry consumed me. I found myself uncharacteristically enraged with the world, resentful that this was happening to me

- a single mother with a young child who depends on me - when there are countless other evil individuals in existence.

The subsequent weeks were exceedingly difficult as I tried to hide my distress from my son. Often retreating to the bathroom for hours on end to weep in solitude so as not to expose my son to my tears.

As the lead-up to my surgery date grew closer, I became unwell with a bad virus and chest infection. This pushed the date of my surgery back another two weeks due to my chest infection taking so long to clear. For two years, I had battled with frequent infections, immense exhaustion, fatigue, bone pain and pneumonia. I always knew in my head something was not right, but doctors could never get to the bottom of what it was.

The surgery date for my hysterectomy had come, and after three days in hospital, I was back at home alone with just my son. This I found the hardest point to deal with. Not only was I still trying to process that I had just undergone major surgery from a cancer diagnosis, but I was also pushed into an early, induced menopause, much before my time, with raging hormones. This was very hard to process.

The next weeks were hard, dark and long. But instead of getting stronger, I got weaker, and my gynaecologist suggested I see a haematologist for further investigations. Over the next two weeks, different blood sampling tests were performed.

Just as I was starting to slowly process everything of the last four weeks, I was somewhat unprepared for how my world was going to be rocked even mor—on the evening of Friday, 4th August 2023, I received a devastating phone call that was about to change my life forever.

The phone call was from my haematologist, who informed me that I had been diagnosed with Hairy Cell Leukaemia (HCL)—a very rare and incurable cancer of the blood and bone marrow. This type of rare leukaemia only affects around 1,000 people a year. Hairy Cell Leukaemia has an excess number of B-lymphocytes in the blood and bone marrow. The bone marrow is not able to make enough normal blood cells and produces too many B lymphocytes, and these cells fill up the bone marrow, preventing it from producing healthy cells, which do not work properly in attacking cancer cells and viruses. Chemotherapy is needed to put it into remission, which can be for several years, then each time there is a re-occurrence, more chemo is necessary. Being diagnosed with HCL can be a shock, especially as most people, and even a lot of doctors, have never heard of it, as it is that rare.

Receiving another cancer diagnosis, alone, via telephone, just five weeks after the first diagnosis, while still recovering from the hysterectomy, was another devastating experience. It was another kick to the stomach while already being at rock bottom.

Part of me was relieved that they had finally got to the bottom of what was wrong with me in these last few years. Yet the other part of me was in utter shock and disbelief- why me out of all the billions of people in the world? Why did I have to fall into this tiny per cent of a fraction? Why is all this happening to me? That weekend, I cried my entire heart and soul, unable to process the news that had been given to me via telephone.

While navigating through Google (that had become my best and worst friend in my weakest moments), trying to learn more about the rare diagnosis I had been given, I found a Hairy Cell Leukaemia support Facebook page dedicated to individuals with HCL. This proved to be a source of solace and support throughout that weekend and the subsequent weeks ahead. It is thanks to this invaluable support network that I have been able to get through this challenging period with greater ease, talking to real people with this condition, some that are many months, years and decades ahead of me.

Over the past four weeks, I have been blessed to have forged meaningful connections with other rare and unique individuals who share my diagnosis, which has made me feel not alone, and I am confident that these newfound friendships will endure for a lifetime. In those moments of utter weakness, it was these people, whom I had never met, that gave me reassurance and, in that moment, I learnt how much we rise by lifting others. For every so-called, unneeded friend that left my life, a new, meaningful one entered, and in this moment, what

I didn't realise was that a great filtering was happening; what I didn't need was giving way, leaving me with the true essence of what I DID need.

I spent the weeks crying for a period that felt like a lifetime. Every hour felt like a day, and every day felt like a week. Some days, it is a struggle getting through the days, so I often have to break it down and just work on just getting through every hour.

During these last weeks, I have experienced feelings, emotions, and situations that I never thought I would find myself in. Regrettably, I discovered that cancer discrimination and cancer ghosting are unfortunate realities. It is a club that no one wants to be a part of. Sadly, I fell victim to cancer discrimination when my kickboxing instructor dumped me upon hearing about my leukaemia diagnosis. They were fine with training me while being aware of my uterine cancer diagnosis. However, as soon as they learned about the leukaemia, they dropped me immediately. I never thought I would experience discrimination because of cancer, but it happened, and it hurt deeply.

I never thought so-called friends would ghost me, but it happened. It hurts and it hurts a lot, especially as it was these things I needed to keep me motivated during the most brutal time of my life. However, it's these rejections and setbacks that define us and make us stronger and more determined. That's why, in the moment of utter weakness, a spark ignited me and I knew I had to turn this pain into my power with a strong will to live. My mindset has always been hugely important to me. Although there have been times when my thoughts run away with me, thinking of the worst, but the only option I have right now is to be determined because I have my little son relying on me; it's me and my son against the world, because somewhere, amongst the stats and numbers, there has to be a survival stat, so why not me?

So I knew this was it. I have to look after myself because not only do I have to look after my body, but my mental health is a top priority too, because the way we think can literally change our brains and health.

I started doing daily affirmations and gratitude. For example, I am grateful for waking up to see another day despite the turmoil. I am grateful for the team looking after me despite the pain. I am grateful for hearing my son laugh despite the tears. I am grateful for the treatment despite the anxiety. I will accept and work with the treatment I will be getting.

I also visualise being able to see my boy grow. I imagine the adventures we still have to go on. I made a mood board of places we want to visit, goals I would like to do, and I envisage ticking these places off that list, as well as adding new places to that list. This is what keeps me motivated during those dark days.

It's not easy being given a cancer diagnosis; it literally tears your heart into a million pieces that you have to try to pick up one by one, trying to find a 'new normal', while I tell my son every day that anything is possible in life because it's during this time I have come to realise just how fragile and precious life is.

My journey is far from over; in fact, my Leukaemia battle is just at the beginning. For now, I am waiting to see the Leukaemia specialist who will tell me when I can start my chemotherapy, but all I can do is stay strong and keep trying to make the impossible possible. This is not the ending, and in fact, this is just ONE chapter in my story/cancer battle.

Hayley Valentino
Hayley is the author of *Making Impossible Possible, The Autobiography of H J Valentino*

Jenny's Story

Grumpy Mr Lumpy

At 36 years of age, I never thought I'd get diagnosed with breast cancer before the year was out. After all, I was much too young even to be invited for a mammogram. I had been pregnant before, I had a healthy BMI, I didn't smoke, I hardly drank, and I did extended breastfeeding for a total of four and a half years! I often wonder how I got this?

I had not long lost my lovely dad on Mother's Day, three and a half months before my cancer diagnosis due to heart failure. I had a vision in my mind of the summer being kind, with longer days and brighter nights. It would be a glimmer of hope during darkened times whilst I was still grieving. Little did I know how wrong I would be.

It all started in June 2023 when I was coming out the shower and drying my body with a towel. I caught the side of my boob with my bare hand. It felt like what seemed to be a hard lump. I had previously been to the breast unit during or after both pregnancies. I was told I have accessory breast tissue, which flared up during pregnancy, but this lump felt very different from last time.

I will be honest; I don't check my boobs very often. In fact, the last time I did was a year previous. There was someone watching over me that day when I found 'Grumpy, Mr Lumpy'.

I immediately made an appointment to see my GP after the weekend, on the Wednesday when I was off. I saw a locum GP who reassured me she felt "pretty confident it was nothing to worry about and most likely a fibroadenoma (a benign breast tumour)". I got referred to the breast unit as an urgent referral. I didn't feel worried until I received a letter from the GP stating, "...this must be a worrying time for me..." and signposting me to my local Macmillan Centre and the Macmillan Cancer Support website address.

Having previously been to the breast clinic twice before, I naively thought I would be in and out. Therefore I took no one with me, despite my mum offering to come. "I will be in and out like last time, Mum. It won't be anything to worry about, then I can go straight back to work," were my famous last words.

The day of the appointment, I saw a very nice doctor, who examined me and once again said she thought it was either a cyst or a fibroadenoma, "But we still need you to have an ultrasound to check," she said. The doctor also found another lump on the adjacent side in my axilla (armpit); she said she thought it was an enlarged lymph node but both areas needed to be looked at properly when I went for an ultrasound scan. The minute she mentioned a second lump, something inside me didn't sit comfortably.

While I was getting my ultrasound scan, the practitioner was so quiet; she hardly spoke a word to me and was taking so many pictures. She was going over my boob with a fine-tooth comb and I could tell something was wrong. She asked me about the lymph node, and if I had felt it? To which I replied, "No." She commented how extremely large it was. "Okay, I have no idea what this is, so I'm going to have to biopsy it and the lymph node too," she said. I started sobbing, telling them that I had not long lost my dad, and since Dad died, everything just seemed to be going wrong. My mind started drifting and I recalled when I was on placement as a student nurse in theatres. From all the breast cancer patients that I had seen having surgery performed, I knew that if it's going to spread, it goes to the sentinel lymph node first. She put a titanium marker into the mass, then later sent me back in to see the doctor.

The doctor asked me what the practitioner had said. "I'm sorry we can't give you the answers you were looking for today. It might be nothing, but I'm just preparing you, as you might have cancer," she regretfully told me. I was then handed the nurse's phone number if I had any questions and told my results would take approximately two weeks or slightly longer to get back.

The wait for the results felt like an eternity! I spent the time researching every possibility. Of those who I'd found to have breast cancer, did their results take longer to come back? What if the reason for my fatigue and brain fog wasn't due to grieving but the fact that I had cancer?

I spoke to the nurse on the phone a few days prior to my next appointment and I could just tell, from being a nurse myself, that at that appointment I was going to get delivered bad news. The day of the appointment, which just so happened to be my brother's 50th birthday, I got told I had cancer. I even knew the type of cancer that I most likely had—invasive ductal carcinoma. I asked, "The biopsy you took of the lymph node, has it gone to that too?" "Yes," the doctor replied. I had so many questions in my head. I was told I would need surgery, chemotherapy, radiotherapy, and a drug at the end to stop it from coming back. I was told due to my age, I needed to have genetics testing, another thing which could potentially affect the treatment plan and I may need further surgery at a later date. But first, I needed to have a CT scan to check if it had spread anywhere else in the body. I knew at present, the chances of me surviving the next five years were 86%, but if it had gone elsewhere, it could drop by as much as 29%.

Of all the waits, the wait for the CT results was by far the worst. I had already convinced myself, after my first appointment, that I had breast cancer. I was unsure if a lymph node that I had felt in my groin was enlarged or not.

"Please don't tell me it's gone anywhere else," I kept telling myself. "I can handle 86%; I don't know how I'd handle 29%."

I had started on some new medication prescribed by my GP and the side effects for the first few weeks were terrible: anxiety, tremors, insomnia, fatigue; it was awful! The day of my CT results is a day I'll never forget, hearing those words, "It hasn't spread, but there is multiple lymph node involvement." I started hyperventilating in the room, which very quickly progressed into a panic attack. I think it was a build-up of stress from the anxiety, lack of sleep and everything that had been going on in my life.

The next hurdle was preparing for the surgery. I was to have a lumpectomy as my tumour was only small and an auxiliary node clearance. I often wondered to myself how best to tell my children. They are only very young: six and three. I didn't want to scare them, but I wanted to prepare them. I made my cancer journey into a bit of a story. I told them that I had a naughty lump and his name was Grumpy Mr Lumpy. I said that Mummy needed to have an operation to get rid of him. My daughter was terribly upset the day I first talked about him, but it lessened her anxiety by being shown and explaining about things along every step of the way.

I planned to donate my hair to The Little Princess Trust, a charity who makes wigs for children with hair loss. I had done this in the past on multiple occasions. I told the children I was donating my hair again but this time it was all of my hair, that my hair would go to a little boy or girl who needed it more than me. Being honest, the type of person I am, I'd never want it to fall out and go to waste. I'd want it to be used to make someone else happy, which I know would make me so happy! I decided I would raise money in memory of Dad for the British Heart Foundation and to Macmillan Cancer Support, who were currently supporting me.

Right from the very start, I always knew that losing my hair and having a general anaesthetic would always be the biggest challenges for me. To get me to cope with things better, I was prescribed yet more medication via my GP to help take the edge of things prior to the surgery. I realised there was no way out, and if I wanted to live, the surgery had to happen. I developed coping strategies I was going to use to prepare me when I went down to theatre. I told the anaesthetist, that I was going to shut my eyes the minute I got on the couch, to please not tell me when I was going to sleep, and that I just wanted someone to hold my hand, as I was so scared.

I remember waking up in recovery and I couldn't believe it was over. I decided I needed to try and eat and drink as soon as I could so I could get home faster, as I really didn't want to be in hospital. I met a very lovely lady that day who was going through a similar journey to me and we've stayed in touch since. The first few days after my op, I stayed at my mum's. This was the first time since both my children were born that I had spent the night without them. My eldest was inquisitive, asking about Mr Lumpy. I think once she saw I was okay and I wasn't in any pain, it had taken away a lot of that anxiety for her.

I couldn't believe how different everything looked and felt. There I was, unable to feel the bottom of my arm, my side, and half of my boob. To this day, the feeling has never come back. I now have one boob bigger than the other, but that's ok, as in the grand scheme of things, at least I am still here! I had a drain and drain bag that I needed to carry around with me for a week before it was able to come out. This made sleeping very difficult at times! Unfortunately, not long after the drain came out and several weeks later, I developed several complications as a result of the surgery. Thankfully, now one has gone but the other complication is still ongoing.

The day of my post-surgery follow-up appointment, I was delighted to know from my histology results that they got the whole thing out and there were clear margins all around! Of the twenty-eight lymph nodes they removed, two were metastatic and one was a micro metastasis. I couldn't thank everyone at the breast unit enough for all they'd done for me. From both consultants, the registrar, my lovely breast care nurse who deserved a medal for always going above and beyond. They had all helped to save my life and I will always be eternally grateful.

Soon after, I decided I was going to "brave the shave" and donate my hair. It's funny how the journey strengthens you, and what I thought would be one of my biggest hurdles actually empowered me. I felt like I had taken something back and got there before cancer was able to. I had all my family surround and support me to help cut my hair. We even got my children involved and they were so happy to help cut Mummy's hair, and this warmed my heart. It wasn't a sad time, it was a happy time and that's what I wanted it to be. I raised an incredible amount of money for my chosen charities. I know Dad would have been so proud, as he always loved helping others.

Not long after this, I got transferred over to the oncology team to discuss what would be next in my treatment plan. I am to have five months in total of chemotherapy, followed by radiotherapy, then either ten years of Tamoxifen or an ovary suppressant. I am still waiting on genetic counselling; I only hope and pray there is no mutated gene, as I would be devastated if I have passed it on to my children. I know now I will never be able to have any more children again. If I take the ovary suppressant, it will shut down my ovaries completely and put me into early menopause. If I take Tamoxifen, I can't get pregnant with that or for a period of time after, which would take me up to almost fifty by the time a third was to come along. I am focusing on being thankful for what I have and not what could have been.

I am due to start my chemotherapy next week, a magic potion to stop Grumpy Mr Lumpy from coming back. My children are aware the 'magic potion' may make Mummy feel unwell sometimes, as it's so powerful. I feel as the time is approaching, the hospital appointments are getting more and more frequent. I only hope and pray I don't get any possible serious side effects and that Grumpy Mr Lumpy truly never does come back again.

I can't thank my family for all the love and support they have given me over the last few months and to everyone who has reached out.

It has been a strange journey, a journey that truly taught me a valuable lesson: that critical illness, including cancer, can happen to anyone and your life can truly change in the blink of an eye. Your time is so precious, so use it wisely. Don't waste it on things that are not worthy of your time. Do what makes you feel alive! Take every opportunity you are given, and don't regret what you didn't do; you never know if you may be given that same opportunity again later. Tell those you love how much they mean to you and make sure you live a life you will remember.

Jenny Kershaw

Angela's Story

My cancer symptoms were sneaky. I never had the classic cancer symptoms of excessive night sweats or unexplained weight loss. I remember developing strange symptoms such as an unexplained large, white patch on my scalp, which took months to get rid of, becoming extremely dizzy while exercising, I would wake up in the middle of the night and unable to fall back asleep. Then my one cup of coffee habit became a five to six cups of coffee a day habit and I also became a raging chocoholic. These symptoms were happening for months, but I always brushed them off with the excuse of being a mother to young children, which was why I had trouble sleeping and needed the coffee and chocolate.

Then my cancer journey began with a misdiagnosis. I was called into the doctor's office after a routine blood test for my results. The first question my doctor asked was, "How are you feeling?" I replied, "Good!" He then asked again, "But how are you really feeling? Your haemoglobin levels are at 106 and your iron levels are at 4! Angela, you must be really exhausted!" Again, I brushed it off and I told him that I felt a little tired due to lack of sleep and having young kids. My doctor then explained to me that I was anaemic, and he was referring me to a gastroenterologist.

I met with my gastroenterologist, and we talked about my low iron and he suggested that I have a colonoscopy and an iron infusion to get my iron levels up. I had my colonoscopy and iron infusion, then I had my six-week-follow-up appointment. At the appointment, the gastroenterologist asked how I was feeling after the iron infusion and if my energy levels had improved. I informed him that there was no improvement in my energy levels. He also suspected after the colonoscopy that he found two tiny ulcers, and I had Crohn's disease, which was causing low iron. He also asked if I had a heavy menstrual cycle, which I did! After hearing this, the gastroenterologist recommended that I see a gynaecologist for further investigations.

Next stop, an appointment with the gynaecologist. During the consultation, the gynaecologist was discussing my latest blood test results, which still showed low iron and low haemoglobin levels but also started showing an increase in my inflammation markers. The gynaecologist decided to do an ultrasound in his office. While doing the ultrasound, he pointed out on the screen that I had Adenomyosis, which is common after childbirth and the cause of heavy menstrual bleeding, which can lead to low iron. After the findings, the gynaecologist recommended a hysterectomy, and this should resolve my low iron issues.

It was six weeks after my hysterectomy that I had check-up with the gynaecologist and to discuss my latest blood test results following my operation. I remembered the shocked expression on his face when he read out aloud my blood test results. My haemoglobin levels were now at 100, my iron levels dropped from 4 to 2 and my inflammation markers were still increasing! He said that my haemoglobin and iron levels should be increasing due to no longer having menstrual periods. The gynaecologist also mentioned the only thing that can cause these results is a chronic disease.

During this whole time through my ordeal, I often caught my husband studying all my blood test results and googling. I would tell him off, to stop googling, that he was going to make himself sick. Little did I know that he was also having discussions with our family doctor about my blood test results and his Google searches kept stating it was Lymphoma.

Then it was on that fateful morning, December 19th 2015, I was getting ready for work and my husband noticed a lump on my chest wall area. He questioned what it was. I felt the area and replied it was a bone. My husband was not happy with my answer and demanded we go to the hospital for a full body scan. I refused and told him that I was going to work; we were then going to go to our family Christmas dinner that night, followed by attending a cousin's birthday the next day. After the birthday I would go to the hospital.

The time had come: a trip to the hospital for a full body scan on December 20th 2015. My husband and I arrived at the hospital with my husband holding all my copies of blood test results in his hands and explaining about the lump he found to the doctor. A CT scan was ordered immediately. After the CT scan. the doctor read my results and said, "We have found masses." I went into shock as I watched my husband crying with the doctor. I then rang family members to inform them of the devasting news. I had to stay overnight for more tests, but I asked the hospital if I could go home to see my kids first, to which they agreed. Then, at 1am in the morning at hospital, the diagnosis finally hit me. "I have cancer." I was shaking and cried like a baby.

It wasn't until the middle of January 2016, after multiple biopsies, that I finally got my correct diagnosis of Hodgkin's Lymphoma Stage 4. This was the real culprit of my low iron! (I didn't even have Crohn's.) I had to endure six rounds of intensive chemotherapy. I remembered my very first dose of chemo; I was so petrified, but once it was administrated, it wasn't so bad. Five days later, after my first round, the side effects appeared, and I ended up having a fever, which caused me to pass out at home and then had me hospitalised. While I was recovering in hospital, I remember flicking the TV channels in my room and Joel Osteen's programme came on. I listen to his sermon and his words, "God's medical report is not the same as the doctor's medical report." This struck a chord with me and gave me the strength to endure the intensive chemotherapy and to fight this battle.

As each round of chemotherapy progressed, my body grew weaker from the toxicity of the treatment. The chemotherapy would knock my blood counts dangerously low, which involved multiple blood transfusions. All my hair fell out and I cried for two weeks. It was so devasting, especially because I was a hairdresser. I wore a wig to hide the side effects of what the cancer was doing to me. I spent six months between home and hospital. The nurses at the hospital were my social life.

Today, I am coming up to seven and a half years cancer-free. I am eternally grateful for God restoring my health back and allowing me to watch my beautiful sons, Domenic and Adrian, grow up with my husband. I am also forever thankful for my husband Marco for saving my life and for attending every medical appointment with me. A big thank you to my family and friends for all your love and support. Plus, a big

285

shout out to Professor To and all the amazing nurses and medical staff at the Royal Adelaide Hospital.

Every day is a blessing!

Angela Laudonia

Lesley's Story

I've hated polystyrene ceiling tiles since the day I was diagnosed with breast cancer. I was lying on a hospital trolley, waiting for what I thought was a minor operation to remove a tiny lump from under my arm, when I was told by the surgeon that the mammogram had shown up a problem. Pre-cancerous cells scattered through my breast "like salt and pepper grains," he said.

I recall my reaction vividly: disbelief, terror, confusion. In the space of a few minutes, on a sunny May afternoon, my world had been turned upside down. What was more, I knew of no one who'd been through it. No one who I could turn to for advice. What was it like to go through chemotherapy and radiotherapy? How would I cope with hair loss? I was terrified.

My family were, of course, endlessly supportive and, despite their own fears, determined to get me through it. My elder daughter, Jane, had just had major bowel surgery and knew what it was like to face a potentially life-changing illness. We would fight this together.

"Stay positive," instructed my doctor. Well, yes, but that's easier said than done. Anyone who says they've never had a negative thought isn't telling the truth. I had to find a way to deal with it and one thing I tried was what we would now call mindfulness. I imagined myself swimming in the sea, with flecks of sunlight dancing on the water. As each one washed over my body, it destroyed the dark cancer cells inside me. "Heal...and relax... heal...and relax...," I would think. I found it relaxing and, to this day, I like to think that it helped.

Hair loss was tough, and I hated my wig. On my first chemotherapy session, I heard the nurse asking a lady who was starting a second course of treatment if she still had her wig. "No," she replied. "It went on the guy on Bonfire Night." I understood exactly how she must have felt. I called mine Ulrika - there was a passing resemblance to Ulrika Jonsson if you closed one eye and it was a foggy day - and I think I wore her about half a dozen times. For the rest of the time, it was jaunty hats and scarves, of which I had many.

My prosthesis has, inevitably, become part of my life and I don't think twice about wearing it now. I soon accepted that strappy tops were a thing of the past and I only forgot to put it on once when I was teaching. My five-year-old charges didn't appear to notice my lop-sided appearance, and my colleagues were too polite to mention it.

Since the day of my diagnosis, 20 years ago now, I've had four friends also diagnosed with breast cancer. For each of us, it was a traumatic experience, which we handled in different ways. I've always done what I can to support them, from going with Pat to her first chemotherapy session to the long phone calls with my friend Carol. I was a survivor and I wanted them to be able to cling to that hope for the future. That there is a future, it's the life raft we all need to hang on to.

Carol had a similar relationship with wigs and boobs to me. I have a favourite memory of meeting her at Newcastle station one hot August day. I saw her striding through the crowds in a long, colourful sundress, clearly without her prosthesis and no wig. Her smile said, "This is me, folks. Take me as I am!" Brilliant and beautiful. She also left her boob in a carrier bag outside the Year 11 boys' toilets at the school where she taught one day. But that's another story.

So, after eight sessions of chemotherapy and five weeks of radiotherapy, 2003 was a year to forget. Although, of course, you never do. Even 20 years on, it can still be raw and make me sad and angry. In that time, I've lost Carol and another dear friend, Nic. Vibrant, wonderful ladies, both taken far too young. Each time, it's hit me hard, both physically and mentally, but all I can do is help those who fight on to find better treatments and hope for a cure in the future. As the mum of two beautiful daughters, that is the most important thing to me. I've done fundraising and can proudly say that my name is included on a wall at the Royal Marsden Hospital in London, along with hundreds of others, including Kylie Minogue. Yes, folks, I've had my name up in lights with Kylie.

Writing this has not been easy. I've never tried to put my experience onto paper before. Maybe I should have done; it feels cathartic in a way. I try not to dwell on the past. I like to think it has made me a stronger and better person, more focused on the joys each day can bring. I know I am very lucky, especially when I look at my young grandson. For the sake of people like Carol and Nic, we have to carry on funding vital research. Live for the moment but create hope for the future.

Lesley Rawlinson

Lesley is the author of a number of children's books, including *Jojo's Star*, *Monty's Blackbird* and the *Woodpecker Tree* series.

Author's Note

There are things that are true, there are things that are not true and there are things that have elements of both. This book is the latter.

It is true that I was at Bangor University in the 1980s and many of the descriptions are true, or at least as true as I remember forty years later. One or two incidents are true and some of the minor characters are based on people I remember, but many are fictional. All the main characters and their stories, however, are completely made up, so no one who remembers me from those days needs to worry. Your secrets are safe with me.

When I challenged myself to write this book in just two months (I started on September 1st and the challenge was to finish it by the end of October, Breast Cancer Awareness Month), I intended it to pay tribute to all those I know who have been on or are still on a cancer journey, but I had to ask myself if I truly had the right. I have never (touch wood) had cancer myself; the nearest I have ever come was the incident described in the book, where Liam has a mole removed from his neck – that was me and it came to nothing. For that reason, I put a plea out for anyone who wanted to share their own cancer story. The response was dazzling, and I am honoured to include those stories in this book. They are all different, all brilliant and thought-provoking in their own way, but all of them contain the overriding message of how important it is to check oneself and to press for information if necessary. I am deeply indebted to Jason, Estelle, Pete, Jenny, Hayley, Angela, Andrea and Lesley for entrusting me with their stories and I hope this book does them justice. I am also extremely grateful to Estelle Maher for casting her expert, critical eye over the manuscript. Any error that remain in the book are wholly mine.

If you've made it this far in the book, thank you too, and please remember to check yourself as part of your daily routine and seek medical attention if there is anything, *anything,* that you don't like the look of. Keep well and my love to you all.

This book was written to raise awareness, but also to raise funds for Cancer Research UK. I am forever indebted to the following lovely people for their very generous donations. In return, I invited them to contribute something, a name, a phrase, a song title (or whatever they wanted) for me to include in the book. I wonder if you can spot any of them!

Anonymous, Hilary Banks, Martin Brooks, Helen Burns, Allan Deaves, Malcolm Dixon, Michelle and Chris Ewen, Lynne and Barry Godfrey, Donna Gowland, Kelly Hannaford, Paula Harmon, Jade Hoare, Alison Jones, Jenny Kershaw, Jude Lennon, Lorraine Lloyd, Jean Lloyd, Estelle Maher, Georgia and Millie Moore, Lesley Rawlinson, Duncan Reid, Lisa Satchell-Foley, Kathy Sharkey, Wendy Stone, Colette Swift, Maddy Templeman, Hayley Valentino, James Walker

Playlist

Music is a big part of this book, so here is a suggested playlist of the songs that are mentioned. Enjoy!

The Rockafeller Skank – Fatboy Slim (Barry/Terry/Cook ©Sony/ATV Music Publishing LLC, Universal Music Publishing Group)

Someone To Watch Over Me – Frank Sinatra (George/Ira Gershwin © Kanjian Music, Warner Chappell Music, Inc)

I Ran – A Flock of Seagulls (Reynolds/Score/Maudsley/Score © Imagem London Ltd)

The First of the Gang to Die – Morrisssey (Morrissey/Whyte © Universal Music Publishing Group, Warner Chappell Music Inc)

Sweet Transvestite – Rocky Horror Picture Show (O'Brien © TuneCore Inc, Universal Music Publishing Group)

The One I Love – REM (Buck/Berry/Mills/Stipe © Night Garden Music)

Sweet Child O'Mine - Guns N'Roses (McKagan/Stradlin/Hudson/Adler/Rose © Universal Music Publishing Group)

How Soon Is Now? – The Smiths (Marr/Morrissey © Sony/ATV Music Publishing LLC, Universal Music Publishing Group, Warner Chappell Music, Inc)

Love and Pride – King (Roberts/King © Sony/ATV Music Publishing LLC)

I'm Your Man – Wham!

(Michael/Jerome © Warner/Chappell Mlm Limited)

No Rest – New Model Army
(Sullivan/Morrow/Heaton © Attack Attack Music/Warner Chappell Music Ltd)

Sometimes - Erasure
(Bell/Clarke © BMG Rights Management, Kobalt Music Publishing Ltd., Peermusic Publishing, Sony/ATV Music Publishing LLC, Warner Chappell Music, Inc)

Suedehead - Morrissey
(Street/Morrissey © BMG Rights Management, Warner Chappell Music, Inc)

Lyin' Eyes – The Eagles
(Frey/Henley © Red Cloud Music)

This Corrosion – Sisters of Mercy
(Taylor © Sony/ATV Music Publishing LLC)

Bela Lugosi's Dead – Bauhaus
(Murphy/Baron © Universal Music Publishing Ltd., Hipgnosis Sfh I Limited)

Sally MacLennane – The Pogues
(Macgowan © Universal Music Publishing Ltd., Perfect Songs Ltd)

Let's Get It On – Marvin Gaye
(Townsend/Gaye © Kanjian Music, Songtrust Ave, Sony/ATV Music Publishing LLC, Warner Chappell Music, Inc)

Into The Valley – The Skids
(Adamson/Jobson © BMG Rights Management)

Don't Leave Me This Way – The Communards
(Gilbert/Huff/Gamble © Warner-Tamerlane Publishing

TAUK Publishing is an established assisted publisher for independent authors in the UK.

With hundreds of titles including novels, non-fiction and children's books, TAUK Publishing is a collaborative-based team providing step-by-step guidance for authors of all genres and formats.

To sign-up to our newsletter or submit an enquiry, visit:
https://taukpublishing.co.uk/contact/

For a one-to-one advice, consider scheduling a Book Clinic:
https://taukpublishing.co.uk/book-clinic/

Connect with us!

Facebook: @TAUKPublishing
Twitter: @TAUKPublishing
Instagram: @TAUKPublishing
Pinterest: @TAUKPublishing

We love to hear from new or established authors wanting support in navigating the world of self-publishing. Visit our website for more details on ways we can help you.

https://taukpublishing.co.uk/

SCAN ME

Printed in Great Britain
by Amazon

32565262R00165